A TOUCH OF

Magic

Enchanted Heiresses

RITA BOUCHER

PROLOGUE

True to their ancient Saxon name, the sentinel rocks of Stonehenge appeared to hang suspended in the waning of the day. Even before the time of Merlin, the standing pillars of sarsen and bluestone had guarded and borne witness to the councils of England's magical beings. With the retreat of elfkin to the Underlands and the decline of druids, only witches and mages were left to gather at the great circle.

As twilight slipped into the sky the former Chief Mage of France, Etienne du Le Fey, tried to turn his attention from the faces in the crowd. Many of them were known to him. A few had once counted among those he might have called *comrade*. Those he might have once named *friend* would not require a full hand to count. Foe or friend, their expressions were almost identical, as harsh and adamantine as the pillars that surrounded them.

Never had Etienne seen so many witches and mages in one place. By his reckoning, it had been more than two hundred years since any Convocation of this size had occurred here. Those of Merlin's Blood had been nearly exterminated by the witch hunts of *The Scourge*,

King James I. Large assemblies were still rare and clandestine.

Seated on a carved chair that was perched upon a platform at the nexus of the stone ring's power, Etienne resisted the temptation to wipe the sweat from his brow. His shirt was plastered to his back with perspiration. There was scant comfort in the realization that the onlookers seemed almost as uncomfortable as he was, wet to the dripping with their own sweat.

The stones did not take kindly to magic other than their own. Even minor, personal spells for relief posed an unwise risk within the circle. Not that it would help him one whit if his brothers and sisters of the Blood were more at ease. Scanning their faces, he could easily read the rage that roared behind their seemingly impassive facades.

They could scarcely be blamed for the anger that permeated the hot summer air. Though this was not supposed to be a trial of nation against nation, all too many of those present had lost kin to the French in the past decades of war.

Ironically, it was only the audience observing him, much like an animal in the Tower Menagerie, which kept him fighting for control. The representatives from England's covens had come to witness the Judgement. They were waiting, if not hoping, to see him transformed into a gibbering spectacle, begging for forgiveness.

I will not give them the satisfaction, Etienne vowed silently.

He schooled his features, forcing himself to maintain a semblance of his customary *savoir-faire*. No magic was necessary to present a shield of complete implacability, to still every quaking muscle, to freeze his expression into a cold bust of rock. Never before had he been so grateful for the harsh lessons his late father, the Devil Comte, had beaten into his very bones.

There was a commotion in the crowd as a woman made her way to the first row of the stone benches.

Circe, his affianced bride, walked like a dream in motion. Attired in yellow, sprigged muslin, she ignored the stares and whispers stirred by her presence and took her seat with a calm poise that would have done credit to the Queen of Faerie. One of his greatest regrets was the pain and grief that he was about to cause her.

If matters had gone differently, he would have been greeting her as his bride on this Mid-summer night. Etienne could only wonder if the avatar of Justice had chosen this date to deliberately taunt him with yet another loss.

Adorned with a wreath of ivy, Circe's unbound ash blond hair, streaked with sunlight, streamed to her waist behind her. Etienne painted the image in his memory, every detail adding one more pang to the aching pile of regret. Yet another chapter of his life was about to end.

Unless the decision of Judgement was death, rendering their betrothal moot, Etienne knew that he would not hold her to their agreement. Those forest green eyes met his for a moment. If there was a message for him in their depths, he could not decipher it before she looked away. Fortunately, there were no tears. They might well have unmanned him. Beside her sat his grandmother, Lady Morgan, who had seemingly aged a decade in the past year.

That crime, too, was upon his head.

There were whispers and rustles as Damien, his wife Rowan, and Etienne's half-sister Giselle entered the forum. Etienne rose with the assembly in a gesture of reverence to England's Chief Mage and its Mistress of Witches. His bow was deep, not just to acknowledge their offices but to accord his true respect to the man and woman who held them. He owed them both his honor and his life. Indeed, his very soul.

Although Lord Wodesby had come to testify for the prosecution, the former Mage of France had come to know Damien and his family well. England's Chief Mage had been charged with monitoring Etienne's conditional release, and making certain that he did not violate parole to intervene on Napoleon's behalf. Strangely enough, Damien was among the few present in this place who actually sought justice, not Etienne's complete destruction.

Mercy was unlikely and undeserved. The charge that had been levelled against the former Chief Mage of France was true. He was guilty of violating one of the most sacred dictates of their kind. His use of compulsion, forcing another of the Blood to use their power under threat of harm, was punishable by either of two penalties. One of them was death. The other, was excision, the forcible, permanent, rending of a mage or witch's magical Gifts.

In all honesty, given a choice, the French mage would rather have Justice put a period to his life.

Etienne raised his eyes to the platform where the others who would testify against him awaited.

His half-sister, Giselle, twisted her handkerchief anxiously. There were tears in her eyes and she looked away when she caught his gaze. Their laws demanded that she would be required to speak against him. If he could have, Etienne would have reassured her once again that he understood and forgave.

Giselle's mother, Rowan, clasped her daughter's hand. Having once been married to Etienne's father when little more than a child herself, the woman who was now Lady Wodesby had been disciplined with the same harsh methods as Etienne. She too, had those among the onlookers who regarded her with ill-concealed disdain because of her previous service to France.

As for Damien, even if he were inclined toward clemency, his discretion was limited in this ancient arena. The fact that the stones themselves had summoned Etienne and the covens to appear before the avatar of Justice was a dire portent indeed. It meant the Council charged by Merlin and Nimue to govern witches and mages could not be depended upon to dispense a fair decision.

When the last rays of the sun faded beneath the horizon, Etienne felt the weight of burgeoning magic.

It had begun.

A scrying pool materialized in the center of the circle, reflecting the crimson of the rising moon at Etienne's back.

It was a Blood moon, an ill omen if ever there was one.

All conversation ceased as the soft chime of bells came from within a swirl of fog. The assembled representatives of the covens bowed their heads in silence as a masked figure seemed to materialize out of the mist.

Swathed completely in a costume, the wearer seemed in constant motion. Ribbons of multi-colored fabric swirled and billowed, their sorcerous nature preventing any conclusions regarding height, shape, age, or gender. A feathered cloak of ceremony, rumored to have once belonged to the Merlin himself, floated behind the witch or mage chosen to act as the embodiment of magical Justice. At the edge of the pool, the standing stone known as the Chair of Judgement shifted into a carved throne as the avatar hovered forward to take the seat facing Etienne.

According to lore, the enchanted regalia appeared

to the witch or mage who was best suited to render a just and impartial verdict. The costume itself was both a sorcerous shield against any form of magical interference and an impenetrable protection of the wearer's identity. Few of those selected for dispensing Justice ever chose to make their names known after the trial.

The penalty for harm to an arbiter of Justice was the permanent excision of power in life and being forever barred from the glory of the Light in death. Even so, most of those chosen to administer Justice remained anonymous forever. The thirst for vengeance often surmounted reason.

Silently, this embodiment of judicial integrity made the signs of earth, air, fire, and water before raising bejeweled gloves skyward toward the scarlet orb above them.

"By Merlin, I give my oath before the Judgement moon." The enchanted voice intoned its words devoid of any identifying characteristics or emotion. *"Truth and fairness here will reign, else all earn Merlin's just disdain. Once sentence be passed 'pon his Blood son, swear we all to peace, and pledge harm to none."*

Judgment's avatar paused, waiting for reply.

"So swear us all!" The majority of voices came as a chorus. Others, a few that Etienne recognized, added their oaths as a reluctant echo.

"I call the first witness. Rowan Rhiannon, born of Peregrine."

At the summons, the heavily pregnant woman stepped forward to the scrying pool. Barefoot upon the sacred ground, England's Mistress of Witches moved with surprising grace as she stepped into the ankle deep water.

Etienne could not help but gasp as the pool roiled, then smoothed to a glass. The silvery surface coalesced gradually into an image of the familiar view of the

6

chateau of the du Le Fey. He watched as Rowan's memories unfolded before them.

Etienne saw himself as his stepmother had seen him. The moving pictures in the water bore visual and verbal witness to his threats against his sister, Giselle and his coercion of Rowan. His heart sank as he was forced to acknowledge the full measure of his own callous disregard, as witness after witness added their testimony.

When the pool was finally blank, the embodiment of Justice spoke once more. "Are there any here who would speak in favor of the former Mage of France?"

Not a whisper disturbed the resounding silence. Never had Etienne felt more alone.

"I shall." To his surprise, Giselle rose and stepped into the pool once more and let her memories unfold. "My brother, he was kind to me."

Damien came forward and took Giselle's place to offer his recollections. "He helped to save my life."

There was an audible gasp from the audience as Rowan herself rose once more and trekked to the water's edge. As she set foot in the pool, her images formed.

Etienne saw his youthful self, his face distorted in a rictus of pain. His body in spasm, he lay sprawled upon the cobblestones of the chateau's courtyard.

"You will not interfere with me when I discipline my wife!" His father bellowed with rage. Hands raised in a spell-casting gesture, the old comte sent blast after blast of debilitating magic at his son.

"You will kill him!" Rowan cried out, running to stand between Etienne and her husband. "He is your only son, your heir!"

"He is mine to use as I please. As are you, my wife!" The band of France glowed menacingly on his arm as he harvested power from a gathering storm above.

There was sweat on young Etienne's brow as he forced his head to rise. Every syllable seemed an effort as he voiced the vision he had deliberately concealed from his father. "Your... w...woman, she is...with ch...ch...child."

The crowd gasped. Mercifully, the pool went blank.

"You preserved my life on that day, and your unborn sister's. Even I did not know myself that I carried a babe until your foreseeing. " Rowan regarded him with a compassion he did not deserve, her voice echoing in the silence amidst the stones. "By revealing that I was with child, Etienne risked both his status as the only du Le Fey heir, and his life."

Once Rowan returned to her place, the avatar of Justice addressed Etienne.

"Have you anything to show us before sentence is passed. You have the right to recount your view of events."

Etienne shrugged and shook his head. "What can I say for myself? Though I thank those who spoke on my behalf, in the end, it was my actions which placed them in peril."

For a moment, it seemed that the representative of Justice was taken aback by his frank admission of guilt.

"Although the Mage of France eschews his right of self-defense, I ask him to stand in the pool, to ask a question pertaining to all of us who are chosen to serve as Chief Mages," Damien asked.

"It is unusual, but you may do so, should you deem it pertinent to the proceedings," came the sonorous reply.

"I do," England's Chief Mage asserted.

Reluctantly, Etienne took his place in the scrying pool.

The liquid had a peculiar texture, less like a liquid than a quivering, gelatinous pudding. It was neither cool, nor warm with the heat. Once, as a child, he had gone swimming in infested waters and emerged covered with leeches. The sensation of a living creature attaching itself to him was much the same, but in this case, entirely painless.

Suddenly, the stone circle vanished and Etienne found himself completely alone, facing the vista of his past. In a way, that gallery of his deeds was even more frightening than the arena of his angry peers. Since his first awareness, he had wasted his years trying to please the selfish, avaricious, cruel man who had sired him. His soul wept with the knowledge that those efforts had been entirely in vain.

"Why did you do it, Mage of France? Why did you commit those crimes of which you are accused?" Damien asked.

Why, indeed?

Helpless before the power of the pool, Etienne watched the past unspool again.

Napoleon rode through Cannes, less than a thousand troops behind him.

King Louis deserted Paris to her fate in the dark of night.

Marshall Soult changed sides and offered his allegiance to Bonaparte once more.

A legion of soldiers followed behind the Imperial Eagles, as the crowds cheered the prospect of revenge and glory.

"I foresaw the flight of the Bourbon King. I had a vision of Bonaparte beginning a new chapter in the destiny of my land. Napoleon was a remarkable man, a more astute leader than the kings and commoners who preceded him." He heard the echo of his own voice. "As France's mage, it was my duty to aid my country's return to prominence by any means that I could. Rowan had not yet surrendered her office as France's Mistress of Witches. I believed it was her obligation as well."

Etienne could have ended there, but he owed Rowan something he had never given anyone before.

An apology.

"I was wrong. I should have found another way. I should never have countenanced the violation of her power and her person as my father did, or used a threat against my sister to coerce her. That is my greatest regret and my everlasting shame."

"But you did these things because you truly believed them to be your duty as France's Chief Mage?" Lord Wodesby's question echoed.

"I did." Abruptly, Etienne found himself standing dry and barefoot on land. The magical watery expanse was gone without a trace.

When the avatar spoke again, there was a marked change in its voice. It was almost hesitant, as if there was a reluctance to continue. "Etienne, Comte du Le Fey. By the stones and the bones, we have seen sufficient to render judgement."

Magic, eldritch and powerful, reverberated against the pillars as the embodiment of Justice spoke.

Merlin's Children harken me.
Upon his head this geas will be.
Ply your Gifts and count them lost.
But fight when evil deeds accost.
Promises broken must be mended.
Else Gifts forever will be rended.
If joy is what you seek to reap,
Give away what you would keep.

A scroll of parchment floated into Lord Wodesby's hands.

"These are the terms of the verdict," Justice pronounced and disappeared.

"Ah," Etienne commented. "Always, there is paperwork."

CHAPTER 1

LONDON, WINTER 1817

*L*ondon was blanketed with a layer of fresh-fallen snow. In the face of the bitter chill, the streets were almost empty. Indeed, there were more than a few who predicted that the Thames would freeze solid as it had years before. Those who had the luxury of a warm hearth and no compelling reason to be abroad were enjoying their good fortune.

Genevieve Dale was not among those so blessed.

She huddled in the cab of her carriage, hoping that the ride would not be much longer. Neither her gloves nor her well-worn wool cloak sufficed against the biting wind that buffeted the vehicle's poorly shielded windows and badly hung doors. Because she had anticipated being delivered directly to the front door of Wodesby House, the clothing beneath was better suited to a ballroom than a journey through a gathering storm.

Her sole concession to the weather had been a pair of stout boots. The slippers that matched her gown sat on the bench beside her, carefully wrapped to prevent them from coming to ruin. The temptation to cast a small heating spell was strong, but she had no jewel for focus and she was reluctant to waste any of her reserve of power tonight. Besides, the illusion of warmth in foul weather was a dangerous one. Many a witch had lost toes or fingers due to frostbite when the desire for false comfort overcame good sense.

"Good sense, indeed!" A cloud of warm breath rose to the roof with her self-deprecating mutter.

She was half-tempted to rap on the box and ask the jarvey to turn around, but then she would be forced to endure the scolding that was sure to come when her familiar discovered that she had chosen to turn craven. There was no feline contempt greater than that of a Chartreux cat raised in the alleyways of Marseille.

They despised cowards.

* * *

"This is absurd, grandson!" Lady Morgan's voice rose above the clatter of the carriage wheels. "I cannot imagine why you need to put a disguise on top of a disguise. You will be wearing a domino and that ridiculously dismal black and white evening garb that somehow persists as *de riguer* despite that man milliner Brummel's exile. No one will recognize you, surely."

"The diamonds you wear are akin to a fireworks display, Grandmama. Only an orchestra in the pit playing Handel is lacking," Etienne said, fastening his borrowed greatcoat. While the smell made it obvious that the footman was overly fond of cheap cheroots, his winter garment was clean and free of vermin. "Despite your mask, they cannot fail to identify you and speculate upon who your companion might be."

"Pah!" She gave a dismissive wave. "For all anyone knows, you are still moldering away in hiding on your Yorkshire estate."

Etienne was about to deny hiding, but it was useless to argue with a statement that they both knew to be the truth. "Those who have been trying to entice me to be a part of their web of intrigue against Lord Wodesby would not dare to approach me openly, especially if I am the meat in tonight's dish of scandal broth. But many anonymous seekers of boons will be present tonight, so I will not be remarked."

His grandmother sniffed in disdain. "The conspirators cannot be possessed of much in the way of brains."

"Was it not you who taught me to never underestimate the power of determined stupidity?" Etienne asked her, winding a knitted purple scarf around his neck. "England's Chief Mage has set the High Circles spinning. His overtures to Outsiders and OutBloods connected to Merlin's children are considered revolutionary by many at the top."

"As if those possessing Merlin's Gifts are so numerous that we can afford to lose a single one of them," she murmured, reaching over to tuck the ends beneath his collar and straighten the drape of his coat. "You have the shoulders of a stevedore now, my boy, and a farmer's hands. It seems to me that all you would have to do is remove your jacket and gloves to proclaim the fact that you are not a member of the First Circles."

"An excellent point! I had nearly forgotten," Etienne declared, peeling off his luxuriantly lined gloves and securing them along with his mage's ring in an inner pocket. "Details are most important. It has been some time since I played a role in *opérations clandestines*."

"Your familiar tells me that you have been laboring like the lowliest Outsider peasant." His grandmother watched with increasing dismay. "You dig ditches and chop wood!"

"Suzette has a lamentable tendency to gossip," Etienne remarked, looking down at his feline companion in rebuke. He would not tell his grandmother that the effort to restrain his caged Gifts was beginning to overwhelm him. Physical activity was the only thing that seemed to calm the roiling power within.

"Suzette cares for your consequence, even if you do not," Lady Morgan retorted, bestowing a pat of approval upon the cat.

Etienne sighed, and looked out the window. He could stay silent or begin to broach the issue that his grandmother refused to acknowledge.

"More than a year has passed since Judgement. It is time that we face the possibility." Etienne clasped her hand between his. "I may never regain my magic. I have decided to learn how to conduct my life without it. This is the way the rest of the world lives."

"Even Outsiders hire servants to dig ditches!" His grandmother protested.

"And I do, when needed," Etienne said, reaching up to wipe away the tear sliding down her cheek. "It is time we face this. Tonight, I hope to pay some of the debt that I owe to Rowan and Lord Wodesby, but I would not have you deceived into the belief that I intend to return to the High Circles."

As they had arranged, the coachman began to slow the carriage to a stop. A knock from the top of the box signaled that they had reached Oxford Street.

"I will be watching you shine, Grandmama." He kissed her cheek and tweaked her diamonds.

"You have as much right to be at Wodesby House tonight as any," the old woman grumbled, restoring the alignment of her jewels. "More than some who drink the wine and eat the viands that the Chief Mage and Mistress of Witches offer tonight, even as they plot against them."

"And that is why I must remain unknown for now," Etienne reiterated. "Only those who are searching for me are aware of where to find me."

His grandmother reached over to adjust the nondescript domino he wore and he felt the familiar touch of her magic as she muttered an incantation.

"A powerful spell for a swath of silk," he observed, as the mask conformed itself to the contours of his face, the openings for mouth, nose and eyes remaining perfectly aligned with his every move. "My thanks, Grandmama."

"I will have you know that I had considerable skills as a needle witch, back in the day," she said, with a nod of satisfaction. "That should prevent any makers of mischief from finding you out."

"I had forgotten this strange game of unmasking that the English play," Etienne admitted.

"Such things were not done in my day!" Her voice rose in indignation. "Every witch and mage playing Ladies and Lords of Misrule! It is no excuse for the lapse of the simple manners that are taught to every youngling. Meddling with another's person without so much as a *by your leave*! Outrageous!"

Lady Morgan shivered at the sudden chill of the open door, pokering up as she surveyed the nearly empty streets beyond. "That coat is hideous and the scarf is the *coup de grace*! There are bound to be footpads about and the snow is growing heavier!" she protested. "You could catch your death!"

A consummation. Devoutly to be wished. Hamlet's words drifted through his head, but to say them aloud would have been hurtful to one of the few people he loved.

Although he would not put a period to himself, sometimes he could not help but wish that oblivion would find him. Etienne forced a smile, hoping that it did not look as much like a grimace as it felt. "Do you think me so fragile a fellow?" He pulled at the handle of his walking stick to partially reveal a wicked blade. "Although I can no longer enspell any who might

15

wish to attack me, you forget that I can still defend myself."

"I forget nothing," she grumbled.

Etienne took her hand again. "This coat is a disguise. While I can deal with thieves, I have no wish to attract them. My garb will likely persuade them to seek more profitable prey. As for the scarf, I would have you know that it was fashioned for me by my sister Giselle with her own hands. I have chosen it as my signal flag for the evening, so that you may know of my safe arrival."

A bitter wind blew as he alighted, making him all the more grateful for the footman's stout wool. It would be far warmer than anything in his wardrobe of finely tailored greatcoats, designed more for appearance than utility.

"Mages!" The word articulated a wealth of contempt, compassion and concern all at once, but she said nothing more until the carriage door was nearly closed.

"Take care, my boy." He barely heard her whisper. "You are all that I have left."

The snow was abating, but the wind was rising as he wound his sister's scarf to shield his face. The moon slid out from between the clouds to glint on the newly fallen snow turning it almost silver, like a mirror.

A scrying pool.

Etienne shivered, although it wasn't from the cold.

It was not a true Vision, but instinct told him that it had significance. Something of import was about to happen.

CHAPTER 2

*T*he cab came to a jarring standstill and a cacophony of curses and shouts exploded from the driver's perch.

"What has happened?" Genevieve asked as the jarvey opened the door to the commotion.

"Can't see it from 'ere, but tell is there be a wagon round the bend got itself a broken shaft!" he explained, punctuating the information with an oath and a swig from his flask. "Narrow road 'ere. No room to turn round. Rigs up front. More linin' up in back!"

Genevieve felt her stomach churning as the ephemeral courage she had been attempting to fix in place came loose from its sticking point. The driver eyed her sympathetically, his breath rising in puffs as he spoke. "Trapped like a rat in a dog pit, we are! Might be another ride to find past the wreck or go by foot the rest of the way. Ain't too far to Portman Square from 'ere."

Reluctantly, Genevieve put her head out the door and saw the truth of it. After gathering up her parcel and adjusting the hood of her cloak, she stepped down to get her bearings. It was a lucky thing that she had often made deliveries for Dale's using this route. The

17

driver was correct about the relatively short distance to her destination.

Even though the snowfall had momentarily subsided, there was no turning back after having come this far. As was the case with so many other aspects of her life these days, there seemed to be little alternative but to move forward and hope for the best.

Declining the gracious offer of a fortifying draught from the driver's flask, Genevieve paid her fare and began the trek to Wodesby House. Passing the bottleneck of a broken down dray, she congratulated herself on having made a wise choice. Some of the trapped drivers had already unhitched their horses, unwilling to risk their animals, or themselves, to what promised to be a freezing cold night on the blocked road.

Unfortunately, she quickly discovered that there was not a hack to be had in the nearly empty street beyond. If she intended to reach Portman Square, it would have to be on foot.

Although snow obscured the landscape, she still found enough familiar markers to point her on her way. After she crossed Oxford Street, she recalled, there was a shorter path through the mews. The temporary respite had ended and the curtain of white was growing heavier by the moment. Even a few steps saved might make the difference between reaching her destination or being forced to seek uncertain shelter.

As Genevieve had hoped, the slimmer open spaces behind the houses helped to provide a break against the driving wind. It was easier going and the drifts did not seem nearly so deep. The snowfall was abating again and the moon began to peer wanly through the clouds, revealing some wagon ruts that gave her firmer treading through the snow. By her reckoning, her goal was no more than a few minutes away when she found herself jerked backward. A man in a ragged coat clutched her arm, peering at her like a raven contemplating a prime piece of carrion.

"Well, well, wha' 'ave we 'ere?" His breath rose in a cloud of stinking miasma as he spoke. Even through the layers of her clothing, Genevieve sensed the evil intent rampant in his touch. His vile thoughts, revealed by her Gift, chilled her even more than the cold and wet. Yanking the reticule from her hand, he shoved her, deliberately sending her tumbling on her back into the road.

There would be no opportunity to run.

"An meself lookin' for summat to keep me warm on a cold winter's night, eh?" The clink of coin drew a gap-toothed grin as he shook the bag.

She rose to her elbows as he fumbled with the drawstrings, embracing the shock of icy wet, letting it feed her anger as she gathered her strength, preparing to defend herself against the oncoming assault. Genevieve knew she would have to move quickly. He would find the empty sheath in her bag and wonder where the blade had gone.

"Now don't ye be goin' nowheres." He eyed her with a sour smirk as he started towards her. "Yer ain't done with old Davy, yet."

Genevieve's chill-stiffened fingers gripped the enchanted weapon that she had secured within the pocket sewn into her cloak. His name was an unexpected gift that would surely amplify the power of her spell. With a soft murmur, she began to activate the charm that would make it strike true.

"Step away from her!" A deep voice declared from the darkness. "She is mine!"

Her would-be assailant whirled and Genevieve saw a swift-moving shadow, heard the swish as a thin blade cut through the gloom to glint momentarily in a wisp of moonlight. Her attacker screamed, clutching at his shoulder as he let the bag drop.

Blood dripped on the snow as Genevieve scrabbled sideways, trying to get to her feet as a cloaked figure interposed between herself and her attacker.

"Beware!" she screamed as the thief pulled a knife of his own. For a moment, Genevieve thought Davy would charge. Instead, he threw the blade. Narrowly missing its target, the weapon landed with a quivering thud in a wooden post behind him. When the swordsman advanced, blade at ready, Davy cursed, turned, and fled, disappearing into the night.

Her savior reached back to retrieve Davy's knife and Genevieve gasped as she caught the first glimpse of a black domino that covered his head almost entirely. Only his piercing blue eyes and the red sensuous slash of a mouth were visible beneath the mask of silken fabric.

Genevieve held her breath, thinking that she was being cast, yet again, from the cauldron into the coals as he came towards her. Her previous use of Davy's name to guide the spell to its target meant she had to remove the personalizing charm. Otherwise, her athame would sail off until it found its objective or lost its power. The stranger turned his back to her, his gaze following Davy as he fled.

She used his momentary distraction to put as much distance as possible between herself and the masked man while she attempted to renew her blade's power. Genevieve had no illusions about the stranger's intentions. Given his appearance, it was likely he was yet another predator who considered her a prize won from the weaker scavenger. He had declared as much, claiming her as his possession.

She attempted to rise, the knife at ready to strike true again, but too much time in the ice had numbed her grip. The weapon fell from her frozen fingers to slip uselessly into the snow. As she stretched to retrieve the blade, a strong hand reached from behind and levered her to her feet.

"Mademoiselle, êtes-vous blessée?" His query about her well-being was delivered in a deep bass. The accents of a Parisian aristocrat were unmistakable.

He grasped her hand and she breathed a silent paean of thanks to the Light. If the man meant her harm, her Gift would have detected it in his touch. There was no trace of malice in this stranger's intentions.

His fingers were bare and cold against her arm as he helped her to rise. Once she was upright, he turned her to face him. Reflected in the bluest eyes that she had ever seen, she saw a mixture of concern, compassion and an emotion that was more difficult to define.

Could it be admiration?

Oddly, she felt no fear, only gratitude when his arms wrapped around her, sharing his warmth, giving her much needed support for knees that had suddenly turned to jelly. There was comfort in the familiar cadence of his words, an unreasonable sense of safety in a strong embrace, feelings she had not experienced since well before illness had ended her husband's life.

She took a deep breath, inhaling the scents of tobacco, wool, mint and man. Closing her eyes, Genevieve indulged herself in the momentary illusion of being sheltered and cherished. Had she imagined the approval she had seen in his eyes? How could he possibly think her to be anything but a worthless fool when she felt as if she were falling apart?

The thought forced her back into reality. The worry in his gaze reminded her she had yet to answer his question.

"Je suis indemne."

21

Even as she assured him she was physically un-harmed, she knew her heart was about to break. All it took was one look beyond his broad shoulder and any pretense of well-being faded. "I am unhurt," she added in English, even though she knew it was a lie in any language.

Spread upon the snow was the wreckage of her hopes. The bundle containing her shoes was partially undone. The delicate silk was likely soaked through. Her reticule was dark with damp. If enough water had gotten into it, the magic within the precious package it contained was probably beyond the possibility of sal-vage. Beneath her cloak, she could feel the clammy, clinging chill of her wet gown and knew it was doubtlessly damaged by her fall and stained by mois-ture and dirt.

All at once, Genevieve felt herself trembling. *A normal reaction to the cold,* she told herself. But as a witch whose powers were based in the detection of truth, she found it hard to believe her own lies. What she felt went far beyond the physical. The strength of her emotions made her shake.

Anger at those who scorned her family and her son because of choices made out of dire necessity. Fury at the need driving her to endanger herself on a freezing winter's night for what ought to have been freely of-fered to any of Merlin's Children in need. Bitterness at being forced to come begging a boon at the Chief Mage's door.

Genevieve realized that the stranger in the domino was speaking to her again.

"*Votre destination, mademoiselle?*" he asked.

She wanted to go home, but she could not. Not in this state. Her mother would think the worst and de-scend into one of her dark episodes. Louis would be devastated with guilt, knowing that she had come to grief for his sake. And Marcel! She didn't even want to think of the hissing fit she would receive from her familiar because she had ignored his advice and left him behind.

There was little choice but to move forward. Lord Wodesby's housekeeper, Tante Reina, would help Genevieve to put herself in order and find a conveyance to carry her home. With luck, the members of her household would be deep in their dreams when she returned. Explanations and repercussions would wait until morning.

In the meantime, her quest was over, even before it had begun. Desolation swallowed her, the word *failure* thrumming through her mind with the force of one of Merlin's great spells. All her plans for Louis, however desperate they might have been, were destroyed.

The combination of cold and misery had her teeth chattering badly. She could barely sputter out the address on Portman Square.

"Wodesby House?" The stranger seemed momentarily taken aback. She barely kept herself from protesting aloud at the bereft feeling when he stepped away from her. Then, he took her hand and removed her gloves. The touch of his bare skin upon hers stunned her. That momentary link provided more than mere warmth and a connection that she could not fully define.

A sense of sanctuary.

She almost moaned aloud when that comforting bond diminished as his fur-lined gloves enveloped her. The addition of his scarf added notes of bergamot and citrus to the masculine perfume that caressed her sensitive nose. His coat surrounded her, draping her in the remnants of his warmth. Genevieve closed her eyes and basked in the cocoon of temporary safety for a moment.

Forcing herself back into reality, she looked around her.

Strewn belongings and the depressions in the snow told the story of the night, the desperation of those frightening moments when she had crawled inch by inch in a seemingly hopeless fight for her life. Despite the added heat of the heavy wool, her shivers grew stronger, seeming to come from the very core of her, as she considered how differently the tale might have ended.

CHAPTER 3

*E*tienne had first noticed the unaccompanied woman trudging through the snow on Oxford Street. When she turned bearing north, it rapidly became evident they were headed in the same general direction. Rather than approach her, he thought it more prudent to keep his distance in order to avoid giving her a fright. Instead, he had been quietly shadowing her, playing an internal variation on the English game of questions, seeking answers based on observation as they slogged along.

Despite the snow, she walked with unusual grace.

Was she a Cyprian in search of a potential customer?

He eliminated the possibility. Even in this foul weather, there were far easier and potentially more lucrative fields to glean closer at hand. Moreover, her determined gait was not the seductive dance of a woman whose profession made every move into a calculated lure. A *fille de joie* would be surveying the area around her, on the lookout for potential clientele.

Was she an upper servant then?

That could be. Her cloak was not *à la mode*, but of excellent quality. A mistress might give such a no longer fashionable garment to her abigail. Moreover, it was not designed to *display the goods*, as it were. A hood covered her head, shadowing her face and the drape concealed her form, providing yet another argument that she was not a lady of the night.

She carried a wrapped, string-bound parcel and a reticule. Might she be on an errand?

What manner of task would be of sufficient urgency to send a lone woman out in such weather on a deserted street where she would be easy prey for all types of London's predators?

The moment after he had posed that question to himself, it was almost as if his Seer's Gift had returned with a Foresight.

A ruffian slithered from the mews to waylay her. Before Etienne could blink, the woman had been knocked to the ground and the thief was rooting through her belongings. The encounter that followed was a disappointment. A true *mêlée*, beating the villain into a bloody pulp, would have been far more satisfying. Instead, the man had been routed too easily and escaped without any punishment for his crime other than the loss of his knife.

Keeping watch on the direction of the coward's flight to make certain that he was not about to rearm and return, Etienne backed up to retrieve the blade. The throw had been close, he realized, extremely close.

Once he was certain the brigand was well and truly gone, Etienne turned his attention to the woman, only to see she was no longer where he had expected to find her. Furrows in the snow marked the path she had crawled.

She was on her knees, focused on the blade in her hand, preparing to fight for her life and honor.

Idiot. He castigated himself internally, suddenly realizing the picture that he must present.

A masked man, coming out of the night!

No doubt, she was expecting to be assaulted yet again. Her struggle to retrieve the knife that had slipped from her trembling hand declared her apprehension. If he did not take care, he might well find himself at the tip of her blade.

Une femme de courage.

Before she could recover her weapon, Etienne was beside her. Gently, but firmly, he drew her up. He prepared himself for a struggle and readied his explanations to reassure her, but the initial look of terrified determination on her face abruptly faded away. The tension in her stance dissipated.

For a moment, Etienne thought that she was going to faint. Hastily, he put his arms around her to keep her from falling. Looking up, as if to study him, the woman regarded him in puzzlement, seemingly not quite sure of what to make of him.

The cowl of her green cloak had fallen to her shoulders to reveal skin like the marble of a statue in the moonlight. Her face, still unnaturally pale from fright, was a frame for eyes of glorious amber that seemed impossibly wide. Shimmers of light reflected from the snow, limning her hair, reminding him of autumn leaves in the deep forest. Browns were traced with glints of gold and auburn.

Her *coiffure* must have come unmoored in her struggles. An abundance of intricate braids and pins dangled against the damp wool. She seemed the embodiment of his grandmother's tales of dryads and fair folk, dancing in their enchanted circles among their trees. Etienne found himself longing to touch that silken softness, to trace the ripe lines of a luscious mouth of a rich red that reminded him of English holly berries.

Then she closed her eyes and took a deep breath,

breaking the unspoken spell that held both his manners
and good sense in thrall. He had not even made a query
about her well-being.

*What a beast she must think him, to touch her so inti-
mately without tendering a single word of reassurance?*

Truly her amazing display of bravery must have
muddled his brain. Etienne rushed to make amends for
his lack of *savoir-vivre*—in French. He was castigating
himself for an oaf and was about to correct his *faux pas*
with a translation when her soft assurance in the same
tongue surprised him.

From the quality of her accent, it was clear that they
shared a native language.

The sound of the speech of his birth held a familiar
music he seldom heard in his exile. As she spoke he realized how much he had missed it. Even a few words
demonstrated a refinement in her address and bearing.
Was she an *émigré* then? Down on her luck? The war
had displaced so many, devoured lives and fortunes.

Before he could ask any more questions, she began
to shake. Once again, he chastised himself for his care-
lessness. Although she claimed to be without wounds,
it did not mean she was unharmed. Her hands were like
blocks of ice, clad in thin gloves, almost glazed over
with melted snow and cold.

He peeled them from her fingers, and tossed them
aside, ignoring her gasp of protest as he pulled his own
from his pocket. His gloves were like large furry paws
on her. The hood of her cloak was damp, so he
wrapped Giselle's scarf around the alabaster column of
her neck and over her head. Lastly, he draped her in his
borrowed coat, but the warmth did little to still her
quaking body. Her look as she opened her eyes and
scanned their surroundings served to explain her
reaction.

This place was her battlefield. Many a time during

the war, he had seen this before, this trembling of the soul when it realizes how very closely it had danced with death.

Etienne assessed their situation again. There was still a possibility her attacker might return, with or without friends, or another of the denizens of the streets might deem them a tempting target. It was time to move on.

"Votre adresse, s'il vous plaît, Mademoiselle?"

He could barely hear her reply for the chattering of her teeth, but to his surprise, the address on Portman Square she gave was Wodesby's. Adding that to his observations, he surmised she was a servant. Tonight's revels would require a surplus of staff beyond those already in residence at the Chief Mage's home.

Etienne grasped her by the shoulders and held her at arm's length, before cupping her face in his hands. *"Nous devons y aller,"* he implored her, emphasizing the need in English. "We must go."

But it was as if she no longer could hear him. The terror was engulfing her.

Although magic was barred to him, he had learned the art of manipulation from a master. Harsh measures were required. *English*, he decided, *with both a sneer and a threat*.

"Can you walk?" he asked. "Or do you wish to be carried like a piece of baggage?"

* * *

IT WAS as if she were observing a character upon a stage, only the actress was herself.

And she was playing the fool.

She could feel the truth of his concern as he told her they had to move on. The feeling of his calloused fingers on her bare skin was rough but comforting in the strength and the determination that he radiated. His speech had the gentle rebuke of an angry parent to a recalcitrant child.

"Can you walk?" he asked. "Or do you wish to be carried like a piece of baggage?"

Although his tones were harsh, his touch declared that her safety was paramount to him.

If he chose to do so, he did seem strong enough to carry her. There was definite appeal in being the temporary heroine of a Minerva Press novel. Those females in perpetual peril were often whisked about like so many lightweight portmanteaus in the arms of their heroes. But that mode of conveyance would pose considerable difficulty, especially given the size of some of the drifts of snow in their path.

Unless he could levitate her? But she immediately decided it unlikely.

Although he was obviously familiar with Wodesby House, he was evidently not of the Blood, not with his work-worn hands, bare of any mage's ring. Perhaps he was one of the Chief Mage's Outsider or OutBlood friends? According to the grumbling gossip she heard in her shop, there were far too many of *those people* hobnobbing with Lord Wodesby these days.

Certainly, none of the mages in her acquaintance would deign to get their hands dirty with manual labor. Few of the Blood pure would have had the desire to intervene in a potentially dangerous situation on behalf of a person who appeared to be nothing more than an Outsider. If any of Merlin's children had, somehow, been moved to intercede, they would have used magic as their weapon of choice.

It was a valuable lesson. Relying upon a single weapon, even a magical one, was insufficient. In the future, she promised to correct that deficiency in her education and better learn how to defend herself.

Those would be useful skills to pass on to Louis, and she vowed to learn whatever she could, since the likelihood of finding him a mentor was diminishing by the minute.

Even though she hadn't wept since Owen's death, she suddenly felt like crying, but there were no tears. Had she somehow depleted the supply? Appearing before the assembly wet and ragged as a guttersnipe would get her laughed out the door.

Her rescuer was speaking again and she sensed a change in the emotions emanating from him.

"Shall we go on to Wodesby House?" he asked. "Or do you want to wait here until your attacker comes back with his friends, *mademoiselle?*"

The question pulled her back from the brink of her brown study.

She was causing danger to them both. If there was to be a future for her family, she would have to move forward.

"Drink." She heard the command and felt a spout of metal at her lips.

"Drink it, now!"

Genevieve sputtered at the first swallow, but the liquor spread through her like molten fire, warming her from the inside out.

"Better? It is excellent, no?" he asked, with the politesse of a man who had offered an aperitif after a formal dinner.

"Courage in a bottle," she agreed, forcing herself to move. She picked up her parcel.

"You have plenty to spare, but sometimes a bit of extra is helpful." She heard amusement in his observation.

"Let me get my things." Genevieve found her voice and fought to keep it steady, forcing herself to step back from the stranger's touch. It made her feel far too safe. Her heartbeat sped with the return of fear and in-security and she used those emotions to move her forward.

"Allow me." Her rescuer offered as he plucked the package from her fumbling hands and neatly retied it for her. "Are you employed at Wodesby House?"

"Upon occasion," she replied, retrieving her reticule. It was no lie. She had helped Tante Reina and Rowan in preparations involving some of the unique and de-manding ingredients she sold.

Genevieve pulled out the empty scabbard, resisting the urge to quickly check the bag's other contents. Whatever had occurred was past now, with no way to change it. The athame's blade gleamed upon the snow and she felt an inordinate pride when she managed to keep her hand from wavering when she returned it to its sheath.

Except for his occasional invective about foolish servants wandering about alone at night, the rest of their walk was mostly silent. Trying to keep up with his long stride while attempting to speak, robbed her of breath. She saw no reason to correct his false impres-sion that she was a servant, even though her impru-dence was entirely her own. In all likelihood, they would never meet again.

As he guided her through the streets, he put her in mind of Marcel stalking prey. Despite the snow, he moved almost like a feline on the prowl, fluid and ready for a fight. Genevieve noticed his evening wear was of far better quality than the coat that had con-cealed it. The flow of fine fabric revealed a powerful, broad-shouldered body owing more to nature than to a tailor's padded trickery.

They were closer to Portman Square than she had reckoned. In a few minutes, she saw a cavalcade of fine carriages lining the street, their owners gathered for the Chief Mage's annual celebration of the Longest Night.

Lord Wodesby had lately revived an ancient tradition. This year, all of Merlin's Blood and their kin were welcome to celebrate the Longest Night and ask a boon of England's Chief Mage. Genevieve no longer had any intention of seeking a favor. It would be completely foolish to walk into the great hall of Wodesby House in her bedraggled state on the arm of a man she could not even name. As a woman who relied on trade with the Blood for her livelihood, she could not afford to be mired in scandal. When they neared the foot of Wodesby House's broad marble stair, Genevieve decided to take her leave.

"I think I will find my way home now," she informed her erstwhile escort. "There will surely be a carriage for hire."

The stranger shook his head and tightened his hold. "If you do not reside on premises, I am sure a place can be found for you to spend the night. In any case, you need to get warm and dry before you venture out again. I will speak to your employer.

"There is no need," she said hastily. "Surely, you have done enough, sir. I am known as Genevieve Dale. The debt of my life is in your hands."

He did not identify himself in return. Although it was disappointing, Genevieve respected his reticence, making no further inquiries of him. Names had intrinsic power, especially among Merlin's children. He owed her nothing. She owed him everything. Perhaps, he was unaware of the significance of a life debt?

But his reaction proved otherwise. He began to chuckle as he led her to the servant's entrance. "A gracious offer, but know you there is no debt of a life between us, Genevieve Dale."

With exquisite care, he unwound the length of

poorly knit purple from her neck and with each glancing touch she felt the force of his amused arrogance. "You did give me a warning which kept a knife from my throat," he said.

"I will not allow you to deny the debt," she said, slipping off the coat to return to him. "You know full well that you were in no real peril, sir."

"You are an impudent wench. There are few women with the nerve to call me a liar. " His eyes glinted appreciatively. "Very well then. I shall have to seek another form of payment. Three kisses. I shall take the first now."

His condescension grated and for a moment, she wanted to tell him she had something of greater value to offer. Instead, she nodded a silent assent.

There was a moment of hesitation as he slowly raised his mask. Despite its seemingly loose drape, she realized the domino was much like the one that she carried, charmed to expose only so much as the wearer wished.

His speech and swordsmanship had caused her to surmise the man was an aristocrat. His clothing beneath the battered coat, well-tailored and definitely *à la mode*, had reinforced that presumption. However, like his outer garb, the reality beneath his disguise, posed a contradiction.

What he revealed of his face, like his hands, told an inconsistent tale. Fading beneath the winter pallor, she recognized the deep tan of a summer spent in the sun. The stranger's physique had been honed by hard labor. Those muscular arms did not belong to an aristocrat who lifted little more than a glass of wine.

His features seemed to confirm her conclusions that this Frenchman was an émigré, fallen on hard times. An OutBlood perhaps? His aquiline nose, sumptuous lips and high cheekbones put Genevieve in mind of the images of the Roman emperors who had gazed haughtily from her late *grand-père's* collection of ancient coins. She wondered if the upper part of the stranger's face matched those long-ago likenesses, but he kept himself partially masked.

He must have realized her frustration and wagged a chiding finger which ended up brushing her cheek. "I am not someone you would wish to know, *chérie*. It is better this way."

His lips touched hers, gently at first, but the caress soon became something deeper, an acknowledgement of the bond of danger they had shared, then a demand claiming all she had promised and more. His hand fisted in her hair, pulling her closer.

Genevieve felt a long dormant part of her flaring to life. Desire kindled and she returned his kiss in full measure, her mouth exploring, sparring with his. Deeper and deeper they plunged, his questing kiss asking for everything he was due. Payment with interest.

A roar of raucous laughter erupted in the street and he thrust her away from him abruptly.

"I would say that would constitute a measure of recompense," he told her dismissively before pushing the door open.

Genevieve would have argued the point, but Tante Reina's exclamation of dismay cut off the possibility of a reply.

"Take care of her." Her savior ushered her inside, making his demand in imperious tones that brooked no contradiction.

Every eye turned to the door. Once again, there was a hollow feeling in the pit of Genevieve's stomach. The huge kitchen was packed to the bursting. She had forgotten the house would be full of servants tonight. Other than the tribe of Romany who served the Chief

Mage's household, there was an abundance of extra staff. From the look of it, a crowd of coachmen and tigers had been invited in from the cold to partake of the Solstice wassail.

Genevieve turned around, ready to charge back outside, no matter what the stranger said. But the entrance was shut. He had disappeared.

Tante Reina ignored her protests as she pulled Genevieve deeper into the crowded room. If her aim was to be unremarked, she had failed utterly. Gossip had a magic all its own. By the morning the tale of her woebegone arrival would be served at every breakfast table in town.

"You will be coming with me," the wizened woman demanded. "There is much to be done."

"Perhaps you can find me a ride home?"

Tante Reina put her hands on her hips and shook her head. "Look outside!"

Through the kitchen window, Genevieve could see the snow beginning to descend in a blanket of white once again. It would be foolish beyond permission to go back out until the storm abated.

"It is your right to be a coward, but I will not allow you to be a fool," Tante Reina declared. "Will you allow me to assist you, milady?"

Although Tante Reina asked a question, it was clear that she would brook no answer but an affirmative one.

CHAPTER 4

*I*n the confusion, Etienne easily made his way upstairs through one of the servants' passages. During the months of his parole under Wodesby's supervision, he had come to know the house extremely well and he was soon in the heart of the celebration. Many others were masked and anonymous to varying degrees. As Etienne had hoped, the less than *luxe* coat and absence of a mage's ring caused those of the Higher Circles of the Blood to give him a wide berth.

Much as Etienne was heartily sick of the war and its aftermath, he could not dismiss the growing evidence of a nascent conspiracy against Wodesby. Although it galled him, he owed the man his existence twice over. Due to Etienne's crimes against Rowan, the unsettled balance on her side of the scale was even more skewed. Hopefully, his efforts tonight would provide some measure of equilibrium. Life debts were a great burden, even between enemies, much more so, between friends.

The thought of life debts brought Genevieve Dale to mind. How was she faring below stairs, he wondered? The very thought of her offer of a life debt had him shaking his head in surprise.

What in Merlin's name had possessed him to seek payment in kisses? He was no stranger to passion, yet there had been something more than mere desire in that brief mating of lips tasting of cognac. A curious mix of sensuality and innocence had demanded an answer from deep within him. For a moment, he had lost himself, forgotten everything but her, the softness of her skin, the scent of her hair, the look in her eyes, the feel of her in his arms. But for the interruption, they would have remained locked in an embrace until—

No, there would be none of that. He was determined not to be like his father, the Devil Comte. The elder du Le Fey had used and discarded people like pairs of old pattens. Unfortunately, there seemed to be more of the old man in him than Etienne thought, if he was tempted to take advantage of a respectable woman's gratitude and treat her like a cheap whore on the side of a building.

Etienne forced himself back to the situation at hand.

Slipping easily through the milling crowd, Etienne found a recessed alcove opposite the grand marble stair and the dais where Damian and Rowan were receiving their guests. Neither of them bothered with the useless pretense of masks. As she turned to reply to a remark from her husband, Etienne could see a mixture of love and magic in his stepmother's gaze.

Perhaps time did heal some wounds. He was surprised to find that there was no longer any spark of desire within him for the woman who had originally been pledged to him. He had never given much credence to the tales of mated souls, but as he watched Rowan and Damien's hands twine, Etienne could feel the sum of their magic coalescing around them. That totality was far greater than their individual Gifts.

Although Etienne had consigned such unions to his mother's fairy stories, he had once nursed hopes for some level of mutual fulfillment in his marriage. But his betrothal to Circe had cured him completely of all such *bourgeois* delusions.

Others were observing the Chief Mage and Mistress. No magic was required to discern the malice lurking behind some of the masks. Etienne had long acknowledged the truth of his father's maxim that the length of a Chief Mage's term was proportionate to the power of magic he held to crush his enemies. Unfortunately, Damien's deplorable tendencies to take the path of diplomacy instead of force were putting him at risk. The traitorous tendrils of covert correspondence which had helped draw Etienne back to London provided clear evidence of that.

On the Longest Night, tradition demanded that all of the Blood and their kin be welcomed in peace. By Merlin's law, any witch or mage, high or low, had the right to approach the chief of their clan, coven, or country to request a boon. Even Etienne's father had forced himself to endure an uncomfortable degree of *égalité* as part of the Yule celebration, and the old comte had been an *aristo* to his very bones. Even so, the Devil Comte had been selective when he opened the gates of Hell.

Despite any pretense otherwise, those of the prominent families of the High Circles formed their own aristocracy. Even though their boundaries were not delineated by the powers of candle and salt, their precincts were far more impermeable than sacred mounds or even the hallowed grounds of the Outsider elite's Almack's. It was much harder to dance within the elevated heights of the covens than to waltz among London's ton.

All pretenses of noblesse oblige notwithstanding, since Damien had unreservedly thrown open his doors to the old ways, some of those scornfully known as *hedge witches* or *cottage mages* actually bothered to take part in the revels that were once exclusive. Etienne was seeking to find out if the Chief Mage's democratic penchant was prompting some of Merlin's Blood to do more than grumble.

As Etienne had hoped, his worn coat was almost like a spell of invisibility amidst those who deemed themselves to be his betters. Nonetheless he kept to the shadows, scrutinizing the crowd, until an unexpected touch on his shoulder roused him from his thoughts.

"Are you sure that you want to be alone?" A masked witch purred the question, her predatory hand creeping up toward the pulse on his neck, attempting to reach beneath the drape of his domino. A ruby naming jewel rested in a valley of décolletage that would have induced a blush upon a Parisian courtesan.

"You have no leave to touch me." Etienne tried to contain his annoyance, a caveat in his guttural whisper. A witch with any claim to proper deportment would know that physically impinging on another without permission was a violation of Blood etiquette. With so many Gifts reliant upon the tactile, only an intimate would dare to lay a hand on another of Merlin's children with such familiarity.

Although he wore no indication that he was a mage, Etienne knew such contact among strangers was frowned upon, even among the Outsider ton.

"Then you must touch me," she whispered.

The words were a demand wrapped in tendrils of magical compulsion, tugging against his will. For a moment, he was tempted to grab the witch by the wrist and drag her before Rowan, proclaiming her perfidy.

Minor compulsions, especially those stirring already nascent emotions, were often difficult to discern. When enacted upon a victim outside one's own coven, especially someone with weak powers or without magic of their own, such spells were nearly impossible to perceive or resist. No Outsider would have been able to withstand her spell and even a weak mage would have unknowingly found his appetites whetted.

Her eyes glittered with satisfaction as his hands moved upwards. But instead of reaching for her breasts, his fingers slid into his inner pocket to slip on the mage's ring he had inherited along with his great-grandfather's estate.

"Take care who you wish to impose yourself upon, witch," Etienne growled, holding his temper in check as he grasped her wrist and pulled her roving hand from his person. He nodded towards Rowan. "Your Mistress looks ill upon coercion."

There was a brief moment of alarm in her eyes, as she wondered how he had detected her ploy. Only the most powerful mages could sense minor compulsions. Despite Etienne's loss of the ring and band of France, many of the passive skills that had come to him as part of his former office still remained. He retained the ability to detect and identify the use of magic by others, as well as the capacity to resist their manipulations.

However, when she saw the trifling jewel upon his finger, all traces of fear immediately vanished. "I thought you were an Outsider in a smelly coat, a no-body," she declared, summing him up with a calculating glance, weighing her expensive gown and jewels against his peon's clothing and ancient ring before dismissing him with a decisive sniff of disdain. "An old mage's ring does not transform a toad to a prince." She turned up her nose. "Tell Lady Wodesby whatever you like, if you believe she will pay heed to your croaking." With a final sneer, she stalked away.

Etienne watched her disappear into the crowd, his hands fisting in contained rage as he memorized every detail of her costume. A few words with one of the Rom would suffice to make certain no other guests were preyed upon.

It shamed him now to admit that any accusations made by a person of lesser power would have been summarily dismissed in his own court in France. The unknown witch had thought him an Outsider, vulnerable, and available for her amusement.

Even here, under Rowan's rule, the witch would likely be correct. If he pulled off the mask, the Comte du Le Fey wearing the *passé* talisman of a long-dead man was worse than the cipher she had named him. It would be his word against hers.

His history would not dispose any to trust him. He was a mage without honor, judged guilty of coercion himself. If he used the Gifts he was born with to defend himself, Justice had declared he would lose them forever. Only the dregs of what he had once been had protected him against the blandishments of the predatory witch.

Promises broken must be mended.
Else Gifts forever will be rended.
If joy is what you seek to reap.
Give away what you would keep.

Etienne had spent over a year trying to decipher that cryptic pronouncement. He was beginning to think elusive hope was part of his punishment.

There was a stir near the stair and he was reminded of his promise. It would not do to miss his grandmother's grand entrance. Lady Morgan's carriage had been among those mired in the congestion out front. So, despite the delay caused by delivering Genevieve Dale to safety, Etienne would be able to witness his grandmother's arrival.

Hastily, he draped his sister's scarf around his neck. All at once the subtle fragrances of jasmine, vanilla, and sandalwood surrounded him. Was it possible Genevieve Dale was somewhere nearby? He stepped out into the open, scanning the crush, before he realized the wool had picked up some of the woman's essence. He inhaled deeply, recalling her valiant nature, her warmth, and the silken touch of her skin.

The memory eased the sting of his reaction to the witch's slights, making him seem a petulant little boy. If anyone could be deemed a nobody, it was Genevieve Dale, but she had defended herself with the courage of a warrior. Etienne wondered if the woman had understood the serious obligation involved in the offer of a life debt. Did she realize he could ask anything he chose in payment for her survival? His father would have been furious that he had let her off so lightly.

Etienne held his breath as his grandmother made her way down the stairs. Every eye was upon her and he was amazed by her enviable *sang froid*. The octogenarian glided serenely into the maelstrom of mages and witches. Other than the slightest of tremors as she lifted her jeweled lorgnette to survey the ballroom, he could see no signs of nerves.

Brewing conspiracies were not the only reason he had returned to London before the holidays. Lord Wodesby had also kept Etienne abreast of the fact that his grandmother was increasingly isolating herself in her London home. Although the old woman would never mention it, Etienne knew his shame was the reason.

After the Judgement, he had planned to keep away from his grandmother. Time would mitigate the damage done by his association with her. At least that had been his hope. As she swept across the room, it was clear that his absence might have inadvertently done her more harm than service.

The challenge had animated her. There was not a family of the Blood without a poorly concealed demon or two in the dungeon, Lady Morgan had reminded him. Despite her assurances that she had weathered far worse social storms than her grandson's disgrace, Etienne had been less than sanguine about her reception in the High Circles.

Head held high, with the Morgan diamonds glittering on her neck and her ears, she inclined her head regally toward those she still considered friends. Her satisfied smile assured old enemies that the years had not erased past slights, nor mitigated future retribution.

She glanced briefly in his direction and took note of the ugly scarf. A light nod signified her satisfaction he had arrived without falling victim to any of her dire predictions. With an arch smile, that put him in mind of a cat in a dairy, she walked across the ballroom, the crowd parting before her like the Red Sea.

A wall of silence rippled around her. The weather outside was balmy in comparison to the chill that spread with the hush.

"Blessings and greetings." Her holiday felicitations chimed through the hall. The grace of her obeisance would have done credit to a woman half her age and her nonchalant air gave no recognition to the waves of speculation beginning to rise behind her.

Etienne let go of a breath he did not know he was holding when Damien and Rowan eschewed the usual ceremony and stepped down from the platform to greet his grandmother. It was a gesture of respect granted to a select few, one which signified their unreserved approval. Henceforth, any insult to Lady

Morgan would be a slight to the England's premier mage and witch.

His grandmother received the homage with her usual reserve, but the sheen in her eyes almost outshone her jewels.

At that moment, Etienne knew his debts to Rowan and Damien would forever be beyond payment.

CHAPTER 5

hile all attention was fixed upon the drama at the dais, Etienne handed off his coat and scarf to one of Tante Reina's grandchildren, and sent a message to Rowan, warning of the predatory ruby-wearing witch. He strolled to the location set for the series of clandestine meetings he had planned.

Rowan had created a gallery of rooms, each decorated with illusions of magical places, past and present. The pyramids loomed in the desert. A series of steps led to a ziggurat in the ancient city of Ur. Rocks painted by nature into glorious reds were vividly rendered. Etienne could almost feel the emanations of power from the stones marking a significant place of power upon the North American continent.

The last of the rooms was familiar and therefore likely to receive the fewest visitors. No one who had not been given notice of his whereabouts would expect to find the Comte du Le Fey there.

The sarsen pillars on Salisbury Plain were reproduced with excruciating accuracy. As Etienne seated himself in a secluded corner of the gallery, he felt the candlelight transforming into moonglow and felt a tremor of trepidation. He told himself it was not an omen, only their plan proceeding as charted.

The sound of footsteps roused him from his reverie. By the time his first visitor found him, Etienne had grabbed two glasses containing fine French brandy and set them on the table. He gestured his guest to a seat.

So long as the silence was unbroken, Etienne could hope that his guess at the identity of the costumed figure was mistaken, but with the first words, his fears were confirmed. The sea-roughed voice of Thomas Cochrane was unmistakable even without its muted Scot's burr. Etienne took a deep swallow of brandy.

"Think ye that our Chief Mage paid the excise?" Thomas asked, pulling up a chair and seating himself in a pool of shadow.

"I have no doubt of it," Etienne informed him softly, wondering what the man Napoleon had dubbed *Le Loups de Mers* was up to now. Unfortunately, if ever a man was a loose cannon, it was the Sea Wolf.

"I believe it myself," Thomas said, moving his domino aside to take a sip of his drink, momentarily revealing a lined visage sculpted by years of wind and wave. "Damien was always a man to take the straight path, even when a detour might better serve. I have to be saying I admire yer cheek, meeting right under Lord Wodesby's nose."

"I still have a few old friends," Etienne said with a shrug. "Between the bespelled tables hushing our words and the masks hiding our faces, some are not even averse to conversing with me while they come to pay their tribute to their Chief. Who knows? I might yet make some new friends this night."

There was a bitter twist to Thomas' smile as he leaned back into his chair. "Aye, a man ought to be grateful for friends both old and new, especially pariahs like ourselves."

"True words, milord," Etienne said, putting his own resentment on display.

"Come, come, Etienne. We dispensed with the honorifics between us, long ago," Thomas waved a dismissive hand. "We two, and Charles," he sighed at the memory. "Yer father was France's Chief Mage back then and ye were sailing with the Comte de Linois when I was captured. Good times, eh?"

"Good times! Leave it to you to make it sound like a pleasure cruise! You wreaked havoc on us before you were obliged to promise your parole," Etienne recalled with a snort of derision. "It took three of our ships of line to capture you, Thomas. How many of ours did that glorified dinghy of yours cost us, eh? Fifty?"

"A fine ship was *The Speedy*. It was fifty-three," Thomas corrected, taking a sip of his brandy. "I kept count."

"You always did." Etienne gave a chuff of laughter. "Do you still have the audacity to claim you did it all without the aid of your Gifts?"

"I might have used a touch of magic to tweak my plans into place every now and then," the seaman admitted. "A bit of fog. A change in the wind. Have ye heard anything from Charles?"

There was no need for Etienne to feign his feelings of regret. Charles' ruin was just one more tale in Napoleon's story of hubris. "He was forced to resign. Court-martialed and although they acquitted him, the glorious naval saga of the Durands is at an end."

Etienne scanned Thomas' face and saw the sparks of anger and bitterness. He knew the man's temper had a tendency to flare and was well aware how easily those embers could be coaxed into a conflagration of impetuous behavior. During the war, Etienne's agents in the English Admiralty had been secretly responsible for more than a few of the incidents that had impeded and ultimately sent the career of one of England's greatest naval minds to wreck on the shoals of bureaucracy. "I have heard England is also less than kind to its heroes."

"The nature of those who give orders without ever having stood on a wartime deck, old friend." Thomas downed the balance of his drink in a single swallow. "Landlubbers, dilettante yachtsmen, and thieves, the lot of them in the Admiralty."

From the look of it, Etienne's old nemesis was more than half seas over. Despite Thomas' impaired state, it would be foolish to underestimate him. The Sea Wolf was a wily opponent. Etienne kept his silence, hoping the whiskey would produce some unintended truth.

"Skim the contracts for profit, grease their palms to ignore tainted grub and feed the honest seamen swill. Then turn around and take a fighting man's prize money, and were that not enough, conspire to steal his honor," Thomas ranted.

"I had heard of your sham trial and conviction. You have made some powerful enemies over the years, *mon ami*." Etienne's sympathy was real. The case against Cochrane and his trial for fraud on the Stock Exchange had been a mockery of justice. The man had lost his seat in Parliament, his position in the Admiralty, his pension, and his honor. As if that did not suffice, his enemies had sentenced him to stand pillory opposite the Stock Exchange. It was little wonder England's former naval hero was resentful, given his futile struggle to restore his reputation.

"Certainly our Chief Mage did not intervene on my behalf when I needed it." Thomas' sneer laid bare his contempt. "'*Trying to keep out of Outsider politics,*' was what he told me."

Wodesby had tried to work behind the scenes to ameliorate Cochrane's sentence, but the man's volatility had alienated too many who would have stood as friends.

"I have come to the conclusion there is little justice in this world. All is in the hands of the capricious whims of the Fates, it would seem." Etienne looked away. Not all of his shame was feigned. "Myself, I had no chance to go to Napoleon's aid when he needed me most. I had given Lord Wodesby my parole. I was forced to stay out of it, or else I might be in France dancing to the Royalist's tune myself."

"And ye kept yer word, as honor demanded."

Etienne met Lord Cochrane's eyes and felt an unaccustomed twinge of guilt at Thomas' indignation on his behalf.

"Even so, when yer parole ended, what was yer reward? Justice bound yer powers indefinitely. Wodesby took the band of France from yer arm, the Chief's ring from yer hand, and gave them to another."

"What use is a Chief Mage without Gifts?" With a Gallic shrug to the whims of fortune, Etienne lifted his drink in salute and took a swallow. "In war always, there are winners, and there are losers."

Cochrane took two more whiskeys from a nearby tray. "And then there are those who refuse to lose." He pushed a glass forward to Etienne. "Bonaparte is no mage, but he is like a phoenix, my friend. I salute them all, mage or Outsider, who rise again despite the odds!"

Etienne forced a smile and held up his glass.

Was Thomas acknowledging a worthy adversary who flattered him? Or was he talking treason?

Surely not?

Then again, when the Sea Wolf was involved, the only certainty was that it was dangerous to be in range of his claws.

* * *

THE SOUNDS EMANATING from the great hall became louder as Tante Reina led Genevieve up the stairs through a hidden passage. Genevieve hesitated at the door.

"You are here for a purpose, milady." The old woman spoke quietly, but there was still a mild rebuke in her words. "Yet now, so near your goal, would you turn craven?"

"I could not have come so far without you and Miranda. It is fortunate she lives but a few doors away and we are much of a size." Genevieve squared her shoulders and took a deep breath. "Whatever the outcome, you have my thanks, dear friend."

"I cannot see the future clearly for those of the Blood, of this you are aware." The old woman held out her work-worn hands. "But into your palm, I would look, before you walk among your sisters and brothers in magic tonight."

Genevieve gave a sniff of skepticism as she slipped off her glove and presented her right hand. "Sisters and brothers, you say?"

"Contention is often the way of families, is it not? Whether they be of the Rom, of Merlin's get, or of ordinary humankind, this is true." Tante Reina stared at the tracery of destiny delineated in the candle glow. With a soft hum, she shook her head. "Is as I thought, I see nothing certain, except the need for courage."

Genevieve swallowed her disappointment and adjusted her gloves. "And you have given me that."

"You have mettle in plenty. If more you need, there is power in your gown beyond that of mere appearance," Tante Reina informed her. "Close your eyes and think of something that gives you pleasure or harmony, a place to calm your fears."

"My mother's garden in bloom." Genevieve obeyed and immediately felt tranquility spreading within her.

It was almost as if she was surrounded by the spring-time swath of the colorful growth she had imagined. Even the reality of the dimly lit passage could not dispel the sense of peace.

Genevieve slid the door open and stepped out before leaning down to give the old woman a kiss on her withered cheek.

"Do not let fear rule you, child," Genevieve heard the whisper as the passage closed behind her.

She stepped into a wondrous landscape of winter. Berry-laden boughs of holly and greenery hung from the rafters, brightening the ballroom with color and the scent of a snow-covered forest. Mistletoe dangled invitingly in corners. Flickering candles were reflected in chandeliers and mirrored sconces fashioned from icicles. Genevieve touched a charmingly decorative frosting of snow that chilled her fingers, but did not melt.

At the foot of the stairs, magical creatures, sculpted from ice, glinted in the candlelight. Some held trays of winter wine in their claws, paws and hands. Others offered dainty morsels which were replaced as soon as they left the platter. Lord Wodesby had clearly lent his elemental powers to help his wife achieve a stunning, holiday display.

Genevieve took a moment to scan the crowd, searching for her savior, but she chided herself for her foolishness. It was ridiculous to believe she had even a remote chance of picking him out from the press of guests roaming the rooms. Most of the company was still masked, their faces concealed by concoctions ranging from outrageously elaborate constructions of feathers, spangles and silk, to simple swaths of fabric like the one the stranger had worn.

Laughter, both amused and malicious, accompanied attempts to bare each other's faces. Genevieve knew that remaining incognito until the time came to shed disguises was considered a coup. Luckily, the domino in her reticule had been undamaged. *Hide me* charms were often difficult, delicate and expensive to obtain from a skilled witch, but it was one of the spells her mother could perform effortlessly. The plain black silk of the unadorned fabric molded to Genevieve like a second skin, but allowed her to see, breath, speak, eat and drink with ease.

Best of all, only Genevieve herself could remove it, so she would remain concealed, despite any attempts to reveal her identity. No one would be able to unmask her, either by accident or intent. If there were any rumors circulating about her untoward arrival, she hoped they would stay below stairs until the morning. With any luck at all, she would be able to remain anonymous, at least until tonight's task was completed.

In a replica of the Temple of Delphi, a substantial crowd surrounded the jar holding the boons. Genevieve opted to wait until the number of seekers diminished. In the meanwhile, she helped herself to hot mulled wine flowing from the mouth of a porcelain dragon into an array of flagons. A babble of languages surrounded her. She understood more than a few from her childhood wanderings across the Continent and easily followed the threads of conversations drifting around her.

Gossip, it would seem, varied little regardless of class.

With more than a year gone by since Napoleon's banishment to St. Helena, many of those who had once opposed each other across battlefields were busily forging their own tenuous accords. The Yule celebration was traditionally a time to seek suitable spouses.

War and revolution had sent all too many of Merlin's children to seek Light before their time, particularly eligible mages. Peace allowed the High Circles of the Blood to cast a wider net for themselves or their offspring. Past grudges were often laid aside in favor of future advantage.

By the time she was finished with her drink, the crowd had ebbed considerably and Genevieve stepped out of cover to make her way across the room.

An ancient amphora stood surrounded by mirrors, the better to display the full circle of painted runes and symbols of Apollo. Beautifully rendered patterns of laurel leaves, bows and arrow laden quivers, sunbursts, and lyres, decorated the vessel. An onyx base in the form of a raven with its wings outspread completed the display. According to rumor, the pottery dated back to the covens of the Pythia, the famous Oracles who had prophesized at the temple at Delphi.

One final time, Genevieve read her request before crumpling the piece of paper and tossing it in with the others, closing her eyes to concentrate on a fervent wish for the help her son needed. It was only when she looked up at her reflection that Genevieve noticed the crowd gathering behind her.

Laid out on Tante Reina's bed, Genevieve's borrowed gown had seemed the perfect garment to avoid notice. Given Miranda's taste for vivid colors, Genevieve had been surprised by the dull blue shade of the cloth, the simple cut, and demure design.

In her focus on her note, Genevieve had failed to notice her own reflection in the mirror behind the amphora. In the glow of a multitude of candles, the hue of the fabric had transformed into a vivid jewel tone of deep sapphire. Her memory of her mother's garden had taken root and clothed Genevieve in a dress that was the work of a mistress of magical needlecraft.

Cunning embroidery had blossomed on the skirts and crept its way up to the bodice. With the brilliant display of stitchery, any hope of passing without remark was dashed. Surrounded by curiosity that was almost a palpable force, Genevieve remembered her friend's advice.

Do not let fear rule you.

With studied nonchalance, Genevieve ignored the looks and whispers, seeking the clearest path to take her leave. Repressing a shudder, she reminded herself a few disdainful looks were nothing. She already had overcome far worse this night.

As she made her way out, witches speculated loudly about her modiste and identity. Mages, many of whom had long lost any illusion of manners in the bottom of a whiskey glass, were making more carnal insinuations. Genevieve had originally planned to find Miranda and give her thanks for the loan of the gown. Now, it appeared it might be best to leave as soon as possible. That was nothing more than common sense, she told herself, certainly not fear.

CHAPTER 6

$\mathcal{E}$tienne rose from his seat, hiding a yawn behind the pretense of admiring the illusion of the stone henge. He had spent the better part of the evening moving about like a pasteboard playing card in a street fair mountebank's game, meeting with conspirators at a variety of pre-ordained times and locations.

More than a few of those whose allegiances had been of concern to the Chief Mage had found Etienne and attempted to enlist him as a fellow traveler. While his magic was under lock and key, apparently the du Le Fey money still made him a somewhat desirable ally.

As Rowan had pointed out to her husband, there were always malcontents no matter what policies Damien might choose to pursue. Most of the complaints that Etienne had been made privy to tonight were not dangerous in and of themselves. The majority of the would-be plotters were small fish, hardly worth the butter for the frying.

The Sea Wolf, however, was a Leviathan and the disunited school of sprats could become a threat, especially if Lord Cochrane was planning something once he got them gathered together into his craw. The problem was there was no telling what Thomas

Cochrane might have in mind. He was, after all, a man who would have used gunpowder and siege tactics to keep the House of Commons from arresting his friend, Francis Burdett.

Etienne's report to Damien, however, could wait for another day. Since the fête had begun at moonrise, the guests had been given more than ample time to drown their powers of discretion in the rivers of wine and fountains of whiskey their host had graciously provided. It was time to hear what the members of the clans and covens had to say when their restraint had been befuddled and their chins were apt to wag unimpeded.

In vino veritas.

With that axiom in mind and a glass in hand, Etienne assumed a John Bull accent and began the task of seeking wine-induced truth among the crowd. As expected, the mere mention of Lord Wodesby's name was sufficient to set tongues flapping. Even those with their masks still intact were not nearly as anonymous as they thought themselves to be. It was relatively simple to match the mage with his name and add them to either side of the ledger of allegiances.

More than once, Etienne was grateful for his grandmother's spellcasting as others tried to unmask a mage of middling importance. His assessment of the evening's crop of Wodesby's potential enemies was nearly complete. Etienne began to think of retrieving his coat and scarf from their cache in the kitchen. With any luck, he might be in his bed with a fine glass of wine and a good book before the boon jar was broached and the unmasking began.

On his way out, he resolved to ask how Genevieve Dale had fared. Somehow, she had become the ghost who haunted his thoughts tonight. Perhaps he would find the opportunity to arrange for the next installment of her life debt? There was nothing better than a cold dose of reality to cure a delusion that was somehow becoming more meaningful and heated with every recollection.

A distinctive bray of laughter reminded Etienne that his fishing expedition was not yet finished. Lord Pendrake had been one of those who had jockeyed to take Damien's place when the Chief Mage's powers had temporarily disappeared. Lord Wodesby's recovery of his Gifts had been a definite disappointment to the head of the Cornwall clan.

Etienne slipped through the crowd, toward the boon jar. From the raucous sound of it, Pendrake and his pack of hangers-on were highly amused. That did not bode well for someone.

The masked Pendrakes hunted in a pack tonight, reminding Etienne of jackals he had seen during his time in Egypt with Napoleon. Acting as a group, they were encircling and harrying their quarry, awaiting their chosen victim's panicked flight. Their appetites were almost palpable as they anticipated that most savory of social feasts—humiliation served with a relish of scandal.

Etienne recognized the gown. He had sent the fabric to Miranda in thanks for her help in trying to solve the meaning of the cryptic sentence meted out by Justice. The bolt of material seemed an almost paltry gift in light of the hours Damien's sister was spending in his aid, researching the records and chronicles of judgements stretching back to the times of Merlin. The stubborn woman had refused any of his more valuable offerings, claiming she was only doing her duty as the Archivist of the Covens.

A witch weaver at one of his mills in Lyon had managed to imbue the cloth with the unique quality of enhancing a body's best attributes. Adjusting itself to position and motion, the drape of blue silk almost seemed to have a will of its own. It caressed the wearer's curves in a simple design that was modest by comparison to the blatantly revealing garments considered *comme il faut* among both the magical and mundane Quality. The panels of sarsnet, and trimmings of velvet stitched with exquisite embroidery, had their own innate magic, starting as a blank slate and attuning themselves to the choice of the one who wore it.

Surely, even Pendrake would not dare to bait the Chief Mage's sister under Wodesby's own roof.

As he moved closer, Etienne realized that Pendrake's target was not Lady Brand. Miranda's whimsy tended to favor fantastical creatures. The last time he had seen her dressed in the garment her modiste had fashioned from the fabric, dragons, unicorns, wyverns and griffins had cavorted across the weave.

The woman being driven into a corner was a lushly figured vision of Demeter, the Mother goddess, waking the earth in spring to celebrate her daughter's return from Hades' domain. This wearer's imaginings had transformed Miranda's gown into a garden of herbs. Delicate flowers, in colors that seemed real enough to pluck, blossomed in seemingly random places. Vines twisted, twining and delineating bosom and hip, drawing the eye and setting a man's mind to wondering what might lie beneath.

Her mask was deceptively plain, but it too, was a cunning magical working. Fabric molded to her face in a taut facial glove making those hidden features seem cast in ebony silk. Covering her entire head and neck like a second skin, the mask accentuated the beauty of high cheekbones, a pert nose and full sensuous lips.

It would have been far better for his peace of mind had he been able to blame her allure upon the use of her Gifts, and thus, easily dismiss her. To Etienne's inner eye, the Unknown had the gleam of a true gem, surrounded by a crowd of poorly made paste imitations. Her liquid grace and genuine beauty made her far more intriguing than any illusion enhanced woman. Etienne's instincts told him there were no spells surrounding her. Save the dress and mask she wore, all of her was undeniably real.

Obviously, the woman had to be a good friend of Lady Brand if Miranda had loaned the gown she claimed as a favorite. Something about the wearer was maddeningly familiar. The mask framed a silhouette of someone he felt he ought to know. Though Etienne wracked his memory, he could not match her to any image in his recall. He moved closer, easing his way into the circle of onlookers.

"No naming jewel I can see," Lord Pendrake's mother observed, loudly. Even without her foghorn voice, her penchant for an over-abundance of ruffles on her gown made her mask a needless piece of puffery. "Doubt she could light a candle without a flint." The lady sniffed in disdain.

"Is Wodesby now allowing Outsiders at our celebrations?" Her older son, Oliver, Lord Pendrake wondered, leaning forward to leer in a manner that threatened to burst the strained buttons on his waistcoat.

"Other than those Outsiders in his own family?" A young mage wearing a Pendrake ring opined before dissolving into a titter of alcohol amplified laughter.

Etienne identified him as Lord Pendrake's younger brother, Octavius. The boy's intellect was as weak as his magic, but from the flurry of supportive nods and loud amusement, his observation was being deemed the epitome of wit.

"Wodesby's sister is actually wed to one of *them*, you know," an older unmasked witch, whose unfortunate features marked her as another relation of Lady Pendrake's, declared with a sneer. "And the Chief Mage's mother is married to one of *those people* as well."

"Ever wondered if that's why Adrienne's daughter is powerless?" Lord Pendrake mused, with a mock whisper that was worthy of a Drury Lane stage. "Wodesby has the look of the sire, but there are those who believe the girl's true father wasn't of the Blood."

"It wouldn't surprise *me* in the least," his mother agreed.

The unknown woman's spine stiffened and her lips thinned in outrage.

"Outsider or not, the gel has the look of a doxy to me," the older matron continued.

"Oh, I doubt that even Lord Wodesby would allow a Cyprian Outsider to his celebrations, though she looks no better than she ought to be," speculated another young witch whose harsh tones of malice belied her look of youthful innocence. "A hedge witch, perhaps, who doesn't know her place?"

"Our Chief Mage does have some odd notions about the company he keeps. Even mixes with Out-Bloods, I'm told," Lady Pendrake agreed. "Perhaps she is a poor relation?"

"Wouldn't mind having relations with her myself," Octavius declared. "She's a comely wench, she is."

Etienne held his breath, waiting for an excuse to strike, but as the insulted party, the Unknown had the right of First Answer, and the license to respond with her own resources.

Even if the Unknown was not a witch or could not stand for herself, there was likely someone at hand in the form of family, friend, or protector, who could be given leave to play her defender. Often the threat of retribution was the best means of keeping the peace at these affairs. Although the oath of *and harm none* was strictly enforced tonight, many a mage had been sent to meet the Light in the morning after the Yule Night truce was ended.

But no one came forward. The Unknown offered no names and no answer of her own but an angry glare.

In the titters and barks of laughter that followed, Etienne automatically braided his fingers in a gesture that would cast a harmless spell to strike the speakers silent until help arrived. But before he could utter the words, he was momentarily deprived of breath by the shock of warning Justice had set as a reminder of the consequences of using his Gifts.

Surprised at his own rising rage and his readiness to jump to her aid, Etienne stepped forward. While harmful offensive spells were strictly forbidden, so long as no weapon was used, physical force was not. Magic users rarely resorted to such brutal measures, but since standing at the stones, Etienne had sought extensive training in the defensive skills of ordinary men and was now quite deadly with his fists and the Eastern fighting arts. Only the knowledge that his intervention might not be wanted or required kept him from rearranging the smug smile beneath Octavius' mask.

He set his glass aside, waiting to take his cue from the woman's reaction.

To his surprise, she did not turn tail or shrink back. Instead she forged ahead into the crowd, dismissing her tormentors with a hauteur that many a jeweled witch of the Blood would have been hard put to emulate.

With each step forward, she proclaimed them to be unworthy of her notice. Her level of disdain actually caused most of them to step aside, confused and cowed by her unexpected dismissal.

Except for Pendrake's brother.

The cur put a hand upon her arm.

She stilled, unyielding as a standing stone, scrutinizing her tormenter as if she considered him to be nothing more than an annoying insect.

Meanwhile, the fool was so fixed in his inspection of her feminine attributes he missed the look of fury in her eyes.

Familiar eyes, now transformed to a volatile mix of whiskey and amber fire.

If looks could have burned, the transgressor would have instantly been seared into a pile of smoldering ash.

"Remove your fingers from my person, at once," she demanded, in a growl that belied her calm expression.

Even muffled by her mask, her words confirmed Etienne's suspicions. He knew her voice, smooth and clear as the finest cognac, blended with a mellow hint of France.

It was Genevieve Dale.

Her right hand had slipped to one of the ubiquitous pockets that Miranda demanded in all of her gowns, the better to hold her books.

The runes of an engraved hilt glowed gold against gloved fingers. In the darkness and confusion behind the mews he had not recognized that the knife Genevieve Dale had used to defend herself was an athame.

Still not apprehending his danger, Octavius gave her a knowing leer and a lopsided smirk in answer. His fingers crawled upward to grip her bare shoulder in a deliberate challenge, daring her to force his compliance.

Much as the drunkard deserved it, there would be consequences, no matter whether Genevieve Dale was a child of Merlin or an Outsider. If she vented her just fury and violated the Peace of the Longest Night by drawing first blood with any weapon, other than her own fists, the penalty would be severe. As amusing as it might be to see her employ a sacred ritual knife to gut Lord Pendrake's brother, Etienne could not stand by and let her endure the repercussions.

"If you wish to keep your hand intact, boy, I strongly suggest that you remove it from this lady's arm," Etienne warned, reaching out and pulling the offending digits away. "If you let off now, I might even leave your nose in the center of your face."

* * *

There was not a hint of France in her defender's blunt declaration, but Genevieve knew his voice immediately. Somehow, she realized he had recognized her as well. Eyes the color of a blue twilight sky caught hers and begged for her compliance. With a nod, she let the athame slip back into its sheath.

The lout who had handled her turned with a snarl, eager to confront the man who dared to challenge him. The force of the stranger's icy azure glare seemed to pierce the veil of the drunken mage's alcoholic haze. Blinking rapidly, as if trying to clear his vision, he took the stranger's measure. Although they were nearly equal in height, six feet of indolence and debilitated living was no match for a man built of solid muscle.

Genevieve noticed a mage's ring on the stranger's fist and felt an odd sense of disappointment. The prospect of the two kisses she owed him gained a sinister cast. He was a mage and likely not much different than the boor who had put his hand upon her. All of them were prone to play games with the lives of those they deemed to be lesser. Was he now protecting her because he deemed her to be *his* plaything?

"Are you declaring yourself her champion?" the oaf

muttered, trying to sidle back into the pack of Pendrakes. He winced, fixed in place by a vice-like grip that tightened with every attempt at movement.

"I am," The stranger proclaimed. "Do you wish to fight me now?"

"Do you know who I am?" the churl demanded.

Genevieve was almost moved to laughter at his besotted attempt at an intimidating stare.

"Your identity will come to you, I am sure, Octavius, once you are sober," a familiar voice remarked acerbically. Miranda broke through the crowd to stand at Genevieve's side.

"L...l...Lady Brand," he stammered. "I did n...n...not know that this w...woman is a f...friend of yours—"

"Friend or not, this witch is a guest of the Chief Mage! Obvious to even the dullest of young blades, by the fact she is under his roof," Miranda snapped. "The youngest child of the Blood knows that to touch uninvited is a violation of Merlin's code." She turned to his mother who stood nearby with her mouth opening and closing like a landed fish. "Clearly, Lady Pendrake, you ought to teach your son some manners before you inflict him on Polite Society again."

Lady Pendrake's lips snapped shut into a tight line and she cleared her throat, as if preparing to protest.

"Before you speak, Lady Pendrake, I will give you three choices of statements acceptable to me at this moment. You may wish us all good tidings. You may voice an apology for standing by and allowing one of my brother's guests to be insulted by one of your kin. You may express your gratitude for my intervention before your son's face was permanently rearranged. If you have anything else to say, I would strongly recommend you keep the words between your teeth," Miranda added, her gaze encompassing all those who surrounded them, stating implicitly that they, too, were culpable.

Lady Pendrake's look was poisonous, but she nodded stiffly, grabbing her protesting scion by the arm and escorting him towards the doorway.

Genevieve took a breath, centering herself, letting the flare of her anger subside. She turned around, thinking to thank the man who had, once again, come to her defense. But he was gone.

"Do you know who that was?" Genevieve asked softly, scanning the rapidly dispersing crowd.

There was a tinge of quiet amusement in Miranda's voice. "If he has not told you, then it is not for me to say, especially tonight before we all unmask."

"You do not understand," Genevieve said. "The man who came to stand with me as my champion? He was the one I mentioned, tonight, behind the mews."

"Bless me blue! He was the stranger who came to your rescue?" Miranda asked, an eyebrow rising in patent surprise. "What a pity I arrived too soon! I vow I would have enjoyed watching him spill Octopus' claret on the floor."

"Octopus?"

"Pendrake's brother, Octavius. His hands would be everywhere if he got you in a corner," Miranda explained with an impish smile. "Your stranger wouldn't have been the first to bloody that bully's nose."

"Nonetheless, I fear you have made yourself an enemy on my behalf tonight."

"Lady Pendrake and her whelps were never on my list of friends." Miranda mimicked Lady Pendrake's treacle tones with deadly accuracy. Her demeanor exactly mirrored the matron's expression of sour faced disapproval. "*Poor, poor Miranda! Not a whit of magic in her.* I refuse to insult a female dog by the comparison to that woman. As a favor, I would ask you to not let

Damien know Pendrake was impugning our mother's honor tonight."

"You heard then."

Miranda gave a rueful nod. "It is a filthy old song whose lyrics I know all too well."

She found them a pair of chairs far enough from the throng to give them a measure of seclusion. Genevieve nestled into the luxuriant upholstery with a muffled sigh, trying to tamp the remnants of magic still churning within her, begging to be released.

"I am certain someone will relay Lord Pendrake's remarks, *with the best of intentions*, of course," Miranda added sarcastically, "but not tonight, I hope. He and Rowan have enough on their shoulders without being provoked to break out in a blaze of blue rage." Miranda gestured to one of the servants. "I did not see so much as a trace of blue in your eyes. I confess my marvel at your control. Even my mother would have lost the reins with such a level of incitement, and she was the Mistress of Witches for decades."

"My thanks." Genevieve accepted a goblet and swirled the golden mead within. "Learning to control myself without a jewel has strengthened my forbearance. But standing behind the counter of a shop catering to the Blood gives me plenty of practice at dodging their barbs and insinuations," Genevieve admitted with a wry twist of the lips at her friend's look of indignation. "For the most part, I deal with their servants, but on those occasions when Merlin's children choose to grace my humble establishment, I bite my tongue and leash my Gift. It is not much use as a weapon, in any case."

Miranda shook her head. "Perhaps, you just don't know how to use it."

"That might be, but tonight's events have taught me that I ought to learn." Genevieve closed her eyes, focusing on letting go the last of her anger, relaxing into the minutia of the moment. There was joy to be found in the company of a good friend. Slowly, the stiffness in her spine relaxed, easing into the comfort as the well-padded chair adjusted itself to embrace her form.

Breathing deeply, she catalogued the yeasty scents in the wassail, a mingling of honey, citrus and the spices that were Dale's stock in trade. Cinnamon, nutmeg and cloves wafted in a cloud of steam. The enspelled goblet containing the brew remained at perfect temperature, warming her hands.

"You are one of the few who knows the nature of my Gift, my friend." Taking a sip, Genevieve imagined the liquid quenching the fire of anger from her spirit. She set her tongue to the task of teasing out the individual identities of the myriad flavors comprising Tante Reina's unique holiday recipe. When the last vestiges of her magic were finally quelled, she allowed herself to be at ease. "If I relax control, I fear I might lose myself. That is why I must find a mentor for Louis. I wish there was some way for me to lead Louis into his Gifts on my own."

"It would be so much simpler wouldn't it? Easier for my children as well." Miranda's sigh seemed to carry the weights of both of their worries for their children's futures. "For all we might wish it otherwise, a mage must train a mageling into his power and a witch must direct a witchling. This has been so since the beginning. But for children of mixed heritage, such as ours?" She held up her hands in a gesture of surrender to an unknown fate with no adequate words for expression, shaking her head in a mixture of pride and dismay. "I thought I was alone, but I am so grateful to you and your OutBlood friends for their welcome. I take it there is still no mage to be found among them to guide Louis? You would not be here otherwise."

"At least the OutBloods would help me if they could, but there are none who know how." Genevieve's gaze of disdain swept the room full of mages and witches. Her huff of dismissal was bitter. "As for my brothers in the Blood, more than one has told me that I've made my bed by marrying an Outsider. The only offers of help I have received thus far would require me to allow others to lie in it."

"That's unconscionable!" Miranda struggled to contain herself. "Damien ought to—"

"Your brother cannot undo centuries of fear and prejudice, Miranda, much as he might try," Genevieve voiced the harsh reality. "Nor can he punish every slight you and I may endure because of what others think of our choices. Maybe it will be different in the future, but I have to do what I can in the here and now." Her smile was rueful as she picked up her goblet again. "And what you ought to do is enjoy the rest of your evening and count yourself blessed that Adam and your Mama are willing to keep watch on your brood so you may savor the Longest Night."

"They were both more than eager to avoid this charade of pretended peace and goodwill." Miranda chuckled. "I highly suspect they may regret their choice to mind my imps by the time I return, well after they are abed of course."

"I was not aware of this evil tendency in your heart," Genevieve said with a sigh, setting aside her drink with regret. "Since I am feeling more the thing, I think I will make my way home."

"But your boon?" Miranda inquired. "Do you not want to stay for the asking?"

"Your brother will do what he can," Genevieve said wearily. "I have no desire to wait until dawn when he finally attends to the wants of us lesser folk."

"You might have need of a ride home sooner than

you think." Her friend raised her goblet in a mock toast as she lowered her voice. *"To my dear brother, who is allowing the magic of the boon jar to make the choices tonight, giving preference by need and not by rank.* Those in the High Circles may find themselves having to take their turn for a favor behind the request of a hedge witch who might be more in want."

"A pity Rowan didn't think to sell tickets. I think that every OutBlood, minor mage, and wise woman would pay just to see the look on their faces when they find out."

Miranda burst into gales of laughter. Genevieve was hard put trying to muffle her own response, but the stress of constant restraint and the strength of Tante Reina's mead overcame her. Hilarity escaped in a gale of uninhibited glee.

* * *

ETIENNE HEARD the sound of untrammeled mirth ring across the room, causing the company to pause with scowls of disapproval at the possibility that the wrong people might actually be enjoying themselves. Clearly, Genevieve Dale was a true friend to Miranda. A light of joy illuminated Lord Wodesby's sister transforming her usually serious expression.

Associating with Miranda was a social statement in and of itself. Many families of the Blood, even those who dared not cut the Wodesbys openly, had no compunction about disparaging them behind their backs. Once she unmasked, her open friendship would place Genevieve Dale firmly in the Chief Mage's camp.

She was a fascinating puzzle, this woman without a jewel who wielded an athame to defend herself. During the witch hunts many who were of the Blood had hidden their Gifts and had married Outsiders, often bearing offspring with diminished or no magic. Perhaps she was OutBlood?

Her bare face was easy to conjure. Etienne guessed she was of an age with him, not much more than thirty years in her dish. Genevieve Dale wore her time serenely. Almost as if his thoughts had called to her, she looked up from her conversation to scan the gathered company. Her smile quickly faded, as she suddenly seemed to recollect where she was, surrounded by those who would not accept her.

Something they definitely had in common.

As if that link sufficed to join them in some way, those wary whiskey eyes were drawn to his for a startled moment.

CHAPTER 7

Genevieve felt a strange tug and looked up to find the stranger regarding her curiously. There were questions in those limpid pools of blue, confusion, curiosity and something she could not define. A tight smile of acknowledgement chased briefly across those sensuous lips. Like one gladiator to another, just as the lions were roaring at the arena's gate, he tipped his head in salute.

But he obviously wanted nothing to do with her. He had come to her defense, which made him better than most, but the man wore a mage's ring and it would appear that he shared the prejudices common to their breed. He had her name and had not given his, had disappeared twice without a fare thee well. Had she become some strange form of amusement for him?

Such peculiar attention could become dangerous. With surprising reluctance, Genevieve tore her gaze away, breaking the connection, hoping to fade into the background once more. If he knew who she was, he knew her place outside the herd. Perhaps it was cowardly of her, but she would not allow herself to become part of some mage's cynical amusement on a cold winter's night.

But you promised him a life debt, her conscience whispered.

And he has made light of it, she reminded herself. *And deems you will pay him with a promise of kisses.*

He helped you again. The troublesome voice of scruples added.

Do not forget you were preparing to help yourself.

"Is something wrong?" Miranda asked.

"He's looking at me, the stranger," Genevieve said. "Don't look at him or he'll know you know."

"Why do I suddenly feel as if I'm back in the nursery?" Miranda asked with a sigh. "Don't worry about any debts you may owe him. He isn't going to make any outré demands."

"He told me I was free of any life debt earlier."

"Did he?" Miranda mused. "How interesting? And what about your confrontation before the boon jar? You would have gutted Octavius with your athame if not for the stranger."

"Anyone could see I was defending myself!" Genevieve protested.

"With a magical weapon. You and your kin would have been declared Outcasts for breaking the peace by drawing First Blood," Miranda explained gently. "But you didn't know, did you? None of the Blood would have ever done business with you again. Louis would find no one willing to be his mentor."

Genevieve shook her head mutely. "He saved me twice," she whispered.

When she looked for him again, he was gone.

"I think it is time for me to take my leave," she declared, rising to give Miranda a farewell embrace. "Thank you once more for the dress. Please convey my gratitude to my champion, whoever he might be, since he obviously has no wish to be associated with us."

"Do not be so certain," Miranda replied cryptically.

"I will have my carriage brought round for you." She held up a hand to forestall Genevieve's protests. "It is nearby and you have already had far too many adventures this evening. Wait here and finish your mead. They will let us know when it is at the door."

* * *

ETIENNE DECIDED it was time to keep his appointment with his book and his bed. But before he took his leave, he decided to see if his grandmother wished to depart with him. She was across the ballroom, chatting animatedly with some of the other elder, wise crones of London. Although she seemed to be enjoying herself, he could detect the weariness in her posture. There was a decided droop to the magically enhanced plumes in her turban.

As he strolled to confer with her, Etienne wondered why Genevieve Dale had turned her face from him so suddenly. There had been a definite look of recognition in her eyes. Had Miranda given her some hint of his unsavory history? Whatever the reason, Genevieve Dale had refused to meet his gaze again.

Etienne tried to control an unreasoning swell of anger. How dare she spurn him? His family could trace themselves back to the times when Merlin was an unknown upstart! He fought for control, tamping back the tide of incomprehensible annoyance, forcing himself to maintain an attitude of calm. It was the contained tide of his Gifts again, stirred up by the presence of the surfeit of magic around him, raging against the inner dam he had fashioned.

Although hope of redemption was distant, it was possible, he reminded himself, but until then the struggle of restraint was all-important. No matter how intriguing the conundrum of Genevieve Dale might be, she was of no consequence. It might be wise to distance himself from her as well. Two busses on the cheek and the life debt would be discharged. He had learned all too well that the so-called *fair sex* was, by far, the most vicious half of the species.

The thought was almost an omen.

His grandmother put a hand upon his shoulder. "Do not turn around just yet, but Circe is just entering the room." There was a hiss of anger beneath her whisper. "Pendrake has gone to greet her. I have heard rumors he was pursuing her."

"She is still a desirable *parti*, with a substantial dowry and connections to half the magical families in Europe." Tucking his grandmother's arm in his, he guided her toward the dais where Damien and his wife sat in state. "Do you wish to take our leave now, Grandmama?" He posed the question sotto voce. "Things may get uglier."

"I will not be driven off by the likes of her." Though there was a trace of a chuckle in the old woman's words, there was also a glisten of fury in her eyes. "The thief is wearing my mother's emerald parure. That is obviously part and parcel of why she has come tonight. To publicly proclaim her right to them, although she was the one who broke the betrothal between you."

Looking at his grandmother's stricken face, Etienne knew it was time to take action. He had been perfectly willing to allow Circe to keep all of the expensive baubles he had gifted to her personally over the course of their connection. However, she had yet to return several magical Morgan and du Le Fey family heirlooms which had been given into her keeping when they had pledged their troth.

"I have already done what I came here to do. Consider me now as your chevalier to command," Etienne confirmed quietly. "Do you wish to retreat?"

"Not an inch, by Merlin's toes," his grandmother agreed. "To withdraw would be defeat."

"Then so shall it be!"

Until tonight, Etienne had hoped to resolve the problem through quiet negotiation. Unfortunately, his grandmother was no doubt correct. Circe was not wearing a mask, which was doubtlessly deliberate. Flaunting the jewels in public was tantamount to a declaration of permanent possession that could not be ignored.

His former fiancée was clothed in a gown of ivory muslin baring neckline and shoulders in a design seemingly fashioned to highlight the spectacular set of emeralds. Thread of pure gold trimmed the cloth in a series of Celtic knots comprising the Donnelly coven symbol. The garment flowed in the Grecian style Circe had always favored.

Etienne knew she had eliminated the bother and discomfort of damping the muslin on a cold winter night. A simple spell temporarily enchanted the thin fabric to mold to the wearer, leaving very little to the imagination. Ash blonde curls framed her heart-shaped face and a touch of glamor gave a blossom of healthy color to her lips and cheeks.

He took his grandmother's elbow and escorted her to the foot of the stairs. A murmur rose in a swelling tide as the crowd gathered in expectation of a skirmish. Lady Morgan had complained loudly and often about Circe's failure to return the jewels.

Etienne stepped aside momentarily to pluck two glasses of wine from a nearby tray.

Circe's startled look told him that she had not expected a confrontation. Surprise was quickly replaced with a triumphant smile.

"Are you about to take your leave, Lady Morgan?"

his former fiancée crowed with mock sweetness. "Do not let me keep you."

From the look of cruel glee on her face, it was clear Circe did not yet recognize him. Due to the effects of months of manual labor, Etienne had been forced to replace his previous wardrobe almost in its entirety. She was under the false impression that Lady Morgan was intimidated, alone and without defenders.

Nonetheless, if Circe believed that his grandmother required anyone to fight her battles, the young witch was obviously less intelligent than Etienne had previously thought.

"Why would I bid *adieu* when the celebration is just about to begin?" the old woman declared with a wicked grin, accepting her glass.

With his hand now free, Etienne swept off his domino and threw it to the ground, revealing a visage that was a perfect portrait of nonchalance.

Almost as one, the crowd gasped in surprise.

When she caught sight of him, Etienne watched Circe's exultant expression pale. She looked to Lord Pendrake in consternation.

So, Pendrake was part of this as well, was he? Interesting.

Likely neither of them had thought he would dare show his face at tonight's celebration.

Circe's eyes narrowed as they met his.

Expected him to falter, did she? For all their intimacy, she had never really known him well at all, it would appear.

"Steady, my boy." His grandmother's whisper was for his ears only and the tight pressure on his elbow was a reminder he was not alone, as if he was somehow the one who needed reassurance amidst the sea of intense hostility surrounding him.

But the onlookers only served to remind Etienne

that if he fell, the old woman beside him might fall as well.

By the Merlin, he would not fall.

He used the silence to contemplate the situation, taking his former fiancée's measure and assessing what she was hoping to accomplish. Though the unexpected encounter was not part of her plan, Circe was hoping he would slink away in shame at her presence or better still, behave like a pitiful shadow in a state of profound decline.

But he had no intention of playing the dejected, discarded suitor. With a wry smile and a shrug, he raised a questioning brow as if to say, *What did you presume? Tears?* Clearly his response was not the dramatic reaction she desired. Had she honestly expected him to be devastated?

From her momentarily bewildered expression, it would appear she had.

Their match had been arranged, of course, a pragmatic alliance between two scions of the Blood with powerful Gifts of Foresight and more. Initially it had been nothing more than a pragmatic agreement to Etienne. As far as his father was concerned, Etienne was the du Le Fey's prime stud to be mated with a prized mare in the expectation of exceptional offspring.

From their first meeting, Circe had charmed him.

He had come to care deeply and she had used his affection to wound him.

Etienne wondered now if his Gift as a Seer had made him so reluctant to consummate their union prematurely. Certainly, his father had urged him to seal the deal before the wedding, making it far more difficult for Circe to withdraw from the bargain contracted with her family. The Devil Comte's marriage to his son's previous betrothed had not enhanced the du Le Fey reputation. Etienne had held fast against the pressure, hoping a proper wedding with its attendant pomp would wipe some of the tarnish from their name.

Still, Circe had certainly been more than willing to anticipate the nuptials.

Barely muffled snickers brought Etienne to the present. Gazes flickered back and forth, like onlookers at a tennis match trying to catch every bounce of embarrassment and emotion as he and Circe confronted each other for the first time since she had publicly repudiated him after the Judgement at Stonehenge.

Oddly enough, that humiliating memory brought a grin to his face.

It was Circe who broke the silence first. "What are you smiling about, du Le Fey?"

Circe was clearly out of practice. First to speak was always the loser in the game of intimidation. First point to du Le Fey!

"I offer a libation to Hecate!" Etienne declared, lifting his glass high. "My thanks for saving me unawares from a lifetime of pain and misery!"

He took a sip and then deliberately turned his back in a blatant cut direct.

The onlookers gasped as one, focusing their attention upon the anticipated reaction of the woman who had once pledged her undying devotion to Etienne.

They were not disappointed. Circe's hiss of outrage echoed in the hall.

Titters of expectation rippled through the room.

Etienne could feel Circe's eyes boring into his back. His spine stiffened with the feel of a magical tug. Was she arrogant enough to use magic against him here in Wodesby's very house on the Longest Night? It was a blatant violation of Justice's edict, forbidding the use of magic as a weapon against Etienne unless his own was first restored.

Those family pieces still in her possession were

worth a fortune, but Etienne knew there was far more than money at stake. His great-grandmother's set of emeralds, and many of the other jewels Circe had refused to return, were powerful talismans. Etienne took a sip of his drink in a private salute to his former fiancée's ability to turn her carriage in a tight corner. Cunning had always been one of Circe's most politically attractive attributes. This on-the-spot scheme to exploit the unexpected confrontation and turn it to her advantage was a formidable ploy.

No doubt, she had calculated that even Etienne, himself, would not realize what she was attempting. As the old comte had often said, *a knife to the back can end a battle faster than an army of archers with full quivers.*

Like the ruby wearing witch who had accosted him, Circe had made the error of underestimating her opponent.

As he felt the righteous anger within him rising, her aim became clear. By stoking his rage, she intended to force him to lose control and confront her.

Touché! What better way to enlist Wodesby's support for her claim? If Circe somehow managed to provoke Etienne to break the Pact of Yuletide Peace, or better still, to violate the Judgement that bound him by causing him to use his magic against her, he would appear the aggressor and she would emerge victorious. Etienne would forever forfeit his magical Gifts making her vengeance even sweeter.

How had he been so blind to the fact that Circe had wanted to be France's Mistress of Witches more than she had ever wanted him?

Since Etienne was not pledged to England's covens, the Chief Mage might not be able to sense this minor use of manipulative magic. Amidst all the other slight spells being employed tonight to maneuver emotions and opinions or mask flaws in appearance, Circe's casting would seem innocuous to Damien. Given the façade of ongoing discord Etienne and Damien were deliberately cultivating between them, the woman was wily enough to wager that Wodesby might choose to ignore her magical interference even if he did detect it.

As his former fiancée attempted to feed Etienne's anger, he allowed her manipulations to succeed somewhat, letting her build false confidence in her level of control over him. Once again, the old comte's lessons came to the fore. *Focus,* his father's voice growled in his mind. *Use your adversary's power to your own end.*

There was no violation of his Judgement as Etienne allowed his consciousness to float on the spell someone else was weaving. He redirected her intent with his own resolve. The memory of the feelings that had once softened his heart became the bedrock of the stuff which made his will impervious to the emotions she was trying to fan within him.

As Etienne had calculated, frustration caused Circe to increase the intensity of her beguilement, burning bright against his unyielding self-control. Wave after wave of her magic flamed against the rock of his defenses. Eventually, he knew that she would overwhelm him and breach the barricades that he had so carefully fortified. It was time to make his move on the battlefield.

CHAPTER 8

*H*e drew his grandmother with him, strolling toward France's former Mistress of Witches, his stepmother, Rowan.

Sitting beside Damien on the dais, Rowan eyed Etienne curiously as he approached. Once unmasked, guests were required to greet their hosts. As Britain's Mistress of Witches, Rowan was well aware of her husband's plan to present the appearance of discord with France's former mage and she barely nodded at him.

"My grandmother has reminded me of my manners. The blessings of Yule upon you, *mon Seigneur, ma Dame.*" His tone was frigid and formal, as if the words were being wrung from him unwilling.

Rowan's lips thinned in a display of obvious irritation at his blatant churlishness, but there was a question in her cold stare. Etienne's father, her late husband, had been a relentless master. The Devil Comte had driven his tactics into his young wife's very bones. Etienne's unexpected approach and his deliberate reversal, putting the mistress of the house last in the traditional formulaic holiday greeting, signaled something was amiss. Rowan would surely know there was a problem Etienne could not voice outright.

Even though she was now pledged to England, he could only hope Rowan's sensitivity to the powers of France had not been fully severed. Circe's magical barrage was increasing in intensity. Retreat would likely mean the forfeit of his grandmother's treasures. But surrender to the tide of rage rising within him would be even worse, resulting in the loss of both the jewels and any prospect of his own salvation.

As he had hoped, England's Mistress of Witches extended a gloved hand. Etienne brought her fingers briefly to his lips, feeling the flare of her power as Rowan followed the stream of the magic attacking him to its source.

"How dare she? Defying Justice and custom both—" Damien growled softly. Doubtlessly, the onlookers took the Chief Mage's thunderous expression as jealousy, but the scowl directed at Circe told Etienne otherwise. Such was the strength of the loving bond between husband and wife. England's Chief Mage knew exactly what was afoot.

"The protection of home and hearth are *my* domains," Rowan reminded Damien gently, rising from her chair and fixing her gaze upon Circe.

A warning to all, kin and guest. The Pact of Peace abides, quarrels at rest.

First to attack, by weapon or Gift, Justice will find you, harsh and swift," she chanted.

Rowan raised her cupped hand and a cool flame glared in her palm, kindling an invisible fuse.

"As Mistress of Witches I call hearth to my will, thus do I warn all who choose to do ill." The sparkling light burned through the air, leading inexorably toward Circe along the cord of her own magic.

"Witchfire," Etienne's grandmother murmured in approval. "Haven't seen the like since I was learning my first spells at my own grandmother's hearth. By

Hecate's hair, all those who speculate England's new Mistress is powerless? That'll give them grist for their rumor mill."

Etienne's former fiancée backed away as she saw magic rapidly barreling towards her on the back of her barrage of compulsion. Circe barely managed to extinguish her casting on Etienne before the counter spell burned its way back to her. As it was, a shower of glistening sparks exploded at her feet. The crowd snickered with delight, craning their necks to try and gauge the reaction of the man who was the most likely to have been Circe's target.

The compulsion at Etienne's back was gone.

"The next time Gifts are misused in this house, there will be more than fireworks," Rowan warned, before taking her seat once more.

"So du Le Fey, if you approach me to request the solving of some matter for you, you may put it in the boon jar like everyone else." Damien provided an opening for Etienne to speak. Sympathy lurked beneath the Chief Mage's angry grimace.

"I make no such requests, milord." Etienne deliberately imbued his bark of harsh laughter with just the right *soupçon* of conceit to gratify the Chief Mage's enemies. "You will not find my name in the urn of supplicants."

Clasping his grandmother's hand, the comte added, "I merely accompany my grandmother to ask for your help in obtaining the return of what rightfully belongs to her. Circe has failed to yield objects of great sentiment which have been in my mother's family for generations. At the henge, many of you heard her public refusal to fulfill our plighted troth. Lady Morgan is a witch who has been pledged to England's Chief and Mistress since birth, yet it has availed her nothing."

"As my grandson says, we merely ask for the return

of family property which this...this...person unlawfully retains, having very openly renounced her betrothal!" Lady Morgan interjected, pinning Circe with steady regard as her voice rose in indignation. "I would not trouble you with this, even now, except this brazen girl has the nerve to wear jewels tonight which have passed from bride to bride in my family. These treasures, which she has no right to claim, were vouchsafed by me only upon pledge of future vows."

"The Comte du Le Fey gave them to me as a gift outright!" Circe claimed, stepping back before the old woman's basilisk stare.

"Did he now?" Damien asked, packing all of his doubt into the question.

Frantically, Circe looked around her for signs of support to her assertion and was obviously surprised at what she found. Curiosity and amusement reigned, as if this was all a drama arranged by the host for an evening's entertainment.

Just when Etienne thought her surrender to the inevitable was imminent, she cast him a venomous look.

"He gave them to me because vows *were* made! They were a *handfasting* present."

There was a hiss of shock and indignation from the assembly.

Circe's move was both bold and desperate. Although the rite of handfast for a year and a day was an old custom, it was viewed in much the same scandalous light as the Outsider ton viewed a Gretna Green marriage over the anvil.

Obviously, Circe was hoping the degree of enmity directed at him would absolve her *faux pas.* Sampling the joys of the marriage bed before formal nuptial rites was not unheard of. Yet, while such acts were often committed, they were rarely admitted. No matter if it was the ton or the High Circles, divorcing discretion from hypocrisy was bad form, with or without the force of magic lurking in a legacy of noble privilege.

Circe ignored the reactions and forged ahead wearing a woebegone look. "The tokens of affection became mine when you took me to your bed. They belong to me now by right."

Her outright lie prompted him to add another silent benison to the Power of Light. It was unexpectedly humbling to acknowledge that he had been blessed unawares. Etienne suddenly wondered if Circe had hesitated to repudiate him before his trial because she had hoped for a sentence of death. Then no one could have disputed any claim she might have made.

"We were never handfasted, nor were we ever lovers," Etienne felt his temper flaring despite his every effort to keep himself in control. "I honored your maidenhood."

"A du Le Fey with honor?" She snickered and there was outright laughter from the audience. "You gave me your pledge in the honorable tradition of the old ways of our people and then took my innocence."

"If your innocence is no more, it was not I who stole it." His fury grew with the grins and chorus of knowing jibes. They did not believe him. Clearly, he had underestimated the degree of prejudice against him.

"Silence!" Rowan demanded. "I have the power to determine the truth here."

Etienne regarded his father's former wife in wonder and dismay. That she would offer to use her Gift of Mind Walking in another's thoughts for his sake? After all the harm the du Le Fey family had caused her?

More than most, Etienne understood the cost of entering the thoughts of someone who was consciously resisting. Circe would fight to maintain her lie every step of the way. He was about to tell Rowan he would not accept a magic boon that might damage the core of her being, when Circe spoke.

"I will not have *her* walk through my thoughts!" Circe declared contemptuously. "She was a creature of the du Le Fey family before she was Wodesby's wife." She smirked knowingly at Etienne. "I would not be surprised if she and my once-fiancé were lovers themselves."

The smell of nascent lightning filled the room. Sparks of fury flared between Damien's fingers at the insult. To publicly impugn the Mistress of Witches, before her own hearth? It was not to be borne.

Etienne's fists curled in impotent anger, only barely able to refrain from a response that would ruin his Gifts beyond recall. Circe dared to imply he had dallied with his father's wife!

The crowd retreated before Damien as he rose from his place at the dais.

Circe stepped back, abruptly becoming aware she might have gone too far.

"Do you truly wish to break the peace of the Longest Night?" A question rose above the murmurs.

Genevieve Dale moved into the empty space between the enraged Chief Mage and Circe.

"You would defend her?" Damien all but roared and took another step forward.

Etienne marveled at the blend of courage and foolhardiness that caused Genevieve Dale to stand her ground.

Clearly, she was aware of her danger. Those deep amber eyes were darkened and wide with terror and her hand trembled.

But she did not yield.

Etienne started towards her himself. This was not her battle to fight.

Lady Morgan put a restraining hand on his wrist.

"Wait," the old woman commanded softly. "Not yet."

Etienne felt the touch of her magic and saw the tell-tale blue tinge of a Foresight in his grandmother's eyes.

"I would protect us all!" Genevieve Dale declared. There was a quaver in her voice, as if she were forcing herself to speak. "Justice and fury cannot dwell in the same circle. Break the peace and you bring upon us your own wife's curse, Lord Wodesby."

Damien gulped a deep breath and forced his power to recede. "You do well to remind us of this truth." He turned his attention back to Circe. "We have all of us felt the discord you have attempted to sow here tonight. For that alone you deserve penalty. And know you this, Circe of the Donnelly clan, your insult to England's Mistress of Witches, my wife, is neither forgiven nor forgotten."

Genevieve Dale drew a deep breath. It was clear she was waging an internal war against an array of emotions. Fear, indecision and determination passed through those expressive eyes. Too late for concealment, she shuttered her gaze. When she looked again, Etienne recognized firm resolve in her stare.

She took a deep breath and spoke. "There is another way to determine the truth, milord," she said.

"Who is this creature?" Lord Pendrake asked with a sneer. "Do you allow OutBloods or Outsiders to give us lessons in our conduct, Lord Wodesby?"

With Pendrake's mockery, all traces of hesitation disappeared. It was as if her fear had been burned away in the furnace of indignation rising in her eyes. In its place, embers of magic began to blaze blue bright, like a flame in a hearth's core.

She was a witch. Etienne felt an unreasonable exultation and at the same time, a measure of trepidation.

"You don't have to do this!" Miranda exclaimed,

forcing her way through the crowd to come and stand beside her friend. "You can walk away and none will place blame upon you."

From Miranda's horrified expression, it was clear that her friend was about to undertake something that placed her at hazard. Genevieve Dale had assumed the stance of a soldier girding for battle, a peculiar mixture of dread and determination that was the stuff of bravery. Slowly, she touched her mask and it slipped into a cowl round her neck.

"My name is Genevieve Dale, a child of Merlin, born of the Blood."

Her hair had been dressed high upon her head and the glow of candles accentuated glints of auburn and gold in the mass of chestnut glory. Even when she had been distressed and bedraggled, she had been beautiful, a warrior. But Etienne could now see beyond the superficial trappings of appearance. Lit from within by the strength of her magic, she was magnificent.

And frightening in the abundance of arcane force that was rising within her.

The control of such power without a jewel to serve as a focus was a grave risk.

There seemed to be a message directed to him in her proud stance, the hint of a wry smile in her gaze as if taunting him for his previous mockery.

Whatever peril she intended to undertake, Etienne knew that she was doing it as payment to him, and it would be a more than ample recompense.

Perhaps deadly.

A babble of voices erupted. Wagers were being made. Information was bubbling forth in a cauldron of confusion and scandal, rumor and questions.

"Upon Lady Genevieve, no guilt will be." The crowd went suddenly silent as Damien's voice, augmented by his Seer's Gift, thundered through the room. Power

flared, his eyes engulfed in an aura of full blue that was the harbinger of a major Foretelling. *"If she seeks no truth, 'tis strife we'll all see. Fathers 'gainst brothers, Sisters 'gainst mothers."* Damien declared in the spell-song tones of a Seer.

He left the platform to face Genevieve. The Chief Mage's eyes returned to their normal shade of emerald as the blue glow of magic faded. He regarded the subject of his prophecy solemnly. "There may be bitter consequences should you withhold your Gift tonight, Lady Genevieve. But the choice still belongs to you, as Miranda has said. What ill may befall here will be to our shame, not your blame."

With a rueful shake of his head, he turned away.

Miranda moved to stand between Etienne and her friend as he approached them. He held his empty palms out in a universal gesture indicating no harm was intended.

"I just wished to give my thanks to the lady for putting herself forward, regardless of what she might choose to do." He spoke softly, surprising himself with his own words. "And to make her aware there are always a variety of interpretations, and few absolute certainties, in a Seer's pronouncements."

"This is true," Miranda nodded, obviously hoping his statement would help to persuade her friend to withdraw.

Genevieve Dale's eyes met his in surprise and puzzlement, but even if the questions within her gaze were voiced aloud, he doubted he would be able to answer. There was only one thing he knew for certain.

"Whatever your power may be, I would not ask you to endanger yourself on my behalf, milady." With a bow that contained both regret and gratitude, he turned back to his grandmother.

Lady Morgan would be disappointed, but he would

not endanger Genevieve Dale, even for the sake of the Morgan jewels, precious as they were. He and his grandmother would have to find some other means of retrieving them.

CHAPTER 9

It took a moment for Genevieve to realize the comte was offering her an excuse to rescind her offer. In her experience, Genevieve had yet to meet a mage of power who would consider anything other than his own welfare and prestige.

Could it be Circe was actually the one who was telling the real tale? Was this a way for him to keep the truth from coming to light? Even though all of Genevieve's instincts told her otherwise, she could think of no other reason than guilt for his gesture.

The whispers were rising into a full-fledged buzz as the gathering speculated. Lady Morgan's eyes glittered with anger and resignation. Circe was doing her best to maintain the appearance of wronged innocence, but with the focus on Genevieve, the comte, and his grandmother, the younger woman's façade slipped to reveal the cold stare of a cobra, ready to strike.

That momentary lapse cemented Genevieve's decision. With a deep breath for courage, she squared her shoulders with resolve. How could she ask others to do what was right and just, if she allowed fear to keep her from doing the same?

Though she was quaking within, Genevieve moved

forward and faced the man she now knew to be the notorious Comte du Le Fey. Judgement had turned his hair silver, making his identity almost unmistakable as one of the few who bore the unique shade caused by experiencing a surfeit of magic.

"I would fault myself for the outcome if I held back now, and those recriminations are the hardest to live with," Genevieve said.

"She speaks wisdom." Lady Morgan inclined her head in acknowledgement. "Are you a Mind-walker then, like our Mistress of Witches?"

"I am a Sifter of Truth," Genevieve said, feeling a peculiar sense of relief at revealing what she had hidden for so long. "Under my power, people cannot knowingly tell me a lie outright."

"I have never heard of such magic!" Circe declared. "Who do you think you are to interfere in the affairs of your betters?" Her look of scorn swept Genevieve from head to toe. "You claim to be of the Blood, but I see no naming jewel upon you!"

There was a murmur of indignant agreement from the crowd.

"You will let this…this upstart…accuse me?" Circe sputtered.

"I accuse you of nothing!" Genevieve raised her head proudly. "I merely ask you to touch my hand and repeat what you have previously claimed."

"Perhaps you may question me first and spare the girl from humiliating herself further?" The comte stepped forward.

Genevieve looked toward Damien, who nodded his approval.

"Very well, milord," Genevieve agreed, as she peeled back her borrowed kid gloves. "Skin to skin would make it simpler, if you would."

Obediently, the comte revealed the rough hands that had guided her through the streets to safety.

The comte's fingers clasped hers. His grip was gentle as before, sure, and somehow comforting. The agitation in her stomach calmed and as those cerulean eyes met hers; she prayed he was planning to tell her the truth. If he did not believe in her power and tried to speak a falsehood, his betrayal of his fiancée would be compounded and revealed to all.

"You will now attempt to lie, Comte du Le Fey," Genevieve requested. "Try to give me another name and claim it as yours."

"This proves nothing!" A familiar voice declared from the crowd. "How do we know that you are not his —confederate?"

Genevieve had never heard so many insinuations imbued into one word. The comte let go of her hand and stepped forward, as if to shield her, but she moved ahead of him to face her foe.

She was done with hiding.

"Aren't you the proprietress of Dale's Apothecary?" Lord Pendrake pushed his way to the fore with a sneer in his voice. He grabbed her at the wrist, as if to restrain her from flight. "Wasn't your late husband an Outsider, *Lady* Genevieve?" He imbued the title with a wealth of doubt.

"Unlike you and your brother, my husband never touched a woman without leave. Unlike you, Owen was a good and honest man," Genevieve declared, smiling with an elation sourced in the release of long held anger and the sweet possibility of retribution. Her plan would have a cost, but it would be worth the price.

Lord Pendrake was one of the men who had hounded her mercilessly, importuning her at every turn, even while her husband had lived. She regarded his fingers with the disgust that one would accord a swarm of slugs crawling on skin, but he did not release her.

"Shall I take off my gloves as well?" he asked.

"I would much rather you didn't," Genevieve speared him with a cold stare. "Even though it will take some additional effort on my part, there are some things I would prefer not to touch."

There was a ripple of laughter and Pendrake's mouth tightened into a hard, humorless line.

A center hit on the target.

The comte's chuckle was an unexpected bonus giving her an extra measure of courage, despite Lord Pendrake's glare. While the snickers of the crowd faded, Genevieve made a decision. If retribution was a surety, she might as well be in for a pound rather than a penny. Once again, she let loose the leash on her Gift.

"Shall we test my Gift on you then, Lord Pendrake? Owen Dale dealt with all in kindness and generosity of spirit. My late husband paid what he owed. Can you declare the same about yourself to me milord? I dare you to say, 'I have no outstanding debt to you, Lady Genevieve.'"

"I owe you...n...no," he sputtered, the falsehood catching in his throat.

"Will you deny the fact that your account is in substantial arrears, then, milord?"

"Tradeswoman!" the mage uttered the word like an epithet.

"Truth!" she declared defiantly.

He released her and stepped back to a chorus of laughter. His scowl was filled with furious promise as Genevieve rubbed her wrist.

"Speaking of tradeswomen, I seem to recall that your Great-grandmother Pendrake began your family fortune selling love philtres and charms in the market of Truro. Had a rat as a familiar, I'm told," Lady

Morgan announced. Somehow, her sour-faced inspection of Pendrake through her jeweled set of lenses was more of an insult than her words. "The type of animal spirits that tend to attach themselves to us says a good deal about the mage or witch we are, I'm told. Did the rats also choose you, Pendrake? Or are they more discerning creatures than I had thought."

"Our tradition says that debts are discharged at Solstice, to start the season in good will." The Chief Mage addressed Pendrake with mock geniality. "If you owe this witch money, I suggest you make good before the New Year. Unless, of course, you wish to try again and say you owe her nothing."

Lord Wodesby's look of counterfeit congeniality swept the guests with almost palpable force. "And if there is anyone else here who wishes to dispute what they owe Lady Genevieve, let them come forward now and do so, that the truth may be determined. If what is due her remains unpaid by the New Year, I shall ask her to bring any open accounts to my attention. Now, if no one else wishes to question our integrity, I believe we shall proceed." His gaze swept the crowd, daring a reply.

The Chief Mage favored Genevieve with a bow. "At your convenience, Lady Genevieve?"

Once again, Genevieve took up the comte's hand. This time, the connection was deeper, well beyond superficial touch. She felt his strength, the sheer power of the magic restrained behind the wall of his will, but there was something more, something that she could not define. Clearing the distraction of her wayward thoughts, she focused on her line of questioning.

Back to the business at hand.

Genevieve nodded at the comte. "Now you will say to me as follows—'I did not make love to Circe daughter of the Donnelly Clan.'"

"I did not make l...l...I did not make...l..." The comte stumbled into a stutter.

"You see!" Circe shouted, the trepidation on her face turning to triumph. "He cannot say it. Our troth has expired since it is well beyond a year and a day. The jewels are mine!"

The Frenchman's face grew pale. "I stole some embraces and the pleasure of a few kisses with the woman I thought would be the soulmate I had hoped for, the witch who would share my life. Apparently, it would seem, my feelings for Circe were stronger than even I believed. Could it be I actually loved her, but did not know it?"

Although his deep bass was calm, and his question prosaic, Genevieve could feel the turmoil beneath his words. He had not loosed his hold on her hand and she knew what he said was nothing less than the truth. This man was just realizing the depth of his feelings for a woman who had scorned and humiliated him.

It was a nasty potion for a proud aristocrat to swallow, even in the privacy of his heart. How much more so in public view? Circe's gloating was adding to the bitter gall of discovering he had been lying to himself.

Genevieve wondered why she had suddenly gained access to the deeper levels of his innermost truths. Never before had her Gift affected anything beyond preventing the utterance of superficial lies, the counterfeit notes that most people proffered as social currency. Yet, she was sharing the newly opened wound of the comte's honest pain. It moved her, stoking a righteous anger against the woman who was blatantly rejoicing at the humiliation of a man who had loved her truly.

How could anyone reject the prospect of a genuine affection for the ephemeral gain of position? Genevieve could understand Circe's desire to sever the connection. The comte had, by his own admission, broken some of their kind's most sacred laws. As a result, he had endured the loss of all he held dear, including his fiancée, yet she was willing to lie, eager to shame him, and demean herself for the possession of a few trifling baubles.

"If you would care to rephrase the statement, Lady Genevieve." His quietly spoken request was barely audible from between clenched teeth.

His visage had grown pale, his brow furrowing, as Genevieve sensed the strain of the struggle happening within him. She could feel the comte fighting to control a surge of soul-deep magic. A pain-driven wave of rage pressed for release, demanding he strike out at those who mocked him.

This time, Genevieve's Gift did more than read his honest emotions. Her power reached out to meet the furious tide threatening to overwhelm the Frenchman. Genevieve braced herself, as if for an oncoming collision, but instead her Gift took a dive into his tossing sea.

For a moment, she feared she would be torn apart and left to drown in the currents. Then, all at once, she found herself drifting gently as the swell of magic abated, leaving her unharmed, but confounded upon the shore. Rapidly, the flood tide receded.

For a moment, she saw her own Gift reflected in his eyes, her blue layered upon his own natural celestial blue. Color returned to his face and calm replaced the tension in his demeanor. There was amazement in his expression and momentary confusion, but he quickly regained his composure. With a brief nod, he indicated he was back in control and ready for her to proceed.

Genevieve nodded her own acknowledgement and found the appropriate words. "Tell me if you would, 'I did not take the maidenhood of Circe, daughter of the Donnelly clan.'"

"I did not take the maidenhood of Circe, daughter of the Donnelly clan." Every syllable was pronounced loudly and clearly as the comte asserted his innocence. "Nor," he added of his own accord, "did I pledge to her in a handfast."

"This is a travesty, as Lord Pendrake has said!" Circe shrieked.

"Curious? You were eager enough to accept the determination of Lady Genevieve's Gift a moment ago, when it seemed to support you. Still, you may end this *travesty*, as you call it, in one of two ways. Withdraw now and undertake to return Lady Morgan's property," Damien advised her, his expression a rigid mask. "Or you may take the opportunity to state your view as you honestly see it and support your claim."

He paused, waiting for her choice, but Circe did not back away. "You will remove your gloves, take Lady Genevieve's hand and say 'Etienne, son of the du Le Fey, took my maidenhood.'"

Reluctantly, Circe came forward, uncovered and extended her fingers.

It was like grasping a writhing snake. "You will have to hold still," Genevieve demanded.

"Etienne son of the du Le Fey took my...my...m... m" Circe tried to force the word from her lips. She drew back her hand as if it had been bitten.

"You shouted it well enough earlier, gel," Lady Morgan pronounced bitterly. "Without a whit of shame before all and sundry."

"We will give you a moment to work on your elocution, Circe, if you would care to make another attempt to state your version of the truth," the Mistress of Witch's acid tones declared the woman a liar without explicitly using the word.

Once again, the sniggers that rippled through the room were further confirmation that the tide had turned against Circe. For a moment, Genevieve turned her focus from her subject. As she raised her eyes to the crowd, what she saw upon their faces caused her to quake at her very core.

Genevieve trembled, but it was more than the unaccustomed and prolonged exercise of her Gift that made her suddenly weak. The Mistress of Witches left the dais to stand at Genevieve's side, tacitly offering her support. With a speaking look, Rowan signified she understood what Genevieve was only just beginning to comprehend.

Genevieve had come forward impulsively, hoping, at first, to prevent violence and then to repay a twice-owed debt to the man she now knew as the Comte du Le Fey. He had saved her from the dangers of the London streets and from the consequences of her own ignorance when she would have wielded her athame against Pendrake's brother.

Now, it became clear the crowd's intense scrutiny was due to more than the entertainment of watching someone publicly pilloried and humiliated. The mages and witches present had found something other than Circe to excite their interest. It was Genevieve herself and the unusual power she possessed rousing their curiosity.

She could almost hear the speculation and calculation running rampant like a rip tide beneath the superficial currents of amusement. How could they use her? How would they be able to gain control of her ability? How could they prevent others from doing the same?

Her sole protection until now had been secrecy, but she had thrown it away. And to what purpose? For some family trinkets belonging to a woman who could doubtless afford to purchase more and better with her pin money? For a man who was infamous among Merlin's children and who had been condemned by the persona of Justice for his crimes?

Why should a woman who had been forced by need to sell her naming jewel meddle in the quarrels of those who deemed themselves to be her *betters*, who held her beneath contempt? She knew the answer lay within the nature of her Gift. To walk away and allow a deliberate lie to stand unchallenged and do harm would be a betrayal of herself. To deny her debt to the Comte du Le Fey, would make her no better than Lord Pendrake.

"Let us explore this matter further, to save ourselves from any future disingenuous claims," Rowan suggested. "With your indulgence, Lady Genevieve?"

Genevieve nodded her consent and clasped Circe's trembling hand once again.

"Try saying these words," Rowan prompted. "'The parure I wear tonight and the betrothal jewels given to my care were gifts given unconditionally.'"

"The par...r...par...r—" Circe choked, snatching her hand back. "This is absurd. It is a conspiracy against me! Can you not all see it?"

Circe surveyed the room for signs of affirmation.

Silent condemnation was all she found.

Donnelly's daughter had forgotten it was not only the Outsider ton who relied upon marriage settlements and their attendant agreements to maintain power and family ties. Those binding pacts stood as the bedrock of the relationships within the upper tiers of the clans and covens as well. Chicanery can, and did, occur in private. However, the High Circles would not countenance it in public.

"With your indulgence, milady," the comte stepped forward. "I would uncover one more truth. Can you say *I did not use my Siren's Gift upon you, Etienne?*"

To Genevieve's surprise, Circe immediately took

her hand. "I did not use my Siren's Gift upon you, Etienne." Her smile was vicious in its scorn. "I had no need of it."

Only Genevieve and Circe herself could see beyond the comte's impassive expression. Fast as a lightning strike, his pain flared amidst the azure of his eyes and then disappeared. Circe exulted in the moment of petty revenge. Her derisive laughter echoed in the hall.

"Lady Morgan, you will give me the list of items due back to you. I will inform you when the daughter of the Donnellys has returned all of the property rightfully belonging to you and your grandson," Rowan commanded, drawing Genevieve up to the platform with her. Waving her guest to an empty seat beside Miranda, England's Mistress of Witches returned to stand beside her husband.

Lady Morgan curtsied deeply. "It shall be as you say, milady."

"If any deficiency remains when the spring begins ascendance, Circe daughter of the Donnellys, I will take your naming jewel from you forever. No contracts of marriage or settlements made on your behalf will be honored because you will be deemed to have completely forfeited your integrity. Do you understand?" Though Rowan's tones were deceptively mild, her eyes flared in a blaze of raw power.

Circe gave a tight nod.

"By Hearth, By Home, By Hecate, so be it!" An aura formed to encircle the comte, Lady Morgan and Circe and the pact was made.

"So be it!" The company echoed in reply.

Circe turned to go, but before she could make her exit, Lady Morgan raised a hand and the young witch was stopped in her tracks.

Rowan eyed the elderly woman with a questioning look.

"On the Longest Night no harm will be done," Lady Morgan assured. "But I would prefer to begin as we mean to go on. With your permission, Mistress?"

Rowan nodded and the comte's grandmother directed a wicked smile at her grandson's erstwhile fiancée. "You have some things on your person that belong to me," she demanded in a timbre that fairly vibrated with restrained power.

The diamonds at Lady Morgan's neck lifted themselves over her head with exquisite control. The plumes that graced her turban stood upright to avoid interference. With a wave of the old woman's hand, the drawstrings of her reticule untied themselves to allow the jewels to snake their way into the silk bag.

"I will have those now." The clasp to the emerald neckpiece at Circe's throat undid itself and the collar of delicate gold filigree floated its way to her grandson. "If you would assist me, dear boy."

With a bow, he dutifully stepped forward to fasten the jewels upon his grandmother's neck. She turned her back to him and addressed Rowan with an impish look.

"Alas, the dilemma of my years. I find, as I get older, I have more of a difficulty with catches of the claw type," she confided. "Adrienne, your mother-by-marriage has told me she is similarly afflicted. And both of us, stricken so young! A pity." Lady Morgan held out a hand and the matching bracelet detached from Circe's arm and floated its way across the room to drape on the elderly woman's bony wrist.

The comte clasped her fingers in his, a genuine joy lighting his face. All at once Genevieve understood that it was not for his own sake he sought the return of these jewels, and endured the humiliation of his encounter with Circe, but for his grandmother. The look he shared with her was the communion of a man who delighted in witnessing the happiness of someone he loved.

He pressed a kiss upon her gnarled fingers before securing the bauble.

Lady Morgan's eyes narrowed into speculative slits as she regarded the earrings that were the last part of the set. "As I mentioned, my *délicatesse*, alas, is not what it once was, Donnelly's daughter. Unfasten those earbobs, if you please, else you risk the possibility that I might accidentally rip them out of those lobes."

With trembling hands, Circe removed the earrings and held them out on her palm.

"Though my grandson has been kind enough to play lady's maid thus far, the fastenings to these earpieces tend to be somewhat fussy, if I recall. I do believe I shall leave off the earrings for now. Don't want to waste the time of the company any further." The old woman magicked her reticule to open wide once again, and the pair of emerald eardrops winked their way into the embroidered silken bag.

"As by my given word, no harm done, Mistress," Lady Morgan dropped a graceful curtsy to the Mistress of Witches. "We Morgans keep our promises, unlike this other baggage, who now has *my* leave to be gone, so she may go home and gather up her other ill-gotten treasures for return."

Circe exited to the sound of mocking laughter, and while she did not dare to attempt any magical retribution at the moment, the dire looks she cast were enough to rekindle Genevieve's sense of impending disaster.

"You ought not to go yet," Miranda whispered. "Do not fear. We will keep you safe."

As Genevieve surveyed the crowd, she wondered if that was a promise anyone could keep.

CHAPTER 10

*C*irce had barely set foot out onto Portman Square before the hasty reconstruction of the façades of comradery and good cheer began. To an even greater extent than its Outsider counterpart, the magical ton of the High Circles was dependent on the veneers of coexistence and shared convention. Deadly internecine feuds had destroyed almost as many clans and covens as the Scourge himself.

Despite Etienne's status as a pariah, everyone suddenly wished to speak to him, to be able to claim that they had rubbed shoulders with the infamous former Chief Mage of France and perhaps share a quote direct from the mouth of the outcast at their dinner tables.

It was the fulfillment of Etienne's worst nightmares. In the hope of helping his grandmother to rejoin society, he had succeeded in pulling her into the ambit of his dishonor once more. Drawing her finally into a space under spell where they could converse privately, he began to discuss their escape.

"Perhaps you could join me in Yorkshire?" Etienne suggested. "You will find your birthplace much improved."

"In the dead of winter? I would rather go to Hades,"

Lady Morgan retorted querulously. "Of a certainty, it is warmer!"

From where they sat, Etienne had an excellent view of Lord Wodesby's table and he used the vantage point to study Lady Genevieve. He quickly realized her reactions were not what he expected. Where most would have delighted in the social consequence of being elevated to the table of honor, Lady Genevieve was obviously less than thrilled by the notice. The food from Wodesby's most excellent kitchen made a series of journeys around her plate, but only a few bites found their way to her mouth.

"She is afraid," Etienne concluded aloud.

Lady Genevieve's pose might have deceived most, but it did not mislead someone for whom the proper measurement of nuance had often made the difference between success and failure, or, for that matter, life and death. In Bonaparte's court a poorly timed word could unleash a storm of temper or worse from the First Consul. The woman's aspect was now wooden and expressionless as that of a poppet.

"Of a certainty she is worried, unless she is thoroughly an idiot," his grandmother agreed, watching her grandson carefully. "Despite her service to the Peace tonight, the gel has made some powerful enemies. If she had understood the consequences of her intervention, and had any sense at all, she would have stayed silent. Alarm indicates that she is not a complete ninny, merely somewhat of a fool."

"Honor often has unforeseen costs." Etienne watched as Lady Genevieve's glass was filled. Instead of savoring the wine, she emptied the rare vintage in a few gulps.

"Honor is a luxury a woman in her position can ill afford. Someone who has no family to speak of standing at her back, and whose continued financial survival depends on the Blood, cannot bite the hand which pays for her bread, " Lady Morgan said with a dip of her plumes for emphasis. "Pendrake is correct when he says that she is in trade. Dale's Apothecary has supplied London's users of magic for more than a decade. Although those who owe her may pay now under the Chief Mage's duress, they might well patronize another shop in the future. There are few things more irksome to those who imagine themselves to be of the Purest Blood than an upstart who holds a mirror of truth and reveals their ugly warts."

As usual, his grandmother was correct. Lady Genevieve's revelation of her Gift to help him was noble, but naïve. Only a woman who was unaware of the morass of High Circle maneuvers would have ventured where Merlin himself might have justly feared to tread.

"Without her intervention, Circe might well have won the day," Etienne commented.

"No *might* about it, dear boy! This is why we are in her debt." Once again, the plumes on her turban reflected her disparaging mood. "And you say she came to your aid tonight, *after* you absolved her of her obligation to you for a *mere kiss*? Whatever possessed you, my boy?"

"Actually, it was three kisses," Etienne responded before he could stop himself.

"Well, *that* makes it an entirely different matter," came the acidic reply.

It did, though he would not dream of telling her so. By no means could the moment he had shared with Genevieve Dale be categorized as a *mere kiss*, Etienne thought, reliving those sensations once again. Though he had thoroughly enjoyed Circe's attempts at beguilement, none of their expeditions to the brink of consummation could compare with the moment of communion he had experienced with Lady Genevieve.

He was definitely looking forward to the repayment of the balance owed to him; far too much for his own comfort, in fact.

His silence only seemed to spur his grandmother's lecture. "You are the image of the old comte, curse his rotten soul, else I might think my daughter had birthed a cuckoo in his nest. I would not have blamed her, mind you; deceived as she was when he wooed her." Once again, the plumes began their swaying to emphasize her incredulity. "Nonetheless, if a dog promised your father a flea, he would have set the duns on the cur for payment! Who knows what she may ask for tonight's favor? Mark my words, it will not come cheap. We are in debt to a nonentity!"

"With respect, I remind you of a fact. After more than a year of useless wrangling, you are wearing your grandmother's jewels tonight because of that *nonentity*, as you style her," Etienne informed her, a chill in his voice.

And thanks to her intervention, I am still in possession of my Gifts, for all the good they do me. He added silently, unwilling to share the horrific moment when Genevieve Dale's power had somehow interposed to prevent a tidal wave of icy rage that might have swept them all away in its fury. Although he had no clue as to how she had managed to forestall the disaster, he knew her intervention was a debt that could never be repaid.

"That is true," Lady Morgan admitted.

"And though she was married to an Outsider, who was apparently not of noble birth, *she is a Lady*. If Wodesby said it in a Seeing, it must be so," Etienne added adamantly.

His grandmother regarded him with an eloquent smirk and he finally realized she had been deliberately goading him. "You leap to her defense, I see. Lady or cipher though she may be, it does my heart good to see you actually caring about something, Etienne."

He was about to proclaim that his interest was nothing more than a matter of self-interest when a chime sounding like the cracking of ice signaled the impending transition of the season.

Glasses were filled. Beneath the table, Etienne's familiar purred her satisfaction as a servant set a bowl of the *crème fraiche* at her paws for her own libation. For Suzette and all cats, the departure of winter was a favorite time of year, a reason to celebrate.

All conversation ceased and the company rose as one. With their glasses held high, they silently drank in tribute to the heart of the dark night and the change in the seasons heralding the chariot of the sun and the coming of spring.

As they set their glasses down, another chime signaled the arrival of the time for supplicants.

The guests began to jockey for position. Those who considered themselves in the First Circles fell in to join the procession following the boon jar to its place before the dais.

Etienne sighed as Lady Genevieve kept her seat and finished another glass. Either she was trying to drink her fear away or she was unaware of the potency and quantity of the vintages she was consuming. From the look of her, she was already half-sprung and at the rate she was swilling wine, it was more than likely that she would be fully inebriated before Wodesby finally dealt with the requests of the lesser folk.

"You may all return to your seats," Damien announced as the amphora was set in its place. "This year I intend to begin a new tradition. The Fates themselves will choose precedence this night. Those who wish to ask a boon will receive their turn based upon need as reckoned by the magic of the urn."

There was a chorus of disgruntled mutters and angry stares as those who had expected the benefits of privilege returned to their tables. Etienne could see smiles dawning on the faces of the lesser supplicants who had thought they would be waiting into the wee hours of the morning until their betters had made done with their requests, usually after a plethora of lengthy speeches.

There was no such relief in Lady Genevieve's expression, if anything, her dismal aspect intensified. Etienne's speculation was confirmed. This was what had brought her to Wodesby House when she had so clearly wished herself elsewhere.

"Before I begin to draw names from the Witch of Delphi's urn," Damien began. "There is one individual here to whom precedence is owed. All of us are indebted to her for keeping the Peace of this night."

Etienne drew a sharp breath as he felt a tingle of foreboding based more on Lady Genevieve's expression than any hint of his Gift.

"Lady Genevieve, is your name and request contained in the Pythia's urn?" Damien asked.

She nodded and started to speak. "Milord, I would prefer if you would not—"

"Nonsense!" the mage's voice boomed, turning his attention back to the other guests and forging ahead, unaware of the growing panic on her face. "I am sure no one here would object if I address her boon first tonight."

Anything further she said was drowned out by cheers.

"Please!"

Etienne read the word on her lips.

She shook her head vigorously; trying to be heard above the crowd, but the mage had already turned his attention back to the other guests.

There was no naysaying from the clamoring audience, only rank curiosity. In Etienne's estimation, there was far too much interest in the request of a witch who had, hitherto, been deemed of little significance.

The slip of paper upon which she had inscribed her wish rose from the jar and floated into her trembling hand. The Chief Mage's command rang out.

"Genevieve Dale, ask."

Her efforts to gain Lord Wodesby's attention ceased in the grasp of the Pythian spell, but her look of panic intensified.

The imperative call to those who wished to seek a boon on the Longest Night contained a compulsion all its own. Its underlying formula had been forged long ago to help encourage the weak so they could eloquently make their wishes known. The power of the invocation was meant to stand as their bulwark against those who might otherwise seek to intimidate them.

Once again, Etienne saw the telltale blue of magic spark in Genevieve Dale's eyes as she struggled against that imperative. Her ability to keep her silence for as long as she had was a tribute to her strength. In the end, he knew any battle against the force of a spell fortified by centuries of custom was a fight even a witch of potent power was bound to lose.

The moment of bitter surrender was easy to recognize. Victims of Madame La Guillotine wore much the same expression when they heard the downward slide of the blade.

"If you please, Lord Damien…I ask that you… choose…a worthy mage to serve as mentor for my son," she blurted out. "**The…final…decision is…*mine*!**"

Never before had Etienne heard anyone delay or falter in the asking of a Yuletide boon. Once again, her eyes met his. She glowed with an expression of triumph before the blaze of her will was doused, a candle in a downpour. Collapsing back into her chair, the woman seemed to deflate like one of Sadler's balloons. The slip of paper with her boon floated to rest beneath the dais.

As one body, a mass of mages had risen to their feet, young and old, powerful and weak. A wave of voices rose, the babbling chorus disintegrating into a raucous cacophony as they all debated their qualifications and their worthiness. Others proceeded to denigrate their fellows as undeserving of the honor of shepherding a young man into magehood.

"Before they knew her to be a Truth Sifter, I doubt there are more than ten among the lot of them who would have volunteered a coin for that collection plate," Lady Morgan remarked as she watched the commotion.

"Your estimate of the number of mages who have the capacity for altruism far exceeds mine," Etienne said, bending down to have a word with his familiar.

Suzette reluctantly abandoned her dish and dashed rapidly through the crowd.

"We are responsible for bringing her to their notice," he continued.

"She was the one who made the decision to put her oar in."

"For a debt whose payment had already been negotiated." Etienne waved a hand in dismissal, keeping a discrete watch on Suzette as she retrieved the scrap he was seeking from the floor. "At a loss to herself. Because of what she did for us, they now wonder if her Gift has passed to her son. Or they seek access to her abilities through the boy."

With all eyes on Lady Genevieve, no one noticed when his familiar returned with the slip.

Etienne read the original words of the boon written in an elegant hand. The difference between the words in ink and those spoken aloud lay in the last part of her request, confirming his suspicions. He marveled at the magnitude of the effort it must have required on her part to add to the formulation of her original appeal so the final decision would be hers alone.

"What are we to do, Grandmama?" He surreptitiously passed the note to his grandmother.

The old woman's eyes widened. "She took the final choice out of Wodesby's hands," she hissed in astonishment. "Not a fool at all, it would appear, is our Lady Genevieve, if she could see this muddle on the horizon."

From his gratified expression, it was apparent Lord Wodesby did not possess that measure of foresight in this regard. Focused on the clamor of eager volunteers, he had not witnessed Lady Genevieve's collapse, nor was it likely that he had fully understood the significance of her hesitation. As Etienne recalled, due to the Chief Mage's duties to Wellington during the war and the temporary loss of his powers, Wodesby's mother had presided over the granting of boons in the past.

Immensely pleased at the response, Damien turned his attention to the asker, his grin transforming to bafflement. Framed by the great window overlooking the square, Lady Genevieve sat, pale as the falling snow outside. Levering herself up on the arms of her chair, she tried to rise, but faltered. Miranda hastened to support her.

From Rowan's expression, it was clear Etienne's stepmother had already grasped the likely consequences of the night's chain of events. The old comte's tutelage had trained her to think in scenarios of the worst case. Lord Wodesby was relatively new to the reins of power. In Etienne's opinion, Damien's years among OutBloods had resulted in a woeful decline in the instincts of suspicion and self-preservation necessary to his office.

He was fortunate in his wife. Rowan had been taught to distrust by default.

She whispered hastily to her husband and then hurried to Lady Genevieve's other side to help her. As the trio retreated into the shadows, Lord Wodesby's voice boomed above the clamor. "It appears Lady Genevieve is overwhelmed by your display of generosity," he announced with barely concealed sarcasm. "We will now proceed with the next boon."

A slip rose and floated to an ill-dressed crone who had the look of a hedge witch about her. There was a plethora of frowns as she hobbled up to Damien.

"Anne Pritcher. Ask!"

"They will be taking her to Tante Reina via the backstairs," Etienne predicted as the old woman gave voice to her request. "They may need help."

"She will need a restorative potion at the least. The poor gel overindulged the drink, not that I blame her!" she declared, forestalling her grandson's angry retort. "I merely say it will exacerbate any ill effects of a surfeit of magic. Send Suzette ahead to inform them to prepare to receive her below stairs. I will have my carriage brought round to the back so it may be ready for her to return home."

Etienne looked at her doubtfully. "In her state?"

"She will want to go home." His grandmother's plumes bobbed in certainty. "She has only just realized her son has been placed at hazard. Believe what I say. She will want to be with him."

CHAPTER 11

*D*espite the support of the two women who flanked her, Genevieve barely managed to stay upright as she left the ballroom. "Do not let them see me fall." Her plea was barely a whisper.

"Never fear," Miranda said. "Tante Reina will mix up something for you and you'll soon feel right as a tripod."

But even with the weariness weakening Genevieve's perceptions, she knew her friend's reassurance contained more than a modicum of doubt. The unaccustomed use of her Gift and the expenditure of magic to reshape the boon were overwhelming. Waves of exhaustion and fear threatened to pull her under. Her eyelids were losing the battle, closing beneath the inexorable weight. Just when she feared she would fall and pull her friends down with her, she found herself literally swept off her feet.

"Down, put me...down!" Her protest came out as little more than a murmur as strong arms cradled her. Scents of lemon, lavender, bergamot and starched linen tickled gently at her nose. For the first time in days, the burden of worry dissipated with an unaccustomed sense of complete safety that went well beyond a mere relief of anxiety. It had been so very long since she had felt safe and warm, enfolded in the comfort of a man's embrace.

Or had it?

The same sense of sanctuary? The scents? Her stranger?

The Comte du Le Fey!

Her mother had warned her of Gifts of this kind. The self-same talents which could soothe a troubled mind and ease an anxious heart could also be employed to lull a victim into a false sense of wellbeing.

Genevieve began a desperate effort to surface from seductive languor. She had to move, to get away.

"Be at ease."

The vibration of the comte's voice rumbled against her as he spoke. "Know you are safe with me. Even if I had the use of my magic, I would do you no harm," he assured her.

She felt the gentle touch of his lips against her forehead, his words so soft, that Genevieve alone could hear him. "Let your Gift see my intent. You may trust me milady. I will protect you." There was a trace of ironic amusement in his voice, as he added, "Circe and I were well matched in that regard. Never yet have I needed to use Merlin's Gifts to charm an attractive woman."

Truth, her magic declared, even as she felt the pang of pain amidst his admission.

The affirmation of her Gift flared far beyond a mere validation of his promise, giving her a glimpse into the strength of his intent. Although her eyes remained closed, she saw a vision of the comte bearing a sword made of light, shielding her from an onslaught of avaricious faces.

At his core, she had seen the capacity to love truly and deeply, despite the wounds he had endured. His words conjured yet another image within her, lurking in the darkness of secret desires. She saw herself entwined with him in the shelter of the shadows, sharing another of the kisses she had promised him.

Was that image the product of his truth or her inner longing? In her muddled state, it was difficult to discern. But no matter what the source, Genevieve dismissed the dream as a wish born of weakness. Ultimately, there would be no one other than herself to depend on. She was, as always, alone.

"Home. Please," Genevieve murmured, unsure he heard her.

"She is in no condition to go back alone," Miranda protested as the comte set Genevieve in a chair, holding her upright as Tante Reina poured a cup of noxious brew into a silver flagon.

"I shall transport her," the comte offered.

"It will not serve!" Rowan argued. "Genevieve can stay the night. We can have a footman inform her family."

Despite her weariness, Genevieve forced her eyes to open at that declaration, but she could not find the strength to argue.

Even so, the mage who held her seemed to read her look. Reflected in those shifting blue depths was concern and strangely enough, she recognized emotions rare among those who deemed themselves to be among the Highest Circles—kindness and compassion.

"What is it to be, milady? Stay here or go home."

"Home." The word was a demand, all the more resolute because it was conveyed upon a sigh.

"Then it is there you shall go, but first you must drink this all."

Obediently, Genevieve forced herself to take another sip of Tante Reina's restorative nostrum.

"We can fetch Louis and your Mama here to stay

with you," Rowan coaxed. "They will be entirely safe under our protection."

"Home!" Genevieve gave a vehement shake of her head and the room went reeling. It took another sip of brew to calm her stomach and stop the spin. "Home," she repeated, too weak to explain how her mother would be frightened. She did not do well in unfamiliar places.

Miranda and Rowan continued their barrage of promises and entreaties.

All at once, she found herself staring into familiar blue eyes as the comte knelt beside her. "Do not allow them to bully you."

"Bully? How dare you interfere?" Rowan declared. "It was you who precipitated this disaster, Etienne!"

"Not truth," Genevieve whispered softly. "I...chose." She looked at him, begging with her eyes. She tried to raise the flagon for another sip but it trembled, threatening to spill.

He took it from her hand and brought it to her lips so that she could swallow.

"Ugh!" She grimaced, gulping air as if it could dispel the taste.

"For a surfeit of magic and wine, potent medicine is needed," Tante Reina explained. "You know well, Lady Genevieve, such remedies, rarely are they pleasant on the tongue."

The comte offered another sip, but she took a bit too much. His fingers brushed her lip gently to wipe away the surplus. Once more, Genevieve felt the peculiar sensation of that connection between them. With each mouthful, she felt a little more of her strength returning.

A cat streaked into the kitchen. *"Coach issss waiting!"* she informed the comte.

Genevieve felt her spirits sinking at the thought of him leaving. "Fare...well," she whispered.

"I am not leaving without you," he told her, setting the empty vessel aside. "Are you ready?"

"Yes," she answered firmly, relief nearly overwhelming her. "Home."

"I will convey you there." There was a promise in his voice.

"Alone in a closed carriage?" Rowan asked. "Do you care nothing for her reputation?"

"Rowan!" Genevieve croaked, feeling herself flushing at the implications of the Mistress of Witches' questions.

"Your friend only seeks to protect you against my foul reputation." There was a touch of sadness in his smile. "My grandmother will accompany us. Will that suit?"

Tante Reina nodded. "A worthy chaperone."

Soon, Genevieve was wrapped in a cocoon of blankets and placed into the wheeled chair Tante Reina sometimes used when her remedies could not fully relieve her aching bones.

"Return...gown...soon," Genevieve muttered weakly, turning to Miranda.

"No hurry," her friend replied, smiling, despite her concern. "I suspect it shall not fit me for the next few months in any case. Perhaps next time I see you, you can find a truth for me."

Genevieve smiled and extended her hand in invitation.

"But you are exhausted," Miranda protested.

"Better now. It will help me," Genevieve reassured her. "Bliss of Gift given. Heals me."

Miranda clasped Genevieve's fingers gently and blurted in haste, "I am carrying a girl." A grin blossomed. "It's a girl! And I see the Bliss in your eyes."

Genevieve nodded, feeling the restorative power of using her Gift to altruistically benefit others. "Want to know if...a witch?"

"You make progress." A damp chill wafted at her back and the comte's voice came from behind her. "You are almost speaking full sentences," he said. "Are you ready to go?"

Genevieve quirked an inquiring eyebrow at her friend.

"Witch or not, it is of no significance," Miranda said.

"This is how you feel truly?" the comte asked, considerable puzzlement on his face as he regarded their fingers still entwined. "With Lady Genevieve's power upon you, you could not say it unless you believe it."

"A child is a gift of love, Etienne." Miranda released Genevieve's hand to caress the nascent bump below her waist. "Adam's daughter will be cherished as much as the other children we share, whether or not she has magic."

The comte lifted Genevieve into his arms with ease. Tante Reina's remedy was having a soporific effect and she nestled into his warmth, the scent of him calming her, and her fears easing with the steady beat of his heart. She closed her eyes, surrendering to a feeling that she had never experienced since she was a little girl, the sensation of being totally shielded from harm.

"Take care of my friend," Miranda called.

"I shall."

Genevieve felt his promise reverberate against her ear and acknowledged its truth even through the layers of clothing and covers between them. The restorative had diminished her already feeble defenses.

"Do you really trust him?" Genevieve heard Rowan ask as the door drifted shut.

The comte's step hesitated, as if he were awaiting an answer.

"He is the only one she can trust," Tante Reina replied cryptically, closing the door behind them.

The snow had turned to a cold rain partially rousing Genevieve with its chill.

"Going out as I went in, through the servant's door. How is that for an omen?" she murmured to the comte. The downpour was like a brisk slap in the face, penetrating the fog of exhaustion and misery that had enveloped her since Circe's departure. He carefully bundled her into Lady Morgan's elegant carriage and seated her on the velvet upholstered cushions beside his grandmother.

"Will you be able to sit beside her and help keep her in place, grandmama?" she heard him ask. "This is likely to be a less than smooth journey and I was warned that our passenger will be slipping in and out of consciousness due to the restorative."

"I can try my best to hold her." His grandmother gave a weary sigh. "But I fear that I have overextended my magic in lessoning Circe."

"Then propriety must give way to practicality," he said. "I will not allow any injury to befall her. If you would switch places with me, Grandmama?"

Genevieve forced her eyes open, wondering at the lie her touch had revealed. Why had Lady Morgan falsely claimed to feel feeble?

The comte seated himself beside her. He rapped on the box to signal the driver. Once again, she was folded in his warmth.

She could only imagine how she looked, blinking and bleary-eyed above a swath of carriage blankets, barely able to keep her eyes open as the carriage began to clatter its way back home.

It occurred to her that her disheveled appearance was the least of her problems, before her wayward thoughts flitted back to the comte.

His curls were cropped in a longish Brutus. However, grey was far too prosaic a description for hair in a shade of silver that was the color of sunlight on ice. Instead of making him look old and worn, his carelessly styled mane bestowed dignity upon a man who had faced the worst and survived the ordeal. A square chin completed the portrait of a man of firm resolve. Somehow, he had managed to contravene the will of England's Mistress of Witches, not an easy feat.

The light of the carriage lantern conferred a flickering aura that was reminiscent of the halos that Genevieve had seen decorating the saints in old church frescos. She stifled a chuckle at the image. This man was no saint. Though his eyes seemed cut from the most beautiful part of heaven, where the sky meets the sea, there was darkness in their depths. He was strong, clasping her steadfastly against the firm plane of his chest as the carriage made turns and stops. Even though he was holding her as no man had since her husband's death, she knew she could trust him.

For now.

She had learned there were all too many people whose inner truths were subject to change.

"Like Lucifer," she whispered. "He was an angel before the Fall. The brightest of all of them."

She could hear a chuckle from across the way and peered blearily from beneath half-closed lids. Lady Morgan. She had almost forgotten her presence.

"I believe that she refers to you Etienne," she said.

Genevieve cringed, realizing that she must have spoken aloud. Merlin's mercy! The potion was robbing her of control. For a moment, her inner fog lifted and the events of the past few hours whirled through her head, a parade of worries marching to the fore of her mind.

What have you done? What have you done?

The question echoed in time with the wheels as they churned their way through the sloppy mix of mud and snow. Although she knew Tante Reina's tinctures were meddling with her perceptions, the ride back home seemed to take much longer than the trudge to Wodesby House had ever been. The disaster of the evening repeated itself like the foreboding leitmotif of a tragic opera, with herself as the fool who brings about the disastrous dénouement.

Never reveal your Gifts to Outsiders. It is très dangereux, ma petite, her mother had warned her.

Revealing herself to those who shared Merlin's Blood was more dangerous by far.

She closed her eyes, trying to hold back the tears.

* * *

THE CARRIAGE LURCHED and Etienne put his arm around the woman beside him. Jasmine, vanilla and sandalwood mixed with the scents of ginger and turmeric in Tante Reina's tonic, teasing at his senses.

"Tante Reina cautioned me that she might drift in and out this way," he commented, adjusting the blanket carefully to keep from staring at the tempting *décolletage* of the warm bundle of woman who was clasped tightly in his arms. He shifted his position, trying to keep her from sliding and his own hands from slipping where they ought not to be.

His grandmother seemed to find the situation highly amusing.

Despite the overall lack of traffic, they encountered a blocked street, forcing them to take the long way around, but Etienne did not begrudge the time. His grandmother seemed lost in contemplation. Every now and then, she would touch the emeralds at her neck as if assuring herself of their reality.

Wandering in his own thoughts, Etienne reviewed the events of the evening, trying to distract himself from fixating upon the feel of the woman he held so tightly. But even as he was assessing the risks Damien's enemies might pose and mentally composing his report, a strange sense of peace stole over him.

Even contemplating his moments of public humiliation did not diminish the feelings of harmony engendered by the warmth of her body. The rhythmic in and out of her repose seemed to ease his spirit. He gently brushed back the curls, fallen loose from her coiffure, savoring the silken softness of the tresses as they slid across his fingers.

Once again, he felt the force of his grandmother's eyes upon him.

"It would not do, to trifle with her," she warned.

"I am not the selfish man my father was," Etienne countered, untangling his fingers.

"I know," Lady Morgan replied. "That is part of what concerns me."

* * *

GENEVIEVE FELT as if she was emerging from a walk in a fog-bound wood. She extended a hand and felt the hard stubbly plane of a man's cheek.

Owen?

But Owen was dead.

A dream then? But her dreams had never possessed a smell before, had they? They certainly wouldn't have had this fragrance. In the end, Owen's odor had been redolent of liquor and laudanum, the former, out of habit, and the latter to numb the pain of his illness. Both the scent and feel of this illusion were different.

And somehow familiar.

126

Genevieve forced her eyes open and was immediately beset by overwhelming embarrassment.

"Ah, you are awake," Lady Morgan's cheerful tone was almost an affront to the senses. "We will be there in a few moments."

"How are you feeling?"

The comte's question tickled at her ear.

Her head was resting on his shoulder.

"What am I...how did...?"

She scrambled to get herself upright, nearly jarring his jaw, wincing at the twinge in her head as a jumble of memories clarified into a comprehensible picture. The comte was eying her in concern.

Reluctantly, she slid herself away from him, feeling a frightening sense of loss at the separation.

"Much more myself, thank you," she finally answered, taking a glance out the window and seeing some familiar landmarks. "I will somehow have to winkle Tante Reina's receipt for that restorative out of her. Between her potion and the wine, I feel like I am floating."

"Do you make a habit of drinking overmuch?"

The comte glared at his grandmother.

Strangely, she sensed more curiosity than hostility in Lady Morgan's question.

"Rarely, especially since it is a habit I can ill afford," Genevieve replied, skewering the old woman with frank evaluation. "Do *you* tend to overindulge often?"

Genevieve heard a hiss from below and found deep blue eyes staring at her in hostility, a claw extended in threat at her ankle.

"*Upssssstart!*"

The comte uttered a strangled sound that could have been laughter.

Once again, Genevieve's feelings galloped, this time to mortification at her unruly tongue. She edged to the farthest end of the seat, curling in upon herself like a hedgehog.

"The potion again. I must apologize for...for... everything! I could die of shame!" Wetness tracked down Genevieve cheeks. A soft square of linen appeared, the comte's from the scent of it, which only increased the flow of humiliation. "I'm so sorry. I rarely cry. It has been years since I shed a tear."

"Then you are well past due! Nothing like a good cry, I say, to expel the angry humors." The old woman snorted. "Child, given what you have endured this evening, I confess myself surprised that you can move at all. Here, allow me to give you a small glamor to make you feel more yourself."

With a wave of her hand, Genevieve felt her face drying. The puffiness of her eyes dissipated.

"I have yet to see anyone expire due to embarrassment." The old woman gave a huff of ridicule.

There was a shuffling sound as she changed places with her grandson. Delicate notes of patchouli and jasmine wafted from Lady Morgan as she rearranged the carriage's robe and blankets. "We shall soon have you home and tucked in safe and sound, never you fear."

"I meant no insult," Genevieve told the cat.

"I will make one more apology and then I declare us done with the expression of regrets this night." The comte's voice rose deep and smooth from the shadows. Their carriage drew to a momentary halt amidst the traffic from an event at Hyde Park Corner and the lights from nearby conveyances illuminated their space. He leaned forward, regarding her with frank amusement, his eyes glinting in a blue that put Genevieve in mind of the lapis lazuli that had once been the centerpiece of her naming jewel.

"I must ask for forgiveness on behalf of my familiar.

Suzette presumed that you would not understand her rude comments. It was not well done of her."

Genevieve managed a smile. "I too have a cat companion and I am quite fluent in Felinish," she explained, glad for the opportunity to break the tension and move on to a more innocuous subject. "Felines are not generally well known for their diplomacy."

She pursed her lips at Suzette's annoyed hiss. They were only a few turns away from the shop. Although the dose of brew had restored her, she desperately longed for the comfort of a strong cup of hot tea by her own hearth and regaining control of her unruly tongue.

CHAPTER 12

They rounded the corner and Genevieve breathed a sigh of relief at the sight of the mortar and pestle hanging above the door of the building that housed Dale's Apothecary and her home. The carriage had barely rolled to a stop when her familiar, Marcel, and her son Louis came charging out the front door. It was only the comte's restraining hand that kept Genevieve from jumping out the door before the coachman deployed the steps.

"Mama, you are back!" The cat's meows of explanation were swallowed by Louis' cry of relief. "Marcel was just about to go and seek you at Wodesby House."

Genevieve eyed her familiar with growing trepidation. Marcel's Chartreux ancestry had gifted him with a double coat of fur, but things were dire indeed if the cat was considering setting a paw out the door in such foul weather. She shepherded them inside, followed by the comte and his grandmother.

Her son was trying to keep from weeping, but his grey eyes were brimming. "*Grand-mère* has disappeared, Mama. We have looked everywhere, Marcel and I, but we cannot find her?"

Genevieve bent and gently brushed the spill of tears

away. "You know how much of an expert *Grand-mère* is at hiding herself, *mon ange*. We shall find her, never you fear."

"It is my fault, Mama," Louis said. "She came to my bedroom and told me the revolutionaries were coming to get us and we must conceal ourselves right away. I didn't want to go hide with her, Mama, and I didn't think the chill would be good for her bones either. It was so cold and the fires had all gone out."

"Quite right, Louis." She squeezed his hand, quietly urging him to continue. "*Grand-mère* is extremely susceptible to this weather."

Louis nodded. Her agreement with his evaluation of the situation seemed to calm him. "So I took her back to her own bed and told her you would be home soon. I went down to get her some warm milk. I was going to sit with her until you returned." Tears started falling again. "But when I went back with the milk, she was gone. I called her and called her, but she wouldn't answer."

"If she is lost in the nightmare, she will not respond." Genevieve tried to speak without letting him feel her fear, although she was ready to scream. It was too much! Too much! All traces of her mentally muzzy state evaporated. "In her mind, we become those who are seeking to do her harm."

"What if she is outside in the cold?" Louis voiced Genevieve's worst worries aloud. "What if she is lost and afraid?"

Marcel rumbled. "*Told the boy. The old witch'ssss cloth fur is ssstill on the peg.*"

"An excellent observation," The comte nodded, agreeing with the cat's assessment. "If her cloak is still inside, it means she is less likely to have gone out."

"May we be of help searching for her?" Lady Morgan asked. "This is not a terribly big place. How difficult might it be to locate her, especially if she is still indoors?"

Genevieve sighed. It would seem all of the family secrets were destined to be revealed this night. "Sometimes, my mother goes back to the times of the Terror, Lady Morgan. They came for our family, when I was very young. Because I was a small girl, she was able to hide me and herself with her magic, but the rest of our family, my father, my grandparents, they were all murdered."

"I remember those terrible times. So many..." Lady Morgan shook her head, sadly. "We will find her, never fear, child," she said trying to comfort the boy.

"How can you say so, when you, yourself doubt we will find her!" Louis cried, breaking into tears. "You don't even understand!"

At Louis' outburst, the comte and his grandmother eyed each other shrewdly. Genevieve gave an inward groan at yet another secret exploded. Louis had unknowingly revealed one of his nascent abilities. She drew her son close.

"My mother has the power to become invisible when she hides," Genevieve explained. "She is an expert at concealing herself. The only way to locate her is to touch her. Even her scent is erased, so finding her is not as easy as it might seem."

"She cloaks herself with magic then?" To her surprise, the comte smiled. "Is she pledged to France and its covens, still?"

Genevieve nodded affirmatively.

"That will make it easier." He began to turn in place, the footman's coat flaring out around him, his hands extended, like a human compass seeking true north.

While they watched in astonishment, he stopped his rotation abruptly, facing the interior of the store. "The fact she is pledged to France and was once allied with my family makes things simpler, much simpler," he said, making his way through the rows of shelves lined with neat rows of jars, labeled by contents and purpose.

"That way." He pointed. "I can still feel the use of magic around me and French powers even more so. This much, Justice has not taken from me." He moved forward slowly, methodically, up and down the rows. "Weaker now." He turned again, seemingly drawn toward the marble counter facing the front of the store.

"Getting stronger, much stronger here," he murmured.

"But we looked under the counter, didn't we Marcel?" Louis asked.

"*Yesssss!*" The cat hissed in agreement.

"But your *Grand-mère*, she is clever, is she not?" The comte asked. "Once she saw where you had already searched, it is to this very place she sneaks back and hides herself, *n'est-ce pas?*"

He moved closer to Genevieve. She could smell the clean scent of lavender and shaving soap as he bent to speak softly. "Will your *maman* be more frightened if a stranger tries to pry her out from her place of concealment?" He asked, pointing to the far corner beneath the marble top.

"She would. Thank you," Genevieve nodded and moved slowly behind the counter to the spot the comte had indicated. "*Maman?*" Her gown formed a pool of flowers around her as she went to her knees and noticed the dust beneath had recently been disturbed. Gently, she crawled forward, reaching out, waving her hand back and forth until she brushed a quaking, invisible body. "It is Genevieve, *Maman*. No one will hurt you."

A hand twined with hers and with that connection, her mother reappeared. The shivering, elderly woman was dressed in a robe, a dark shawl draped over her head. Huddled in the corner, she kneeled, hunching over upon herself to become as small as she could possibly be. Even without the added concealment of invisibility, it was little wonder neither Louis nor Marcel were able to find her.

As Genevieve tried to help her mother to her feet, the old woman's eyes opened wide. *"Le Diable est ici,"* she whispered staring at the comte in horror and confusion.

The comte had been leaning forward to help, but he drew back abruptly. "It is better, perhaps, if I should go," he said, his face losing all expression. "It is possible your mother had some encounter with my father. I look much like him. Those who called my father the Devil Comte had ample reason to do so."

Louis reached out and clasped her wrinkled hand. "It will be well, *Grand-mère*. The comte means us no harm."

"Thank you, Louis, now I see he is not the same," Genevieve's mother blinked rapidly, as if trying to banish the visions of the past. Etienne thought he caught a momentary spark of magic in her eyes, but when she looked at him next, it was gone.

By the time they had raised her to her feet, there were tears of embarrassment tracking down her cheeks. "I am sorry, Genevieve, so very sorry. Again, I have done it, have I not?" She tried to draw the shawl up to cover her face. "I am so much trouble."

"Do not ever think so, *Maman*," Genevieve bent and draped her mother's arm over her shoulder.

Louis went to his grandmother's other side, but although they had succeeded in getting her to her feet, she pitched forward when she tried to take a step, nearly bringing the three of them down altogether.

"If you would allow me, Madame?" the comte asked,

rendering a bow that would have done credit to a chevalier in the king's court.

To Genevieve's surprise, her mother nodded her assent.

"Build the fire up in the sitting room, Louis," Genevieve commanded, "and heat up the milk."

"I will help you with both, boy, if you show me the way," Lady Morgan said. "We will have the room toasty in no time at all and the drink hot and ready before you can say *Merlin's moustache.*"

"Merlin didn't have a moustache." Louis chortled. "Did he?"

"You think I would know, boy? Do I appear so very old?" Lady Morgan asked with a disgruntled sniff. "On second thought, do not answer that question."

Despite her petite size, Genevieve's mother was a substantial woman, yet the comte swept her easily into his arms. The superfine fabric of his evening clothes went taut against the ripple of muscle beneath. Certainly no effete ton beau could have carried her so easily up the stairs to the private area of their home above the shop.

As Genevieve followed the comte into their sitting room, she realized how shabby its appearance must seem to a man of his station in life. The upholstery on the chairs had thinned at the armrests and the tables were piled with a disorder of books and papers. A clutter of empty dishes provided evidence that Louis and her mother had enjoyed the holiday supper she had left for them but failed to tidy up afterwards. Surprisingly, Marcel abandoned his favorite nook close to the fire in Suzette's favor.

When she saw herself reflected in the mirror above the mantle, she was all the more mortified. Miranda's dress was streaked with dust. Her cheek had a smear of dirt that went from chin to cheek. A cobweb adorned her hair, which had escaped the control of its pins.

What the comte must think of her!

Still, as he carefully set her mother on the sofa and tucked blankets around her, Genevieve could not help but be grateful for his presence. Even with Louis' help, she could not possibly have brought her mother safely up the stairs. The fire was crackling merrily in the hearth and the room was already warm and toasty, no doubt due to the aid of Lady Morgan's magic.

That too, was a matter for gratitude. Within the space of minutes, Genevieve's mother began to be more herself. When Louis and Lady Morgan arrived with trays, she began apologizing and clucking over the mess, even as she directed the placement of the tea service. Genevieve breathed a sigh of relief. If her mother had revived sufficiently to act as a fussing chatelaine, it was the best possible sign all would be well.

To Genevieve's surprise, Lady Morgan and her grandson made no move to take their leave. At first, the comte was subdued, allowing his grandmother to bear the full burden of conversation. But, to Genevieve's surprise, her mother made deliberate efforts to draw the mage into what became a badinage exploring the possibilities of mutual connections.

Living as they had since their long-ago flight from the revolutionaries, it was easy to forget that Maman had once walked in that world of aristocracy and privilege. Lady Morgan's French was excellent, and the conversation soon flowed easily. Genevieve saw a growing respect dawning on the faces of their guests as the two older women began to score palpable hits in the game of matching acquaintances.

Her mother blossomed under their attention. She actually blushed when Lady Morgan turned to Genevieve and declared, "You do know, Lady

Genevieve, that your mother once ruled the drawing rooms of Paris? There will be many who will rejoice to hear that she survived. An invitation to your *maman's* salon was more sought after than an invitation to Versailles."

"I can barely remember those times," Genevieve admitted. In truth, Genevieve found it difficult to reconcile that image of a Paris doyenne with the terrified woman who had raised her. Her mother had always seemed like a frightened sparrow, protecting her nest, constantly scanning the skies for the hawks that would inevitably come. Now, watching the confident woman seated before the fire, listening to her speak familiarly of Marie Antoinette, vague memories of another place, another time drifted into Genevieve's mind.

Louis proudly set the pieces of bread and cheese he had toasted upon plates. The comte and his grandmother complimented him as if he was worthy of usurping Prinny's chef, Careme. With her mother's permission, the comte produced a flask and he added a tot of fine brandy to the warm milk and the tea. Under the circumstances, even Louis was permitted a thimbleful. The excellent liquor warmed them all from the inside out. Soon, the comte had them all laughing with stories of his boyish mischief.

Genevieve was not quite certain when she gave Etienne leave to address her by her first name. Laughter spilled from his lips as he eloquently mimed the reactions of the officers in a rollicking tale involving a cat who stole a squab from Napoleon's table. Lady Morgan was giggling and her mother was clapping her hands in delight, the dread that always haunted her eyes, temporarily chased away.

Genevieve's gaze met Etienne's in silent gratitude. For the first time that evening, she was truly glad she had come to his aid.

What might have happened, she mused silently, *if she had kept her silence at Wodesby House?*

Finally, the liquor and the events of the evening took their toll. Etienne seemed to be lost in thought. Lady Morgan was recounting an amusing anecdote about Prinny importuning her for a spell to control his weight. "So then I said, *'your Highness, you do know that to perform such sorcery upon a head of state is absolutely forbidden. However, I could bespell Careme's food and make it taste like sawdust.'*" She looked toward Genevieve's mother. "Lucille, you would not credit what Prinny..." Her voice trailed off into a smile and a nod of approval.

"*Grand-mère* is asleep," Louis whispered. "She will get the aches if she stays the night here, Mama."

* * *

ETIENNE LOOKED AT GENEVIEVE INTENTLY, his mind a clutter of unasked questions. He shook his head, trying to clear the cobwebs from his head. "If I may help convey her to her bed?"

At her nod, he carefully lifted the sleeping woman into his arms and carried her to her room and held her until Louis had run a warming pan beneath the covers. The elderly woman sighed, snuggling close to him for heat, her gray head resting upon his shoulder as she smiled in her dreams. "*Bonne nuit mon coeur,*" she murmured softly, as he set her down gently and helped her grandson lay the quilt atop her. Although he knew he was not the one that she referred to, there was a touch of magic in the warmth of her dreamy expression of love.

"Thank you, for making yourself our porter tonight. All of this carrying to and fro must be exhausting," Genevieve said as they headed back to the sitting room.

"I perform a great deal of physical labor at my Yorkshire estate," he informed her. "It helps control..." his voice trailed off as he remembered that the boy was listening. "Controls the anger," he completed and waited for her reaction.

"So that explains the callouses on your hands," Genevieve said matter-of-factly. "I clean house to control mine, though you might not think it so from the state of the house tonight. I must thank you for your kindness to my mother. She was quite mortified, you know, that strangers would see her like this."

"But that embarrassed feeling disappeared so quickly," Louis mused, sounding more than a little puzzled. "What made her so happy? She was laughing, Mama! She smiles sometimes, but I don't think I have ever heard her laugh so before."

"It has been a long time," Genevieve admitted, tousling his hair with a sad sigh.

"That is why we must find the reason for her joy," the boy continued earnestly. "I want to hear her laughing again."

Genevieve's son had a good and innocent heart. Etienne felt a renewed determination to help her find the right mentor for the child, someone who would try to preserve that purity of soul. It would be a difficult search.

When they opened the door, they found Lady Morgan quietly staring into the fire. At their approach, she rose. Momentarily losing her balance, she reached out to steady herself. His grandmother hissed with pain as she clasped at the hot poker and sent it clattering to the hearth's apron of stone.

Etienne rushed forward to examine the old woman's palm and gave a gasp of alarm. Even if he had his magic at hand, there was nothing he could do to help her. The Gift of Healing was the stuff of legends.

After the Scourge, only the Rom had retained some of that talent.

"We must get you back to Tante Reina at once," he declared, as the familiar wartime stench of burning flesh evoked gory memories of gunfire and battlefields. Burns such as the one his grandmother had sustained could kill. He had seen strong, young men die from less. "Have you any salve? Bandages?" Etienne asked, battling the feelings of helplessness by searching for something to do.

"Getting to be...a careless...f..fool, I am," Lady Morgan stuttered with pain, falling back into her chair to stare at the fiery mark on her skin.

To Etienne's surprise, neither Genevieve nor Louis made any move to fetch the supplies. Anger was starting to mix with fear when Etienne noticed that Louis was regarding his mother as if asking a silent question.

Genevieve took a deep breath. "Help her, Louis."

The boy reached out and gently touched his fingers to Lady Morgan's palm.

Tears began to stream down Louis' face.

"You must not tell anyone of this, you know? You must swear it to me by Merlin's bones afterward." Louis spoke slowly, as if every word he uttered was an agony.

And the boy was suffering indeed, Etienne realized. The look of intense pain in the child's eyes mirrored Lady Morgan's misery as the grey of his eyes transformed into a transcendent blue.

"Oh my," she whispered, her grimace easing as the shimmer of magic enveloped her hand.

Slowly, the field of blisters which had already begun to form shrank and faded. After a few minutes the angry red of her palm paled to the peculiar pink of healing skin. Within a few blinks of the eye, there was no sign of the injury. The haze grew brighter.

"My hands? The wrinkles? They are disappearing!" Lady Morgan cried in wonder, clutching the child tighter.

"That is enough Louis!" Etienne declared, hastily pulling the boy's hand from the old woman's grasp. "You will cause yourself harm if you give her too much."

The blue glow in his eyes faded leaving a look of unsurpassed joy, the Bliss that came with helping others through his Gift. Etienne marveled at witnessing it in one so young.

Genevieve rose and hugged the boy close.

"She was hurting so badly, Mama," the boy said, his voice muffled in her skirts. "I know you told me that I can't—"

"There are exceptions to every rule," Genevieve said. "Now you must lie down before—"

"Before I fall down, I know," he said as his mother tucked a blanket around him. "It didn't hurt nearly so bad this time. Maybe I don't need...a...mentor." His eyes closed as he fell back against the cushion with a soft sigh.

"He exhausted himself for me, poor lad," Lady Morgan said.

"This is not the first time he has drained himself to the dregs," Genevieve said, her eyes dark with worry and pride as she sat beside her son and ran a hand through his hair. "Last time, my *maman* broke her hip in a fall. Louis slept for two days. I feared he might die."

"It has been a long time since I have seen the Bliss that comes with true giving on a child's face, or on a full grown face, for that matter," the old woman said. "You have a remarkable family."

"As you can see, Louis does not have the control he needs. He would not know when to stop."

There was dread in Genevieve's eyes and Etienne knew that she spoke truly when she said that the boy had already skated too close to the edge of the Light.

"And you are rightly aware there are many who would keep hold of him until he had expended himself unto death," Etienne added grimly, stretching out his hand. "I know that you are weary, but I ask you now to use your Gift to weigh the veracity of my words, please."

Her fingers twined with his and Etienne felt a surge of pure joy beyond the thrill of the touch of her magic. "I swear to you now, a sacred oath upon the bones of Merlin. No word of your son's healing Gift or any of the other Gifts I have witnessed here this night will be disclosed by me without your express permission."

Lady Morgan placed her healed hand in Genevieve's and repeated the same oath. "You know we have sworn truly tonight. But even though we will keep our peace, eventually others will suspect or find out."

"Your family is a treasure, Genevieve. From what I see, your son has more than one power that others will covet. After tonight, everyone will be aware of your power." His shrug indicated a cause already lost. "We will keep our peace regarding Louis, but others will be looking for signs," Etienne said, dividing the remnants of his flask into three glasses. "I am only sorry I have brought you and your son to the attention of those who might do you harm because you came to my aid. He needs a worthy mage to teach him, and protection until he can protect himself. You are wise to guard those you love fiercely, but you cannot do it alone."

"I shall, if I have to," she declared.

Etienne knew there was the power of a mother's vow in that simple statement. The smile upon

Genevieve's face seemed false. She looked ready to cry herself and Etienne found himself wanting to hold her, comfort her.

He envied his grandmother as she reached for Genevieve's hand.

All at once, he wished that he could offer her more than advice. With the Gifts once at his command, no one would have dared to do ill to her or her family. Never had he felt his helplessness so keenly.

His grandmother voiced the thought. "After what you have done for us, we will offer you whatever assistance may be at our disposal."

"It is I who owe you true life debts, not just twice, but thrice over." Genevieve ticked off the incidents as she spoke. "You saved me in the mews, Etienne. You kept me from using my athame on Pendrake's brother, although the satisfaction of gutting him might have been worth the price."

The glow of firelight burnished her hair and she smiled at him. "I am no Seer." Genevieve spoke slowly as if she was giving words to an understanding that was only just becoming clear to her. "But I do not have to see the future to know what might have been the outcome, if I had failed to come forward tonight."

She smoothed her son's hair. "If I had played the coward and remained silent, Marcel might still be making his way to Mayfair to find me."

She lifted her glass of brandy, took a sip, and then sighed. "Knowing Louis, my boy would be out in the streets alone, searching for his grandmother. With all the dangers abroad in London at night, he would likely have come to grief himself."

Etienne watched mesmerized as she stared into the liquid, almost as if she could scry within what might have been had she made a different choice. Her eyes met his, and he could see the touch of flames reflected in their amber depths. "Had I not come to your aid, I might still be at Wodesby House waiting for my boon to merit the Chief Mage's attention."

Meeting his quizzical look frankly, she raised her glass in a silent toast to him. "Without your ability to detect her, my mother would probably have spent the night in the corner beneath the counter, afraid unto death, shivering in the dark and cold until her magic failed. You can see how frail she is. She might not have survived. So do not speak to me of what I have done for you. By my reckoning, the larger debt tonight is mine."

"No, child, 'tis not true!" His grandmother shook her head. "If we are totting up ledgers, I fear the largest obligation owed for tonight's work can never be repaid. Had you chosen to stand aside, I have no doubt that Lord Wodesby's predictions would have become reality and every one of us would have come to grief." She raised her glass in salute and smiled. "My mother used to say that even when you choose the darkest way, if it is the true one, the Light provides a beacon. Tonight, you lit that torch."

Etienne stared into his empty glass for a moment, wishing he could find a way to express this strange feeling. Admiration was too tame to describe it. Genevieve Dale was magnificent, but he knew better than to tell her so. She was too wary to accept praise. No matter how sincere the compliment might be, she would label it an ephemeral truth at best. He would not have her believing that he dealt in Spanish coin.

Although he could not use his Gifts to help her, he began to think of other plans that might be set in motion. "We will talk of settling debts another time." Their eyes met momentarily and he knew that she was thinking of the kisses that remained uncollected. "Tonight we must all think upon the best means to protect you and your family. Once you left France, did you or your mother pledge to any coven or mage?"

"My mother has no belief in such loyalties. When we asked for help, they gave us none. We have relied only upon ourselves for a very long time." Genevieve eyed him warily. "Do you want us pledged to you?"

"You would be a fool to ally your family's future to me, Lady Genevieve, a mage with neither influence nor power." She was wise to question his motives, he told himself. She had no reason to trust, especially with all the rumors surrounding him. Still, he could not help but feel disappointed.

"You must go to Damien and his wife and initiate an alliance with them," he continued. "Whether you do so, or not, they will help you to find the right mage to fulfill the terms of your boon."

His grandmother nodded her agreement. "Etienne is correct. The Wodesbys have the wherewithal to provide protection, and after tonight, they too, are indebted to you. Since you chose the words to reserve the choice of mentor to yourself, you need not fear."

"Still, you cannot afford to choose poorly," Etienne said. "Because the one you select to bend your twig will influence the way he will grow."

CHAPTER 13

"*H*er mother is a Brisbois by marriage," Etienne's grandmother had barely seated herself in the carriage before she began assembling the details that she had gleaned from Genevieve and her family into a coherent whole. "If I recall correctly—"

Etienne smiled. "I would sooner rely on the accuracy of your memory than the pages of *Debrett's Peerage* grandmama."

Lady Morgan gave a disparaging snort, even as she looked inordinately pleased. "Flatterer! Had I a fan at hand, I would rap you across the knuckles," she remarked. "According to her mother, Genevieve's grandfather was a *chevalier* of some renown, an advisor to the fifteenth Louis. He and his wife were fixtures at the French court. There were rumors—" She tapped her forehead in a motion that stated *but of course*. "Rumors that the *chevalier's* family had an uncanny knack for judging the reliability of investments."

"Truth sifting, more than likely," Etienne observed, looking out through the glass as they were approaching Wodesby House once again. By the count of carriages waiting idle and the lights in the windows, it was obvious few who were wealthy enough to own equipages had chosen to depart early.

His grandmother chuckled as she noted the direction of his gaze. "Looks like the high and mighty are still fuming around the boon jar."

Etienne shrugged. "Not the most politically astute move, but a necessary one, I think." Etienne deliberated aloud. "Change is inevitable if Merlin's children wish to thrive. Unlike my father and the old men who wish to turn the clock back to before the Bourbons surrendered their heads, Damien is taking a lesson from France."

"Gradual change is far superior to the guillotine," Lady Morgan agreed. "Poor Lady Brisbois, to lose everything so horribly."

"You saw her reaction to me." Etienne shook his head at the recollection of Lady Brisbois' terror. "It seems clear that there is a connection."

"Even if the old comte is the devil that haunts her, you cannot atone for all his evil, Etienne. But that does not signify, in the end," his grandmother observed. "You do realize that Genevieve denied her debt to us. By right, we could hold her to her words, since she has clearly stated her belief that it is discharged."

"You think I would do that?" Etienne rounded on his grandmother in barely contained annoyance. "The High Circles are about to pursue her like hounds on the scent of a vixen, and we are the one who put them on her trail."

"And there you make my point." Lady Morgan peered at him, squinting in the light of the carriage lamp as if to better read his face. "Your father would have denied the debt in a mage's minute and then calculated how he might use her power to his own ends. You are not the old comte, my boy, and it is well past time you acknowledge that."

Etienne laughed bitterly. "There are those who would say that I am fighting off the other hounds so that I may claim her myself. Clearly she thinks so."

"I doubt it. But if she did, would you blame her?" his grandmother asked, frankly. "She and her mother have hidden their talents for a long time and now the boy manifests a healing skill that not even the Rom can match. You must admit, you have something of a reputation."

"Ever the mistress of understatement."

Etienne's evening had begun with a growing sense of futility. The feeling that he had no purpose to his existence had been increasing steadily since the Judgement. He had ventured forth from his isolation in Yorkshire due to his debt to Wodesby and his concern for his grandmother.

"From the time I was barely out of leading strings, I was groomed to inherit the Mage's band of France," Etienne began, trying to explain what had been his *raison d'être*. "My teeth were cut on politics and I was tutored by a man who was an expert in the art of the lie. I may not be Lucifer, but I am his son."

He looked out the window, unable to bring himself to meet his grandmother's look of pity and sympathy. "Without my Gifts, what am I?"

"Balderdash!" He turned to face her at the force of her utterance. Her glare blazed with fury. "I have yet to hear a bigger pot of self-pitying poppycock!"

He could only stare at her in open-mouthed shock as she shook a scrawny fist at him. "Since your arrival in London, you have been haunting Morgan Manse like a ghost. The only saving grace until now has been you were not loudly bemoaning your fate like one of Byron's brooding heroes! Gall is what it is! Absolute gall! You are wealthy enough to offer Croesus a loan. Charlemagne was an upstart when the first of your ancestors rose to nobility! I will tolerate no more of this nonsensical self-pity. France is on someone else's plate now, may Merlin have mercy upon him."

The coach had halted for a moment and Lady Morgan leaned forward and cupped his face between her hands. "Tell me truthfully, Etienne, if you could have it all back, would you truly want it? The intrigues in the ballrooms, bedrooms and parlors? Gambling with lives to gain power and influence?"

There was no magic in her piercing gaze. Eyes of a blue that matched his demanded honesty. "No," he admitted at last, finally allowing himself to say the words out loud. "I miss my Gifts. It is like the loss of my limbs, I think. Before, when I truly believed in Napoleon, I did my duty to France. I worked toward a cause. But the great game? I miss it not at all."

"And tonight, I believe that you may have found something else." She released him, but held him with her look. Etienne thought of Circe being immobilized earlier and wondered if his grandmother was employing her Gift. "Tell me, are you interested in the Dales because you think to use them?"

It was a reasonable question.

"I will try to guide them, but I would not use them, though I can think of many ways that I might," Etienne declared. "While Genevieve may deny it, I still have an obligation. Until she and her family are safe, and young Louis is set on the path to proper training, I will do what I can. Part of fulfilling that duty is to make sure Genevieve and her family can defend themselves."

Lady Morgan nodded her head in approval. "So let us take stock of what we know. It would seem that Lady Genevieve's Gift can determine the truth with a touch."

"All of us, it seems, were unaware that she was of noble birth until Damien addressed her as Lady

Genevieve," Etienne confirmed. "However, as of tonight, Genevieve's anonymity is at an end. Everyone will be seeking information to use as leverage."

"Or attempting to attach themselves to her," his grandmother added. "Her previous *mésalliance* is irrelevant. She is a young widow with a mageling son who is a proof of fertility and power."

"Add to those virtues the facts that she is beautiful, and a witch of unusual Gifts," honesty compelled him to add with surprising reluctance.

"Her father was a mage of limited skills, it seems, but of the Blood and a Marquis to boot."

"To me, it makes no difference," Etienne told her, turning his thoughts back to the celebration still in progress at Wodesby House and debating his next move. Originally, he had intended to return home with his grandmother and his delayed rendezvous with words and whiskey.

"At one time, it would have mattered a great deal to you," his grandmother persisted. "For many of the sticklers who fancy themselves Merlin's select, she is still merely one more impoverished émigré they might use, despite her title."

"She is a woman who has put herself at risk to help us!" Etienne turned to find that his grandmother was smiling enigmatically. "What?" he asked.

"I may smile if I wish, if only to confuse you. I have found it to be an excellent tactic." She shook her head. "We will have to move quickly. I doubt the Dales have any inkling of what they will be facing come the morrow."

"It *is* the morrow," Etienne pointed out. "I will set you down at the Manse and report to Wodesby. Perhaps we can come up with a plan."

CHAPTER 14

Genevieve awoke with Marcel's hairy paw gently batting her nose. The meow in her ear was insistent.

"I told you before I left that I intended to open late in the afternoon today," she grumbled, using her pillow to cover her head. "Go away. Let me sleep, you meddling mouser."

Marcel's volume elevated.

"Hush!" Genevieve warned him, popping up from her nest of pillows and blankets. "You will wake Grandmère and Louis. What do you deem to be so urgent that you demand I must immediately leave my bed?"

The cat hooked a calculated claw in a piece of lace that peeked from beneath the covers. Unless she followed him, the delicate edge she had tatted for her nightdress would tear.

"I could have chosen a hawk," she grumbled. "Hawks are pleasant animals who mind their own business, Lady Morgan told me. They look elegant on your shoulder. They are useful creatures and can catch mice as well as dinner for the pot in a pinch. But did I listen to my mother who warned me cats are troublesome

153

creatures? Not me! I chose an arrogant French Chartreux who—"

Marcel began to hack insistently.

"No, I will not get out of bed!" But at the threat of
Marcel coughing up on her linen, she emerged from
her cocoon of quilts, shoved her feet into slippers and
donned the lacy confection that was her robe. Her intimate lingerie was one of her few vices, sewn with de-
tailed care by her own hand, the fine fabric chosen for
the feel against her bare skin rather than the utility
characterizing her outer wardrobe.

"Sssssseee!"

At Marcel's hissed behest, she followed him to a
window at the end of the hallway overlooking the
street in front of the shop. She lifted a corner of the
curtain and peered out. A crowd of witches and mages
was milling at the door of Dale's.

Even on a typical day, the shop was not due to open
for another hour. The hand-written sign she had left
on the window plainly, in letters writ large, stated her
plans for a late start his morning.

"Oh my! What in Nimue's name is going on?" she
exclaimed with a gasp. She heard footsteps on the
stairway behind her. "Have you seen what is happening,
Maman? Come look!"

"I am looking!" At the sound of a male voice, she
whirled.

"My sincere apologies for the intrusion," Etienne
said, his face lit with frank male appreciation, as he
came up to the landing. "My familiar informed me that
Lady Brisbois was in need of assistance getting down
to breakfast, and I am standing here making excuses
for my rude behavior when I really ought to be going."

Genevieve blushed from head to toe at the thought
of the sight she must present in nearly sheer lawn and
lace. "Yes, you ought to before my mother conjures a

bolt that will leave you smoking!" she declared pulling the sash more tightly around her.

"Milady, you have no need for magic to make a man go up in smoke," he said. "Behold, I burn at the sight of you."

"But h...how did you get in?" Genevieve sputtered. "Why...?"

"Because your locks are a waste of metal and will do little to hold back any determined mage or witch." Lady Morgan burst into the hall, interposing between Genevieve and her grandson. "You are shivering child. No wonder, given what you're wearing! Or not—as the case may be! As for you!" She turned on her grandson. "*Burn at the sight of you!*" She snorted and waved a dismissive hand. "Get away with you and stop embarrassing the gel with your French twaddle, or I will turn you into kindling myself! I may be more the Crone than the Maiden, but do not doubt my proficiency!"

"Grandmama, in my eyes, you are ever young." He planted a kiss on her nose and her cheeks came close to matching the film of rouge that adorned them.

"These du Le Feys," she groused, but Genevieve could see the pleasure beneath her annoyance. "They will flirt with any female on two feet."

"Is Lady Brisbois ready?"

"You may assist her downstairs in a moment. She was feeling a trifle stiff after last night's adventures. Now at least have the grace to turn your back before I bespell you, boy!" Lady Morgan commanded. "And as for you, Genevieve, you will show me your wardrobe so that I may help you choose something appropriate."

"I don't understand—" Genevieve began.

"With my grandmama, it is wiser to obey first and hope for an explanation later," Etienne said.

"Eyes. Elsewhere!" Lady Morgan warned.

"Spoilsport!" Etienne accused laughingly, as his

grandmother grasped him by the shoulders and directed him toward Lady Brisbois' door.

His mirth rang in the hall as his grandmother shepherded Genevieve back to her room.

"You were so exhausted, I was leaving you to wake until last," she informed Genevieve briskly. "Really I am at fault for Etienne's *faux pas*. I thought you still abed when I sent Suzette to fetch him. I confess, though, I would gladly put you to the blush again to hear him laugh like that once more."

Lady Morgan sat down on the bed. "Forgive me. Last night was the first time since...and then again this morning, to hear him so merry—" She sniffed, trying to regain her composure.

"I was, after all, standing in the hall, so your grandson cannot be wholly faulted for the trespass and his flattery." Genevieve attempted a matter-of-fact tone, even as she felt herself warming from head to toe at the memory of the heat in his look.

"Something elegant, but not too elaborate, I think," Lady Morgan mused, throwing open Genevieve's wardrobe. "Let us see what we have to work with." She pursed her lips in dismay at the thin array of garments.

"What in Nimue's name is going on?" Genevieve asked, as the old woman examined one dress after another and tossed them aside.

"You cannot mean to attend a private audience with the Chief Mage this morning looking like a poorly attired upper servant, my dear." Lady Morgan's expression puckered in a frown as she surveyed the scant totality of Genevieve's wardrobe.

"This morning? But you said last night it would be a week at the very least before he might see us."

"Etienne and Rowan convinced Wodesby of the matter's urgency. And they were entirely on the mark. What you beheld out there is just the trickle at the beginning of the flood. Many of those who are gathering at your doorstep have little patience. A few of them are here just to pay their debts as Lord Damien commanded, but more have come to try and importune you for the use of your powers, or to bribe, coerce, or convince you to choose their supervision for your son. Your mother agrees."

"But—"

"Is this everything you own?" Lady Morgan asked pulling out a faded, blue muslin dress and peeking under an unravelling hem to reveal its original shade. "Was this indigo when it was new?" she asked.

"I wouldn't know. I never saw it in a state other than worn," Genevieve admitted in embarrassment.

"Hmmm." Lady Morgan considered, running a finger over the fabric. "Quality goods! That will help."

"When I purchased it, it was only slightly darker than it is now." She shook her head. "I wear it for gardening mostly. It is far too shabby to wear in public."

"I agree. However, we must make do with what is available." She held the dress out imperiously. "Off with your night things and put it on."

Genevieve hesitated and Lady Morgan regarded her with a frown. "Time is limited and I will not waste my magic when you can undress yourself."

Genevieve obeyed. "But how—?" Her question was muffled as she scrambled into the dress.

"My grandmother could make a ball gown out of soot covered rags. She did, in fact, do just that, with legendary results, I might add. Made her a fortune and got her husband a title when the cinder maid became a duchess," Lady Morgan informed as she helped with the buttons. "It was my grandmama who insisted that I become proficient at thread witchery, although that skill has fallen out of favor with the younger set. A pity, that! A magical gown is far simpler and more foolproof than love philtres, in my way of thinking." She tapped a thoughtful finger to her lips, before pinching the waistline to create a gather. "This should do nicely. It will be a good shade for your complexion."

Lady Morgan sent a spark of color into the trim and nodded her head in satisfaction. "Getting the tint right is the hardest part, you know? Nonetheless, it is far easier to renew than to recreate."

* * *

AFTER A FINAL GLIMPSE in the mirror, Genevieve descended to the kitchen. To her surprise, she arrived to find her mother presiding over a laden breakfast table. Plates of buttery brioche, flaky croissants, pots of preserves, and pastries, crowded the board alongside platters of sausage, and kippers.

"There is more in the hampers," Lady Morgan said before polishing off the last of large hothouse strawberry. "I thought we would need to fortify ourselves."

"This is absolutely splendid!" Louis declared, smearing a spoonful of jam on the rich buttery bread. "Thank you so much, milady! I never have had a breakfast half so fine."

"Mages do not live by magic alone." Lady Morgan beamed at the boy. "Such a polite child, Lucille! You have raised him well!"

Lady Brisbois' casual shrug was belied by her obvious pleasure at the praise. "We have tried our best, my Genevieve and I," she said modestly, looking toward her daughter, who stood in the doorway.

Etienne, whose back had been toward the entrance, rose immediately. His gratifyingly gobsmacked expression confirmed what the small looking glass in her room had only partially revealed. There would be no need for her to feel embarrassed at her appearance. The last traces of her annoyance at Lady Morgan's high-handed magical meddling faded.

"However did you do it?" Genevieve's mother exclaimed.

With a casual wave of her hand, Lady Morgan dismissed her triumph as little more than a trifle.

"Restoring the gown's original indigo color was far easier than I expected," she explained. "It was the threadbare state of the jaconet posing the problem. And the satin? Well, I admit that required some coaxing to bring the trim back to its proper bright shade of canary."

"*C'est magnifique!*" Lady Brisbois exclaimed.

"I would certainly agree," Etienne declared, inclining his head to his grandmother in acknowledgement, before turning the full warmth of his regard on Genevieve, putting her in mind of the moments in the hallway. Although she was no stranger to lust-ridden looks, it had been a long time since she had felt a yearning echoing within her. Her cheeks flared with embarrassment.

Even his own grandmother has decried him as a flirt, she reminded herself. Genevieve was determined not to be a fool.

Purposefully, she tore her gaze from Etienne's and jumped into the conversation.

"It is the lutestring spencer that is the *pièce de résistance*, Mama." She walked to the sideboard and examined the array of offerings. "Do you remember that the rag-woman threw it in with the gown as a buy-the-lot for a few pennies more? Much-mended and worn as it was, we thought the piece was beyond salvaging, but Lady Morgan renewed the stripes to the same yellow as the silk trim."

"You look like one of those costume plate in that Ackermann's magazine *Grand-mère* favors," Louis exclaimed, emulating Etienne's gentlemanly bow and hurrying to help his mother seat herself "Prettier than a queen!"

"A queen indeed!" Genevieve's mother agreed. "Come; join our feast, your majesty! Do you remember the *Galette des Rois*? My mother would insist upon baking it herself every year."

"Was it as good as the one you make, Grand-mère?" Louis asked.

"Much more elaborate. She would fashion crowns of *pâte d'amande*," she replied with a sigh and a bitter-sweet smile at the memory.

"I remember helping her grind the almonds for the marchpane," Genevieve said. "She said helping with the preparation made luck. It must have worked because I was always the one to find the *fève* and be declared queen." She clasped her mother's hand. "I always wondered. Did Grand-père use magic to help me?"

"No, of course not," her mother said with a chuckle. "It is ill luck to use magic to cheat the fates. Your *Grand-mère* and I, we took care to have a favor baked in every piece. You remember this? You were very young."

Genevieve nodded. "I'm surprised that I haven't recollected it before. It was a good time."

"Yes," Lady Brisbois agreed softly. "Yes, it was. Lady Morgan has reminded me there were many good times."

"Is that why I am always the one to find the *fève*, Grand-mère?" Louis asked, looking at her suspiciously.

"Alas, my secret is discovered!" Lady Brisbois laughed and there was a twinkle in her eye.

"No more, please," Louis' tones were chiding. "Only one favor and all of us have a chance."

"Do you not wish to be king of the *fête*?" Etienne asked.

"Not if I cannot get the crown on my own," Louis

told him, earnestly. "I will not cheat to win." He looked at his grandmother apologetically. "Not that I am accusing you of cheating, mind you. I am just not a baby to be coddled anymore."

"A most laudable thought." Lady Morgan nodded in approval. "The greatest gains are achieved through our own merits and skills."

"This is true," Etienne agreed, exchanging a significant glance with Genevieve. "By your own words you show us that you are ready to become a grown mage, Louis. That is why we meet with the Chief Mage today."

"Has he already found a mentor for me?" Louis jumped up from his chair in excitement. "Truly?"

"Not quite yet," Genevieve prevaricated. "If you would go upstairs and fetch the hat from my bed. You will see Lady Morgan worked wonders upon it as well."

"I suppose you mean I must stay there until you are done talking about me and whatever else is going on," Louis grumbled, helping himself to another croissant before starting for the door.

"Wait," Lady Brisbois put a hand on her grandson's shoulder. "If he is old enough to begin his study of higher magic, then he is of age to understand the situation and take part in the decisions affecting him." She looked at Genevieve expectantly.

"I don't know," she began.

"You will not be able to protect him forever, Genevieve." There was a deep sadness in Etienne's expression as he spoke. "We cannot always shield those we care for. My stepmother was deliberately kept in ignorance of how to practice her craft, and that lack of knowledge was used against her."

"We sometimes make mistakes out of an abundance of love," Louis' grandmother added. "To spare our children from our pain, we unwittingly make them less capable of dealing with their own difficulties." She regarded her daughter with a look of regret. "I know I have done so. Try as we might, we cannot alter the future to suit our desires or cheat the forces of destiny."

Genevieve met her son's gaze. Even though she knew he would obey her, no matter what her decision, there was no denying the plea for respect in his look.

"You are right. He should be with us," Genevieve said with a sigh.

Louis' delighted grin confirmed her choice. "The Chief Mage!" He whistled in awe.

"If you would be so kind as to show me what Louis has in the way of clothing, I shall see what may be done." Lady Morgan started for the stairway.

Genevieve rose, but her mother waved her back to her seat. "You have not yet eaten, and I feel much refreshed. I will show you Matilda."

"Come along, young man!" Lady Morgan commanded. "You cannot meet Lord Wodesby looking like a well-dressed crossing sweeper. You must be garbed appropriately."

Louis looked at his unfinished treats longingly.

"But you always say that good food is not to be wasted, don't you *Grand-mère*?"

"I will save your plate for you," Genevieve promised, patting him on the shoulder as he passed. "Now hurry along."

* * *

TRUE TO HER WORD, Genevieve cast a spell to keep her son's plate from going cool. Etienne watched with interest while she completed the short working. Elegant in its simplicity, with barely a flicker of power to fuel it, it was a bit of magic Etienne had never encountered before.

"I'm sorry. That was thoughtless of me," she said, obviously misinterpreting the look on his face.

"Does it trouble you to see others doing magic when you cannot?"

"*Au contraire*," Etienne declared. "I am quite fascinated by what you have wrought."

"It is what the OutBloods call a *weaving*," she explained. "It is a magical means of preserving food, somewhat like the new method of canning, but far more temporary."

"Never before have I seen a spell such as this." He touched the surface of the plate and a filmy shield yielded.

"How many mages or witches among the Highest Circles worry about food spoiling when they can easily purchase more?" Genevieve said, extending the magic to cover the rest of the comestibles. "Necessity often forces us to seek solutions."

"Ah, but not everyone has the strength to pursue the path of necessity, milady," Etienne declared with a bow of admiration. "You are quite remarkable."

At his praise, her cheeks turned rosy.

"Ah, again that blush of yours!" he remarked. "It tempts a man to shower you with compliments, just for the delight of watching the lovely cloud of color sweeping your face."

Her embarrassment deepened and she turned away, ostensibly to get some food from the sideboard. "I have found compliments are often the prelude to insulting suggestions, milord," she murmured softly. "They are rarely genuine."

"Have I become *milord* again because I have spoken the truth?" he asked, moving to stand at her side. "I am sorry if my words have gone into the same purse as all those other bits of false coin."

She would not look at him, regarding the rashers of

bacon on the tray with the fixation of a victim fascinated by a medusa spell.

"Please, believe me," he asked, wanting to physically compel her to look at him, to touch her, so she would know that he would never deliberately hurt her. But in the time since his Judgement, he had come to understand what it was to be without power, to have no defense against others who had no compunction about crossing personal boundaries without leave.

Etienne would not join those interlopers. However, persuasion did not come easily when force had long been his family's favored method of inducement. "We du Le Feys are not known for honesty, but for your own protection, you must become aware of the power of your own attraction. Do you know how rare an innocent blush is among the Blood, *chérie*? How potent it might be if you could somehow harvest its magic?"

Genevieve set her plate down and looked at him, her head tilted as she listened. This morning, while waiting for his grandmother to be ready, he had searched for information on truth sifters in the library at the Manse. Even without their Gifts, they were said to have a sense that detected lies. Luckily, Etienne had no intention of lying to her.

"Do you know when I last saw the honest blossom of rose on a cheek, Genevieve?" he asked. "My sister Giselle still retains that delightful naiveté. Blessings on Rowan for preserving her childhood despite all those who conspired to steal it from her, myself included!" Her lack of surprise at his statement told him that she was well aware of his reputation. "The girl will soon come into her powers and Damien's mother, Adrienne has undertaken to train her in the ways of the witch, but I hope this does not change her."

"You love your sister. I hear it in your voice."

Etienne nodded, trying not to be offended by the

note of surprise in her observation. "Giselle is one of the true joys I have left. I miss her very much. It was her scarf I wore last night."

"Are they keeping you from her?" Genevieve asked. "Because of the Judgement against you?"

Was that a hint of indignation he heard? Etienne wondered. She seemed almost outraged on his behalf.

"No, no," Etienne denied hastily. "Although after all I have done, I would not blame Rowan if she forbade any connection. Her mother, she permits me to see my sister as often as I wish, but—" He hesitated, finding the admission of the shameful truth harder than expected. "In years to come, she will be seeking a partner in life. Bad enough she is now burdened with the disgrace of a member of her family."

"Surely your sister would want—"

He had hoped that she would understand what he was trying to say without the need for him to actually say it, but he held up a hand, asking to be allowed to finish.

"You have seen last night what it means. The curse I carry is like a plague. I would not have Giselle bear my malediction." He shook his head in adamant denial. "Can you imagine what it would cost her to walk in public, on her brother's arm? To remind everyone of our connection? I think not." His voice dropped to a near whisper, as if he was speaking to himself. "Even when she someday bears the name of another, it will better for me to keep my distance. For now, at the very least, I would give people time to forget what I have done."

Genevieve shook her head in disagreement, but Etienne decided to plunge forward. There was another related subject that needed to be raised. "I have thought much on this. After today, it might be better that you should avoid all association with me. At present few are aware that we have spent any time together and that is best for you. You will always have my gratitude and all the protection I may give, but I will not do your reputation harm."

To his surprise, Genevieve burst into gales of laughter. "You? Harm *my* reputation? By Merlin's toes and whiskers!"

Her unexpected reaction discomfited him. He had been formulating his speech since sunrise.

"How very noble of you!" Her tone calmed from hilarity to a mild sarcastic humor that was belied by the angry fire in her eyes. "You seem to forget that I married a man who was not of the Blood." She scanned his face for a moment. "I can see you are puzzled by my choice."

Etienne was startled by her perception. He could not recall a time when he had lacked the ability to mask his true feelings. After his mother's death, fortifying the privacy of his innermost thoughts and seeking the shelter of his own mind had become his only defenses against the volatile whirlwind of the old comte and his manipulations.

The façade that Etienne had built and reinforced for so many years was a bastion he had deemed nigh on impenetrable, yet this woman had pierced those walls effortlessly.

"Until last night, the Brisbois family had disappeared from the ken of those in high circles, and now..." With a rueful look, she directed her attention to the sideboard, but not before he saw the flash of fear in her expression. "I had best take care of the rest of the food before we go."

As she began the weaving, Etienne stepped forward to pick up the empty plate she had set aside. "Before you bespell the food, it might be wise to eat something yourself, Genevieve," he coaxed, sliding an elegant fruit tart on her plate. "Here, you must try these. Grandma-ma's chef has surpassed himself."

As he had hoped, the routine of choosing her meal had a soothing effect. Only after seating her and taking a croissant for himself, did Genevieve renew the conversation.

"We wandered across Europe for years, moving from place to place, always changing our names, until we moved to England. I was never quite sure what my mother was afraid of, but after I married Owen, she seemed to be less fearful, as if—"

"Mama, Mama, look at me!" Louis flew into the room, ending the conversation to Genevieve's obvious relief.

"Well, you are quite the young gentleman!" Genevieve put her hands upon Louis' shoulder and surveyed his attire. "Fine as a brand new sixpence!"

"A guinea at least!" Lady Morgan sniffed. "He does look quite elegant, doesn't he?"

As they all lauded his grandmother on her thread working skills, Etienne recognized a transformation happening without so much as a drop of magic. Lady Morgan was becoming more like the grandmother of his childhood memories, younger and vivacious.

Less sad.

As she turned Louis this way and that, so all might better admire the subtle nuances of her working, Etienne understood the spell wrought by having people who needed her, others to care for. He knew she had once eagerly anticipated his marriage and the prospect of his children.

But his actions had robbed her of that sense of purpose and would do so again, once their connection to the Dales was severed. Somehow, he would have to make it up to her.

CHAPTER 15

*I*n the end, it was decided that Dale's Apothecary would open its doors as scheduled. "We tell them first they must pay what they owe before they will be granted any audience with Genevieve," Lady Morgan suggested. "This is not to say we will guarantee they may speak to her, of course. But this way, we shall collect your money."

Genevieve had wanted to keep the shop closed so that her mother could join them and pledge herself to Lord Damien. The old woman had continued to insist, however, that she would ally herself with neither mage nor coven. Despite pleas and arguments, she could not be persuaded to do otherwise.

"I am done with hiding!" she declared.

Their clerk was due to arrive before the doors opened and Etienne's grandmother had volunteered to remain, ostensibly to assist. However, they all knew her real purpose was to make certain no magical force was employed against Madame Brisbois. No one would dare to step over that line in Lady Morgan's presence.

An hour before their appointment with Lord Damien, Genevieve, Louis and Etienne slipped out the back door, cloaked by a temporary *see-me-not* charm that Genevieve's mother had insisted upon spinning herself. They had decided to walk some distance to where Lady Morgan's coach awaited them since Marcel advised that the entrances to their shop and house were under surveillance.

The Chartreux cat had also warned that he had caught a number of intruders attempting magical workings in the area. *"Thossssse I discovered wear my mark,"* he rumbled, demonstrating his methods with a deft swipe of his claws. *"Ssssadly, I am but one feline. I cannot find them all."*

The cat's caveat enabled the comte to detect a series of magical trip-traps which would have betrayed them. His ability to sense their locations allowed them to be evaded handily.

On the way, they nearly collided with several pedestrians. Louis' delighted giggles disconcerted more than one passer-by. Marcel had gone ahead to confirm their rendezvous. When they finally reached the vehicle, Genevieve lifted the spell.

At Wodesby House, they were ushered in to the Chief Mage's study by Angel, Lord Wodesby's canine familiar. He barked an apology for his lordship's delay, explaining how the mage's three puppies were growing teeth at last. The tedious and painful manifestation of baby dentition was one more indication of canine superiority in his opinion. Nonetheless, it was obvious that Angel had experience with older boys, since he exited with a promise to Louis of cream cakes for his patience and obedience to the warning against touching objects without permission.

Magical relics lined the shelves, telescopes and astrolabes sat side by side with crystals and amulets. Upon one wall a collection of athames seemed to whisper of centuries of deeds both dire and benevolent. Ancient flint blades fixed to engraved wood and sharpened horn bound with thongs of leather, shared pride of place with jeweled handles tanged to keen blades. A seeming hodgepodge of leather-bound grimoires and scrolls filled a variety of nooks, shelves and niches that rose from floor to ceiling.

Louis looked around him with open-mouthed awe and Genevieve barely kept herself from gawping like a green country bumpkin. She reached out to touch a dual edged blade of Damascus steel.

"You won't get a cream cake," Louis warned. "Angel said no touching."

"I give your mother permission." The Chief Mage entered, favoring them with a weary smile as he seated himself in his chair. His look of profound fatigue was such that Genevieve doubted the man had slept at all. "That's a bloodthirsty piece, Lady Genevieve, so I would take care if you are more accustomed to an herb woman's athame."

Louis snickered, but was silenced by his mother's raised eyebrow.

"I am sorry, milord," he began penitently. "I had no intention of being rude. It is just that Mama—" He shrugged abashed, but unsure as to how to properly explain himself. He looked at Genevieve in a silent plea.

"What Louis means to say is his mother is somewhat skilled." With a sigh, Genevieve gestured the athame to her hand, testing its heft and its balance with a few experimental swipes. Satisfied, she flowed into the first measures of the daily routine she had been forced to skip in the morning uproar. She began the dance with a lunge to pierce her invisible opponent's heart.

Angling the blade from above, she swept downward with deadly force in a move to open an attacker from collar to gut. With a graceful dip, she reversed the motion, carving her way upwards from below. With a quick turn, an imaginary attack from behind her was deflected and she whirled slicing and striking, laying waste to an invisible horde of assailants, before coming to a halt. With a curtsy, she sent the athame back to its place of honor.

"An excellent piece, milord," she commented, taking her seat.

The look of open-mouthed astonishment on the men's faces was more than gratifying. An herb woman's athame indeed! As if an herbalist's blade was anything less than deadly when wielded by a knowing hand.

"Mama is usually much faster than that," Louis declared proudly, "but she left her own athame at home today because—" He halted at Etienne's infinitesimal shake of the head. "And I have not yet greeted you properly, Lord Wodesby." He bowed. "My name is Louis Dale and I tend to talk too much."

"Greetings, Louis Dale," Lord Wodesby said ruefully, running a hand through his silver mane in a gesture that bespoke embarrassment. "I warn you to beware of condescension, lad. It leads to false assumptions. Now, I must tender two apologies to your mother. My wife and sister have pointed out the error of my ways in the granting of your boon, milady," the Chief Mage said, shaking his head in dismay. "My attention should have been fixed upon you and your needs. And you obviously can handle a blade."

He turned his attention to Louis. "So, I hear that you are trying to earn your mage's ring, young man?" he said, trying to put the boy at ease.

Genevieve winced at her son's sudden scowl. Lord Wodesby had stepped on a sore spot.

"Perhaps you are unaware, milord, there are no rings from my mother's family, since they were stolen from us," the boy said, his chin rising in a gesture of defiance. "My father was an Outsider, so there are no mage jewels to be had from his line."

Genevieve took a breath, recognizing what her son was trying to do. "Louis!" She made the name a warning and a rebuke, but Louis had determined upon his gambit to gain the truth from the Chief Mage. "I don't think—"

Etienne gave an infinitesimal shake of his head, reminding her they had given their word. Louis could speak for himself. But never had she thought her son would be forward to the brink of incivility.

"If that means no one will deign to teach me because I am an OutBlood, then I must apologize for wasting your time." The boy rose from his seat, but a wave of the Chief Mage's hand stayed the child in his tracks.

"The first lesson that a mage must master is control," Lord Wodesby said. "I must say restraint was likely the hardest lesson for me, young Dale, so I will forgive your display. Know I brook no insults to Outsiders. My stepfather is an Outsider and one of the finest men I have been privileged to know. My sister is married to one as well."

"My apologies, milord." Louis hung his head in embarrassment.

The Chief Mage rose from behind his desk. "Know you this, young Dale. When my sister, the Archivist, heard of your healing powers, she was up till dawn, digging in her mound of dusty papers and flaking tomes for all she could find. From what she claims it is rare for your kind of magic to pass from generation to generation with only one magical parent."

Louis began to blink rapidly, trying to fight tears and the Chief Mage seemed to recognize he had stepped wrongly again. He began to speak hastily. "What I am saying to you is this; the healing skills you possess likely come in part from the Time Before, Louis. They were presents from the Fae who gave Merlin and his Blood the first Gifts of Magic. Your Da was likely of Elven blood."

"Is that a good thing?" Louis asked.

Damien groaned. "By Merlin's Beard! I knew I should have had Rowan here with me! She is far better at explaining these matters than I am. But between last night and the babies the poor woman is worn to a frazzle and so am I."

Genevieve heard a sound beside her.

Laughter? Etienne was shaking with contained mirth. He tried and failed to suppress a snort.

"You knew it! I thought so, but now I know for sure," Lord Wodesby rose with a roar and pointed accusingly at the comte. "You knew Rowan carried three babies! By Merlin, a Seer's task is to give warning of impending disaster and you let this event catch me unawares."

Etienne coughed to cover one final snigger before composing himself. "Rowan was months along when it was revealed to me she carried a coven complete within her, so it seemed your doom was sealed no matter what I foretold."

Louis was beginning to squirm impatiently.

"If I may answer the young man's question, milord?" At the Chief Mage's nod, Etienne proceeded. "Yes, Louis, Fae magic is a very good thing. All those of the Blood carry the magic of the Fae. It was their final Gift, shared with Merlin and his descendants before the elven kin departed the realms of man. Healing is one of the rarest skills among our kind. Almost none of Merlin's children are so blessed. To carry such magic?" He stretched out his palms as if trying to hold something beyond measure. "This is an abundance of blessing."

"So Da was of the Fae then?" Louis looked to his mother in wonder.

"Your father always had a knack for making people feel better," Genevieve said, feeling the obvious truth in what Etienne had said. Perhaps it was the reason for her late husband's sadness? She knew well what it felt like to be trapped in a world where you were always something other. "There were recoveries and healings we could never explain. It might be it was more than his potions?"

"Quite likely it was. During the days of the Scourge, many of Merlin's children and their Fae kin went into hiding," Lord Damien explained. "Out of fear and caution, some kept the knowledge of their heritage a secret and concealed their magic, even from their children. But Gifts are given by the will of the Light and they do not always pass from generation to generation."

Genevieve saw the sadness in his eyes and knew he was thinking of his sister, Miranda. "There are many kinds of Gifts, milord."

He smiled. "Yes. My sister would be the first to tell me so," he agreed. "In these troubled times, we cannot afford to spurn any of them. That is why I am hoping you might help me to build bridges to the OutBlood community."

"You intend to go forward with this publicly?" Etienne raised a brow, his expression concerned. "You know it will inflame many of those who already oppose you."

"Some," Lord Damien admitted. "But Miranda's refusal to remain secretive has already opened many doors. My sister's inability is not as much of an aberration as we had thought."

"I do not doubt every coven has someone they hide to maintain the illusion of purity and power," Etienne agreed. "I am aware of more than a few in France.

There are more instances of children with Gifts who appear outside the covens than those in the High Circles would wish to admit."

"Like me." Louis eyed the Chief Mage warily. "Why do you want us if we are not as good as you? At breakfast the comte told me to be careful, there will be those who want to use me. Are you one of them?"

"Louis!" Genevieve colored in embarrassment.

"Legitimate questions," the Chief Mage admitted. "It is my job to protect and serve England and *all* of Merlin's children. If you choose to ally yourself with me today, you agree I may someday call upon you for help if there is need. So, the answer to the latter question is *yes*. I will use you to keep our people safe. The war may be over for now, but as a Seer I know there will be need in the future. I tell you in all honesty and with great sadness, more than a few witches and mages under my protection have gone to the Light, for England's sake."

It was obvious the boy was weighing his words carefully. "As they say you almost did?" Louis asked. "Was it true that you danced with lightning?"

"I confess myself amazed at what people will tell to children," the Chief Mage said with a groan. "I did my duty and yes, I danced with a storm and saw the Light but a step away."

"You would be horrified to know what we hear milord, especially when you don't know we listen," Louis told him with a shrewd smile which rapidly slipped into a thoughtful expression. "You made an apology when you thought yourself wrong. You risked yourself for what you believe in. That is good." He nodded, as if crossing off items on his own internal list. "Mama says my family will be safer under your shield. Is this true?"

"If you declare yourself to me, I pledge to do my best, as I do for all my people, young mage." He placed his fingers upon the band of England, signifying his oath and bond.

"Then I would do so gladly, milord." Louis rose eagerly from his chair, and took a step forward, but then he hesitated.

"You have a question? A concern?" Lord Damien asked.

The boy nodded slowly. "I am afraid for my grandmother." He looked anxiously at his mother. "Will they not try to get to us through her? How can we leave her defenseless, Mama?"

"Unfortunately, my mother refuses to swear fealty to any mage or coven," Genevieve told Lord Damien ruefully.

"What if I agree to include your grandmother as well?" Lord Damien asked.

"Could you, milord?" Louis asked excitedly. "We would be ever so grateful, wouldn't we, Mama?"

"So long as your grandmother doesn't conspire with my enemies or act against those I have sworn to shield, then she will have my protection through her connection to you, young mage, just as your mother does," Lord Damien agreed.

At Genevieve's nod of agreement, Louis eagerly stepped forward and knelt to kiss the Chief Mage's ring.

For a moment, through her bond to Louis, Genevieve felt like a bird, soaring over the land. Fields and lakes, valleys and mountains passed beneath her inner eye until she felt as if her very soul stretched from sea to sea. Although England had been her home for most of her life, she now felt that it was truly a part of her.

"That was amazing, milord!" Louis' voice brought her abruptly back to earth. "Angel said there would be cakes, after. Is it *after* now?"

Louis was eying her eagerly. Genevieve looked toward the Chief Mage who was chuckling.

"So he is still a little boy after all. Heaven and Earth linking in a mystical binding, but the cakes are what come to his mind!" Lord Damien waved Louis off. "A mageling after my own heart, this one. Go on with you and bring back two for me."

As soon as the door closed behind Louis, Etienne began to laugh.

Lord Damien watched the Frenchman's amusement with increasing puzzlement.

"I admit that the child is quite charming," Lord Damien declared when the merriment ceased. "But I have never seen you lose yourself to that extent. What did I miss, Etienne?"

Etienne wiped a tear from his eye. "By Merlin's teeth, that boy is going to lead us all on a dance. First, accept my apologies, Damien, but I gave Louis my word that I would be silent until his decision was made."

Lord Damien scowled suspiciously. "And why do you feel the need to tender your regrets?"

"Please do not take this ill, milord," Genevieve interjected with a sheepish look on her face. "Louis does it all the time. It is how he protects himself and our family."

"If it is any comfort, Damien, the boy has played me as well," Etienne said. "Like a violin on the concert stage."

"So just how have I been gulled here?" the Chief Mage asked, his fingers in a thoughtful steeple. "I felt no magic at work. Louis received nothing that I wasn't ready to give."

"And my son knew every offer you made had truth behind it," Genevieve said, shaking her head at the Chief Mage's sudden frown. "I was not assaying your

178

words, milord. Never would I do so, without your consent. However, Louis was. He cannot help it. My son would have known the instant a falsehood left your mouth."

"Merlin's Bones! A twice-Blessed! I was not aware that he shares your Gift as well as that of healing!" Lord Wodesby was momentarily nonplussed. "Does this mean he does not need touch, as you do, for his power to manifest?"

Genevieve's sigh was his answer.

"You see now why he needs a mentor so badly?" Etienne said. "And why we must choose a mage who will be scrupulously honest with him? You cannot lie to that child. Have you reviewed the list I gave you?"

"I wish that I could bring the boy to his ring myself, but my duties are many." The Chief Mage gave a sigh of regret. "Rowan helps me as much as she may, but with the triplets and her own responsibilities, I could not possibly ask her to take on more than she already does."

"I know one of the candidates I propose is financially challenged. If it is a matter of the ring, I am possessed of several that have been passed through my direct line," Etienne proposed. "It would be my honor to gift one to Louis."

Genevieve's expression must have conveyed her shock at his proposal. Mage's rings were rarely allowed to pass out of the family.

Etienne's lip curled with wry regret. "Given my recent history, it is unlikely I will be presenting a ring to a son. I would that someone worthy had the use of it."

Before Genevieve could find the words to thank him, there was a knock at the door and Louis returned to the room with a plate of cakes.

"Tante Reina sent enough for two for everyone, see?" Louis said delightedly. "And there are lots more downstairs."

"I can see that you have already sampled at least one. However, *lots* does not give you leave to make yourself sick with greed," Genevieve said, wiping a trail of cream off his upper lip. "We were just discussing who we ought to choose to teach you about mage's magic."

"That's simple," Louis said, after taking a bite of another cake. "The comte should be my teacher."

After a moment of shocked silence, Etienne began to explain. "Louis, you do not understand. There are many reasons why I should not—"

The Chief Mage held out his palm for quiet. A tinge of magic touched his eyes.

"Why should the comte be your mentor, Louis?" Lord Wodesby asked.

"He has never lied to me, for one thing and grown people lie all the time," Louis said, his head tilting in an attitude of serious consideration. "He is a very powerful mage."

"Was," Etienne interrupted his tone bitter.

"Is," Louis contradicted him. "That is the first untruth you have told me, even though you believe the lie yourself.

"Who better to teach the boy how to control power than someone who is doing it at every waking moment?" the Chief Mage mused aloud.

Louis set down the plate of treats and looked earnestly at Lord Wodesby. "But I haven't yet mentioned what is most important. He doesn't *want* to do it. The comte doesn't want to use me or Mama. He feels like he owes us a debt of honor and he wishes to pay it."

"This is a means to discharge last night's debt, Etienne. Had Lady Genevieve not intervened, it would have been almost impossible to prove your family's right to the jewels."

The glow in the Chief Mage's eyes had not completely dissipated. Genevieve realized he was still speaking as a Seer. "It is your decision," he said as the blue finally faded.

"In the end, it must be up to Lady Genevieve and her son," Etienne countered, seeming to pull the words from the depths of his humiliation. "You must know what I am, milady, from the rumors and the whispers of your friends, but does the boy?"

He stepped forward to stand before the boy like a criminal in the dock. "This is my truth. You see before you, a mage in disgrace, Louis Dale. My name is a by-word for treachery. Think upon this decision and ask yourself, would you have a mage of such infamy associated with your family? Ask of me what you will and I will respond. My answers may well dissuade you."

"There is one thing that I must know before I make my choice. Are you truly working against the Chief Mage, as they say?" Louis asked, turning his attention to his mother at her audible gasp.

"Where did you hear—" Genevieve began.

"As I said, I listen to things. You don't have to be like *Grand-mère* and use magic to be invisible," Louis declared, looking back at Etienne for his answer. "There are many who believe you are still loyal to Napoleon."

The Chief Mage sighed. "It would seem our plan is working, Etienne."

"Indeed," Etienne agreed with a sigh. "*Non.* I am not Lord Wodesby's enemy and Napoleon no longer has my allegiance."

"I thought not, especially since the real reason you did not tell Lord Wodesby about the triplets was to spare him worry."

"Louis!" Genevieve scolded. "What have I told you about repeating private truths?"

The boy blushed and eyed Etienne warily. "I apologize, milord. I will try to be better, if you will show me how. There are so many things I do not want to know, but I can't help it."

"I will do my best," Etienne promised.

"I know you will." Louis gave a satisfied nod and eyed the empty tray on the nearby table. "May I be excused, please? Tante Reina told me she needed someone to help take care of a batch of raspberry tarts. They came out less than perfect."

"Before you go to destroy the evidence of this regrettable error, I will ask you to tell me why you have chosen me," Etienne asked.

"I know you have not lied to me, even when you were not aware of my Gift," Louis answered with conviction. "And my *Grand-mère* has told me sometimes, learning from what you have done wrong is almost as important as knowing what is right."

When the door closed behind Louis, Damien sighed and put his head in his hands. "When I remember that we are thrice-blessed with Gifted babies, I don't know how Rowan and I will survive their childhoods."

"Such is the fate of parents," Etienne opined, as he reached for the brandy decanter on the side table. "Still as one who finds the path barred, I envy such problems." He contemplated the drink, before returning the stopper to its place without pouring a drop. "If I am to be the boy's mentor, how will we maintain the fiction of this contention between us?"

Lord Wodesby shook his head. "A conundrum indeed. But I may have a plan, if Lady Genevieve and her family will consent to assist us. I believe a betrothal might serve to protect Madame Brisbois and the Dales until her son comes into his own, and to forward our plans as well."

In Etienne's opinion, the look in the Chief Mage's eyes as he bit into his cream cake was far too merry.

CHAPTER 16

At the Pendrake town house on Grosvenor Square, a late breakfast was being served with a generous portion of indignation.

"And if you would believe, Oliver, Lady Morgan was standing at the door! Collecting pennies like the veriest shopkeeper. *That Woman!*" Lady Pendrake vehemently stabbed at her kipper as if it were indeed, *That Woman*. "Then she had the gall to inform me that I would have to wait my turn in the queue, along with the rabble that had arrived before me to pay their debts, even though I am certain we owed far more than most of that lot!"

Oliver, Lord Pendrake scowled and stuffed a piece of toast in his mouth, reminding himself that it was always wiser to let his mother's tongue have its gallop before attempting to seize the reins of the conversation.

"I have always thought that she was a parvenu. Her grandmother was a thread witch, I'm told," she added before shoveling a fork full of eggs into her mouth.

Lord Pendrake stepped into the breach of the monologue. "Did you see Lady Genevieve?" he asked.

"I refuse to give that upstart a title that she does not merit!" Fluffy fragments spewed, making it seem almost as if she was frothing yellow at the mouth. "Despite the rumors Edgar brought to my attention." The squirrel on the back of her chair chittered in protest.

"Yes, yes, I know you heard it direct from Lady Jersey's weasel, dearest," she gave the squirrel a fond pat, "but you know full well that Silence's sources are often Outsiders since she is a Patroness of Almack's."

"What rumors?" With a bleary-eyed blink, Octavius raised his head from the table.

"Lady Jersey declares Mrs. Dale and her mother are of French nobility, which does not signify even if it is true." She snorted derisively. "With the Bourbons restored, every émigré in England is claiming to be kin to the King of France."

"Wodesby did name her as *Lady*," Pendrake said thoughtfully.

His mother pursed her lips and skewered her son with a fulminating look. "When I finally came before the counter, the old Frenchwoman consulted her books. It would seem we owe somewhat more than I anticipated. I gave her what I had, but apparently her daughter will accept no communication from anyone who has not fulfilled Wodesby's command to pay their account in its entirety."

Pendrake eyed his mother, his suspicion increasing as her rant abruptly ceased. "I gave you more than enough to wipe the slate."

Lady Pendrake looked away. "I may owe a small sum to Dale's for some unguents no one else sells. Their youth cream is—"

"Might just marry Lady Genevieve myself," Octavius declared. "Have to give up the business of course! Can't have a wife in trade. Get another to run it with all the money rolling in. Or sell it! Sure it'll fetch a pretty penny. And she is a pretty piece!"

"You are a Pendrake!" his mother declared her chins

aquiver. "Tell your brother, Oliver, why this scheme is out of the question!"

"Actually, Mother, Octavius might have hit upon a good idea." Pendrake rubbed his chin in thought. "To have a Truth Sifter in the family? Especially once Wodesby gives up his office?"

"Woman doesn't like me though." Octavius frowned.

"I don't particularly like Circe, but I fully intend to marry her," Pendrake reminded him.

"Might be better to have a wife than a mistress. A mistress has to be paid to like me." Octavius pursed his lips as he considered the possibility. "I'm eligible. Next in line, after Ollie. Step up for her, isn't it?"

"I will not have it!" Lady Pendrake shook her head, aghast.

"Think of it, Mama," her younger son declared. "Always asking me to economize, you and Ollie. All the wrinkle cream you want and you won't have to pay a penny for it!"

* * *

Once Lord Wodesby's plan had been debated and agreed upon, the announcement of Etienne's betrothal to Genevieve appeared in the papers within the week.

Young Louis' training began on the same day. Uncontrolled magic was dangerous to the wielder and everyone around him.

To his surprise, Etienne found himself enjoying his lessons with the boy. Time flew by quickly and they settled into a routine. Remembering his own boredom with rote memorization and tedious tomes of theory, Etienne alternated lessons with activity. Thanks to Genevieve's teachings, Louis was already adept with a knife and he was quickly picking up the essentials of swordplay. He was a bright pupil and usually required little more than a brief explanation to master a skill or a concept.

Despite Etienne's initial misgivings, the lessons in mage craft caused no difficulty. The boy had galloped his way through *The Grimoire for Novices*. Etienne's inability to employ his own magic was less of a problem than anticipated. Louis' Gift for truth made matters almost simple when it came to providing examples of spell casting. If Etienne understood the boy correctly, magic had its own inherent veracity. Etienne had only to think upon how he would perform a particular spell and Louis claimed he could see the process within Etienne, almost like the drawings in a book.

It was a memory of the diagrams in one particular primer that sent Etienne down from the schoolroom to scour the shelves of the Manse's library. However, locating the volume was far more difficult than he had anticipated.

After a few minutes of useless searching, he closed his eyes and envisioned his grandfather. As Etienne called up the memory, he realized the room had not changed at all. The warmth from the hearth, the well-stuffed chair in the corner, the Constable landscape above the piecrust table all seemed to be fixed in time. He could almost see the old man, sitting in his nook, waiting patiently for his grandson to recite the previous day's lesson before floating the next chosen book to hand.

Etienne smiled as the reminiscence finally supplied the title that had eluded him. *A Young Mage's Guide to Mastery* had been an essential text in his early training. It had also been a favorite, with beautiful illuminations and instructions that guided each step. Grandpapa had deliberately shelved it up in the farthest, highest corners of the library as something of a test.

A promise had been made.

When you can summon it for yourself, I will purchase you a pony, boy.

His mother's ghostly laughter echoed in the empty room. *You are spoiling him, Papa!*

Someone ought to! The long-ago retort spun into the silence.

Scanning the shadowed upper shelves, Etienne thought he could see the familiar tooled leather binding. With a wave, he automatically began to beckon it to him when he felt a warning.

"It would seem I may never quite manage to merit that pony," he muttered to himself, moving to fetch the ladder.

More than a few smashed bits of pottery had attested to his failure to safely summon objects to hand during that holiday. The end of his childhood was marked by that long-ago visit. It had been his mother's final trip to England.

Etienne realized he was standing and staring into space. He was forgetting himself far too often lately, getting lost in thoughts of the past.

Or the present, for that matter.

Memories of Genevieve would occur to him at odd moments. Etienne often found himself dwelling on her smile, contemplating the color of her hair in the firelight, reliving the sound of her laugh.

There was no doubt in his mind. When Louis finally completed his studies, Etienne would leave London, at least until Genevieve found herself a husband. With a pang of sadness, he shifted the ladder to the corner and began to climb.

The top shelf was finally within reach when he heard the door to the library open. Due to his distraction and the lack of magic, it was taking far beyond the "no more than a moment or two," Etienne had estimated it would require to fetch the book. He could not blame Louis for growing impatient.

"I begin to discover I miss the small things almost as much as the greater Gifts that were once mine," Etienne mused aloud as he pulled the primer for young mages from its place and opened it to the familiar first page illustrated by an exquisite depiction of Merlin addressing King Arthur's court. "The everyday magics in particular, the ones we learn in our youth, are precious." He shook his head with regret. "Never take them for granted, Louis."

"Wisdom, indeed."

Startled at the unexpected sound of Genevieve's voice, Etienne snapped the book shut, raising a cloud of dust that set him to sneezing.

Genevieve stood before the library window, framed within a pool of sun that made the motes seem like minute flakes of snow. The emerald green of her gown contrasted with the mahogany paneling creating a rich burst of color amidst the wan wintry light.

"My apologies. I didn't mean to disconcert you," she said. "I'm here to fetch Louis. Your grandmother sent me to wait here while she sent word upstairs."

"I had just come to the library to seek this out for your son." Etienne made his way back down the ladder. "Please forgive the dust."

"I would be glad to assist you," Genevieve offered, "unless—" She hesitated, her embarrassment obvious.

"No offense is taken. If you would not mind, I would be grateful for your help."

With a graceful sweep of her hand, all the specks of dust made their way up the chimney.

He bowed his thanks and gestured toward a chair near the hearth. "Please have a seat near the fire while we await Louis. It is a chilly day and I suspect we might see more snow before its end."

"Excellent, you are now discoursing upon the weather. Your grandmother will make a proper Englishman of you yet," Genevieve quipped with an arch of her brow.

"Ah, but I am a Frenchman at heart, Genevieve," he retorted, eying her with candid admiration. "As such, I would be remiss if I did not remark upon the fact you are in excellent looks today."

Genevieve gave a delighted sashay. A billow of skirts and petticoats twirled as she invited him to admire her finery. "It is a new gown. Lady Morgan dragooned me, as well as *Maman*, into a visit to her modiste. Your grandmother has been so kind, taking my mother under her wing. Lady Morgan insists she is only seeking to elevate our betrothal by reminding society of the Brisbois name."

"Your family is nearly as old as my own," Etienne said, "and far more respected. Grandmama is most astute in these matters."

"Whatever her reasons, I have never seen my mother so self-assured," Genevieve declared. "She and Lady Morgan actually got into a bit of a row when your grandmother insisted upon sending Madame Bouchard's bill to herself! I agree with my mother. This is a sham betrothal, after all."

Never before had Etienne known a woman to complain about a purchase paid with someone else's credit. "My grandmother has demanded that I introduce Louis to my tailor. Sham or not, it would not do for my fiancée's family to present a shabby appearance. It will be my pleasure to provide him with an appropriate wardrobe." Setting the book aside, Etienne gestured Genevieve to a seat.

"Well, I cannot like it and I have told your grandmother as much." Her moue of displeasure delighted him. "As *Maman* said, the Brisbois have always paid our own way. Certainly, we can afford it now." She shook her head in disbelief. "Nearly a decade's worth of debts, even accounts Owen had long despaired of, are now paid in full. And the shop is constantly busy with people who are buying something in the hope they may speak with me and change my..." her voice trailed off in embarrassment.

"Change your choice of mentor?" Etienne forced a chuckle. "Or your choice of fiancé? Or both?"

As usual, her blush blossomed full force. It was sad to realize her honest expressions of discomfiture were like the roses of summer. They would not last. If she wished to someday move among the High Circles, she would have to learn to hide those telltale signs of her emotions, but in the meantime, Etienne meant to enjoy them as long as he could.

"I cannot understand why they are still tendering offers of marriage, despite the announcement of our intention to be wed!"

"Because they believe you would gladly throw me over for what might be considered a better offer," Etienne admitted, forcing himself to be truthful. Etienne felt a tinge of regret when she frowned. It was not well done of him, to burst the bubble of her happiness at her good fortune. He hastened to reassure her.

"Do not fear, once I, villain that I am, give you your *congé*, as Damien has suggested, there will surely be other offers, more honorable ones, I would venture to say. You are Gifted, of good birth, and beautiful besides. You have the favor of England's Chief Mage and Mistress. Louis' extraordinary Gifts will cause many to overlook the circumstances of his birth."

"As you do?" There was bitterness in her voice and her eyes held a trace of reproach. "Do you compromise your standards by associating with my son?"

Honesty. He reminded himself. He had promised her

no less when she had agreed to the sham engagement Wodesby had proposed. Fortunately, this was a feeling he could share without equivocation. "If you would, milady," he asked, extending his hand to her.

Once again, a flush of embarrassment colored her cheeks. "There is no need, truly. I am just angry at them all, their hypocrisy, and their greed. A part of me is not sorry I was not raised in their world, otherwise I might be just like them."

"Forgive me if I doubt that, Genevieve. Your Gift would never allow you to become disingenuous or false," Etienne said, stepping towards her, his hand still outreached. "But it is you and Louis who honor me with your trust."

She shook her head. "Such proof is unnecessary."

"I believe it important you be sure of the facts so that Louis will not accidentally become aware of your misapprehensions." *And because I want to touch you, if only for a moment.*

"Very well." She removed her gloves and placed her fingers in Etienne's hand. Immediately, a peculiar peace enveloped him. Somehow, the serenity seemed to intensify each time she touched him. He could not bring himself to ask Genevieve if this was a sensation she could routinely engender with mere contact. It was troubling to admit that he preferred to remain ignorant because it allowed him to pretend those moments of harmony between them were unique.

A spark of her Gift lit her eyes, prompting him to speak. "Once I was the kind of man who would have disdained you and your son. I am no longer that man, Genevieve." There was a deeper truth within him, one that he was only just beginning to acknowledge, an honesty whispering *I find myself wishing you and Louis were mine in truth.*

But he had no right to give those words a voice.

Once said aloud, the accord between them could very well be destroyed. "You are both worthy of my deepest respect." He raised her hand to his lips and kissed it lightly before letting her go. "I hope this does not count toward my promise of payment," he added with a deliberately roguish air.

"I will think upon it," she said, trying to match his mischievous tones. "We are, after all, affianced."

Honesty, Etienne adjured himself. Nonetheless, he turned away, resting his hand upon the carved mantelpiece before he spoke again. "Few would blame you if you set me aside, especially if you find someone better suited, including me." The final two words did not truly constitute a lie. He would regret, but not blame. "Damian and I will contrive another means of accumulating the information we need. Until then, your presence provides me with a pretext to attend entertainments and garner information whereas before, I could not."

"But there was no need to purchase an entire wardrobe for me," she protested. "I doubt I could wear everything we have chosen before this charade comes to an end."

"My grandmother is having a wonderful time helping to outfit your family. Please do not deprive her of the pleasure of providing your costumes for this masquerade." His throat suddenly felt tight at the thought of the inevitable severing of their connection. He reminded himself their parting would be best for the welfare of her family.

Damien had made the case that a temporary betrothal would be an excellent move on all fronts. Although Genevieve and her family were pledged to England, they would still be vulnerable until Louis was shepherded into his maturity. Lady Morgan was a witch to be reckoned with, her arcane power amplified with the wisdom of age.

Moreover, although Etienne was without Gifts, it did not mean he lacked resources. The du Le Feys had invested wisely and broadly with assets around the globe. Money could often solve problems when magic could not. Between his wealth and his grandmother's magic Lady Brisbois and the Dales would have a formidable measure of protection against those who might plague them.

"Well, I will certainly need at least some of the gowns." Genevieve pulled a pile of envelopes from her reticule. "The invitations keep coming. I do not understand, Etienne, why do they want us at their entertainments if we are both of us notorious?"

"For now, they want us because we *are* the entertainments because we *are* infamous. Novelty will often trump good taste," Etienne explained, shuffling through the invites and sorting them into stacks. "Were it not for you, though, many of these invitations would cease. It is your attention most of them crave."

He handed her an elaborately engraved piece of vellum that sparkled with a family crest when opened. "Lady Martel's son is a widower with a hellion of a boy whose Gifts are unknown, but dangerous. She sees you as a potential lion tamer and hopes you will favor Lord Martel over me. He is quite handsome and it is a respected family."

"Why do you persist in promoting suitors for me?"

"A Seer comes to recognize some events as inevitable." He tried to maintain a tenor of light amusement. "Once you acquire a degree of what the Outsiders call *town bronze* any mage with a measure of discernment will come to recognize you as a witch worthy of being wooed. But I can help you to easily eliminate some of those who are beneath your consideration." He pulled out another invitation and shook his head in disbelief. "This mage once courted my grandmother. He is an aging stallion seeking a broodmare to give him an heir, but he accounts himself an excellent catch."

Etienne picked up the next invitation. As he felt the magic radiating from it, he dropped it immediately. The source was not the usual decorative spells, but something foul. Malice was sealed beneath the wax. Etienne picked up the tongs from beside the fireplace and used them to convey the envelope to the stone apron of the hearth.

"Something is wrong, I take it?" Genevieve asked. "May I help?"

"In a moment, if you will. The counter-spell must be framed just so." Etienne chose some wood from the basket and carefully began to add it to the fireplace. "I find myself missing the physical activity of the country." Etienne tried to keep his tones matter of fact. "I have found it helps me maintain my control. Chopping wood works best. This is why we have timber aplenty in this house, rather than coal. It is fortunate because living matter serves better to contain and consume this type of malicious spell. Now I will place it here." Etienne used the tongs to move the envelope to the top of the corral of wood he had constructed. He moved a nearby chair aside.

"Would you be so kind as to accelerate the fire in a moment? Stand back." He pushed the envelope into the makeshift enclosure where it began to glow. "Now, Genevieve, if you please."

The flames rose and a shower of red sparks erupted from the heart of the flame.

"Bespelled," he explained, inhaling a relieved breath. "It was likely set to react when you broke the seal. You do not want to know what it could have made you do.

From now on, please, open no correspondence on your own. Bring it to me first so I may verify its safety."

"But wouldn't it harm you instead?" Genevieve asked.

She was genuinely concerned for his welfare. The knowledge touched him deeply.

Etienne shook his head in answer. "That too, is part of Justice's sentence. I cannot be killed or badly damaged by magic. Those who use their Gifts against me may do me some mild harm, but Justice has warned them they will pay a larger penalty."

Genevieve looked into the hearth and the shower of angry sparks still roiling in the flames. She backed away. Her expression of horror evoked a feeling of guilt within him. Unfortunately, without guidance she would be a lamb unwittingly presenting her throat to the edge of the sacrificial knife. "Information is power, Genevieve, and I will give you all at my disposal, so you may make educated choices. When I give your *congé*, you will be flooded with suitors. You will have friends who may advise you, but ultimately, you must learn how to deal with them."

The very thought was painful.

To distract them both, Etienne took up the volume he had been seeking and caressed the leather binding, riffling through the pages, before presenting it to Genevieve. "I find myself surprised by the satisfaction teaching gives me. It is my hope your son will enjoy this as much as I did. Louis may bring it home."

"*A Young Mage's Guide to Mastery.*" Genevieve read the title and turned the page. "This is quite old and extremely valuable from the look of it. Perhaps you ought to keep it safe here. Louis can be somewhat careless with his things." She handed it back to him.

"Books are meant to be read, not to sit on shelves to gather dust," Etienne said with a shrug. He fingered the leather binding and remembered lazy autumn afternoons and the sound of his grandfather's voice. Etienne knew Lord Morgan would never have approved letting the book languish in a library hoard of dusty shelves. "This volume is almost indestructible and has survived generations of little boys. Perhaps Louis will pass it on to his son someday."

"You mean to gift this to him?"

"After we complete our studies." The voicing of that impending finality brought another surprising pang. "We are making unexpectedly rapid progress, so you may be rid of me soon enough." Etienne busied himself with some quills on the desk, setting them in order as he trotted words out to obscure the sudden void that seemed to yawn ahead of him. "I confess, I am somewhat looking forward to finishing the story. It is told in the form of a quest, you see, the tale of a young mage who seeks mastery over his Gifts. The actual lessons are well-hidden within. My grandfather and I had only reached the middle of the story where the young mage meets a beautiful witch who is on a quest of her own."

He was able to muster a smile as he turned to face her again. "At that point, my attention began to wander. I was at the age where dragons and dire wolves were of more interest than females, and grandpapa promised we would continue the story on our next visit." He caressed the leather lightly. "We never did get that chance."

"The war?" Genevieve inquired softly.

"In part." Etienne shook his head, surprised at the sting that those memories still held. "My mother died in childbed that year. While she was alive, my father had never dared to keep us from my grandparents. *Maman* was a formidable power in her own right. After her death—" He shrugged.

Genevieve's eyes held a world of sympathy when

she spoke. "It is always a dangerous journey, bringing a new soul from the Light, particularly when a babe carries Gifts of its own."

"And your son is one of those with unusual Gifts." Etienne seized the change of subject with relief. "Precocious, in fact. I only wish he had a more adept teacher. As I said, if Louis changes his mind, and wishes to study with someone who can better demonstrate the skills he must learn, I will yield the honor of being his mentor." *That was fully the truth, at least.*

CHAPTER 17

"*M*ama! Mama! Lady Morgan said that you have come to take me home!" Louis was a whirlwind bursting into the room. "I am learning so much! Watch this!" He pointed to an unlit taper on the desk and it flared to life.

"Louis," Etienne's voice was stern. "What is the first pillar upon which all power must rest?"

Louis looked at his feet. "Control," he recited quietly. "Impulsive mages court unnecessary risk and may harm themselves and others. I should not have run in like that and lit a fire without thought."

"Nonetheless, it is quite an accomplishment," Lady Morgan said, bustling into the room behind him.

"Indeed it is," Etienne said, tempering the rebuke with approval. "It took me nearly three weeks to master the techniques of fire and Lady Morgan was quite ready to send me back to our stone chateau in France because I burnt so many things."

"Did you? Truly?"

Excellent, Louis is applying today's lesson, Etienne thought, sending the boy an encouraging smile.

Genevieve's eyebrow arched inquiringly at her son's unnecessary question.

Etienne said nothing, deciding to allow Louis to tell his mother of his most recent triumph.

Lady Morgan laughed. "I can assure you, your tutor has made more than his share of mischief. I will show you, if you like." With a gesture, a small writing desk slid away, revealing a significant burn hole in the oriental carpet beneath.

"You moved the desk to cover it until it could be repaired. At least, that was what you said at the time." Etienne shook his head in disbelief. "You told me that it would be simple to mend."

"It would have been, and I did mean to do it," his grandmother said with a wistful smile. "But then your grandfather became ill and after—" Her hands fluttered as if the gesture could somehow encompass the bounds of her sorrow. "Those scorch marks became a memory of a wonderful time that I didn't wish to erase."

Genevieve broke the melancholy silence. "Louis, why did you ask the comte if he had truly done what he had said?"

"I will show you." Louis's expression glowed with pride. "Touch me with your Gift, Mama, if you please."

Genevieve took off her gloves and grasped her son's hand in hers and let loose the rein on her Gift.

"I am the Duke of Wellington." Louis giggled.

"You have taught my son how to lie to me?" Although her tone was humorous, her expression was difficult to define.

"He is learning to shield himself from the magic and feelings of others," Etienne explained. "A mage who cannot create and maintain a personal shield is vulnerable."

"Etienne showed me how to build a fortress inside me, just like his," Louis explained. "Well, not quite. His is really big and very strong because he has to keep his magic locked inside now, as well as keep others out, but he let me see how it's done."

Genevieve's face was usually an open text, easy to read. But for once, she seemed closed, distant. Was she angry? Etienne was about to explain the necessity of the skill when Louis spoke up.

"Are you mad, Mama? You can lie to me now, if you want to, and say you are not angry. And I don't have to know it isn't the truth anymore unless I want to. But it's not polite to read people's truths without permission, so I won't."

"No, I'm truly not upset," she said tremulously, bending down to sweep him into her arms. "Come and read the truth of my happiness for you. I am so very delighted!"

"She is!" Louis informed Etienne in a rush of joy. "Mama is thrilled for me. I can see you are happy, Mama, but you are crying. Why is that?"

Genevieve tried to speak, but her answer was a sob.

Louis was nonplussed and looked to Etienne for an explanation. The older mage ran a hand through his hair. How was he to explain the ways of women to the boy, when much wiser men had contemplated the mysteries and found no answers?

"Grown witches do this sometime, Louis," Etienne explained. "It is a confusing thing I know, but it is something that happens every now and then, when they are particularly pleased."

"Your tutor is right. Come with me, Louis," Lady Morgan said, her voice gruff. "You must not forget the *gateau* that we promised your *Grand-mère*. She wished to taste my chef's formulation so we can decide if it is equal to her mother's recipe. And we will choose some nibbles as well, in case you become hungry on the ride home."

"And it is such a long ride sometimes!" Louis said,

trying to make his mother smile. "Half of an hour, right Mama? I get ravenous!"

"Go now, you cheeky child, and assist Lady Morgan with the *gateau*," Genevieve said with a watery smile.

With his mother's permission, Louis took his leave.

"Just like a man, eager to abandon ship at the first sign of emotional storm." Genevieve sniffed, trying to make light of the situation. She had never believed herself to be one of those women who were prone to turn weepy, especially in the presence of others. Her tears were mostly shed in privacy, in the heart of the night, on her own pillow.

"Your son shows excellent male instincts for survival," Etienne parried with a wry smile, drawing the chair closer for her. As she seated herself, he pulled a handkerchief out of thin air and proffered it to her with a bow.

Genevieve inhaled in surprise and wonder. "Etienne! Your Gifts. Are they returning?"

"No, unfortunately," he said, shaking his head as he went to the decanter and poured them each a glass. "I wish it were so. Have you never seen *léger de la main?*" Setting their drinks on the piecrust table, he plucked a sixpence from behind his ear and handed it to her for examination. "Look at this coin carefully and keep an eye upon it, because it tends to wander. Minted in 1815, a propitious year for Britain, a lucky Waterloo coin one might say."

She gave the coin back to him and he closed his palm. When he opened his hand and spread his fingers, the sixpence was gone.

"With your permission, I think this sneak of a sixpence, he does not like to be in the hands of one who fought for France. Perhaps he may be hiding on your person?" He leaned toward her and a thrill speared down her spine as she felt his hand sweep quickly behind her ear. "Ah, such a lucky sixpence, I do not blame him for wanting to be with you."

He put the coin in her hand. It was the 1815 sixpence with the same nick above the cast of the crown she had noted before. Etienne presented his palm with a beckoning gesture and she returned the sixpenny piece. Up into the air it went and down to be closed in his fist.

Once again, the coin had vanished when his fingers unfolded.

"Perhaps he hides under your glass, eh?"

Taking the hint, she lifted her drink to find the missing coin once again. "But if this is not magic, how did you do it?"

"This is something that Miranda's husband can do, far better than I, even though I learned these tricks almost from the time I could be depended upon not to take the coin and swallow it," Etienne laughingly told her. "Sleight of hand was a useful skill during the times of the Scourge, a means to fool Outsiders and explain away the seemingly unexplainable, especially if we were discovered using our Gifts. The Pythia of Delphi knew how to produce voices and project them elsewhere."

His words suddenly seemed to emanate from the fireplace. "The Greeks called it *gastromancy*, but since Outsiders have begun to learn its secrets, it is known as *ventriloquism*."

As he spoke the coin seemed to travel faster than her eye could follow. It sped from hand to hand, to beneath his glass. Finally, he seemingly dislodged it from her nose with a light tap of his finger.

"Even after King James' witch hunts, this tradition of false magic continued as a means of teaching our children and preparing them for using their magic when it blossoms. It helps preserve power when true sorcery is unnecessary." His hands moved in a graceful dance. "These days, men like Lord Brand use the skills gleaned from Merlin's children to entertain at fairs, or to cheat the unwary in sham card games of skill, like three-card, *Find the Lady*." Etienne bowed before opening his fists to reveal four identical coins, each with the same flaw.

"Aha! So that is how it is done." Genevieve took up her glass and raised it in a salute. "I've never been to a fair, but I know an excellent performance when I see one."

Etienne seated himself and took up his own drink. Genevieve took a sip of the amber liquid. "And speaking of excellent, this is the best I have ever tasted."

"From my own vineyards." Etienne's pride was reflected in his smile. "You are one of the first to sample the vintage. I have tried something new."

"Spices and flavors are an herbalist's bread and butter. Let me try to guess." She closed her eyes, savoring the flavors on her tongue. "Caramel, I think and oak casks? And something else that's sweet. Could it be apricot?"

"I must take care lest you discover all my secrets!"

Her eyes flew open and she set her glass down in a rush of consternation. "Oh, no, I would never dream of—"

The delight in those cerulean eyes darkened to dismay. "*Non, non*, dear Genevieve. I was not accusing, just complimenting your discerning palate." He drew his chair closer. "I know that you would never use your gift thoughtlessly."

"But sometimes I do. Sometimes I cannot control… That is why I was overcome before. I never thought…I never dreamed Louis would be able to—" Tears began to flow again. "That he would be able to shield himself against the thoughts of others."

Etienne produced another handkerchief.

"How many handkerchiefs do you have?" she asked with a watery smile.

"Hopefully as many as you require. And if needful, I will walk up the stairs and fetch more myself just as Outsiders do."

"When I first realized Louis doesn't need touch to know the truth, I was terrified," she explained, trying to make Etienne understand the depths of her gratitude. "If I absolutely don't want to feel a lie, I am careful not to make physical contact, and the façade of social false-hoods we all hide behind usually remains intact. And even I, ignorant as I am, could see my son's Gift is un-usually strong."

"And that, of itself, should reassure you." He tilted his head in an attitude of confusion as he tried to un-derstand what she was trying to tell him. "It is a funda-mental thing. Those who are given great strength of power have a greater capacity to protect themselves from their Gifts. As they mature, they learn to employ those shields. This is why Louis can deny you access to his truth. His shield must be much like your own..." He looked at her and seemed stunned. "Can it be you do not know how to confine your Gift? Or fully shield yourself from others? How is this?"

She turned away from him in shame. "My mother didn't know how to bring me into the Gift. It was my papa's mother who had the ability."

"Genevieve, look at me please." He set aside his glass and rose, extending a hand, and she got up to face him. Gently, he caressed her cheek as if she was a child in need of comfort. Her fingers reached for his in a ges-ture she knew was beyond a sharing of truth. Etienne was pulling her from the brink of despair.

"Any witch may show you how to build your shield, regardless of their own Gift, just as I have shown your

Louis. The only magic it requires is trust. This is why such things are usually passed from generation to generation among Merlin's children." His honesty resonated as he spoke. "It is easier to open one's innermost self to family and to teach this to a student whose gifts are similar to one's own."

"But *Maman*, she never—"

She felt his sympathy, his regret for the years of unnecessary pain she had endured. "Your *maman* was so young when all was lost, she might not have known that she could help you herself. All of us build walls, *chérie*, be we Outsiders, OutBloods or of the Blood pure, but it is not easy to let another in."

"I was so afraid," she whispered, "so frightened Louis would have to spend his life alone, away from the constant deceit, hidden from the well-meaning lies of those who love him. You have saved him from a hermit's existence."

"Perhaps we are saving each other," Etienne murmured. "I want very much to kiss you, Genevieve. Will you allow me to claim my second kiss?"

Genevieve felt a thread of certainty reaching from her center to the very core of his being.

She stepped into his arms, gazing up into azure eyes alight with something that was not quite magic but certainly a kind of gift.

"Yes."

He smoothed the stray curls from her face, his fingers brushing her cheeks and slipping around to the nape of her neck.

"So tense," he whispered, caressing her shoulders and rubbing lightly inward to the tip of her spine. Genevieve's rigidity eased with his touch. Tentatively, she reached up, feeling the rough afternoon growth of beard on her fingertips, watching his eyes as he encouraged her wordlessly to make her own move.

He sighed with pleasure as she reached up to tangle her hands in his hair, disarranging the immaculate Brutus, savoring the texture of spun silver slipping between her fingers. He allowed her to take control, letting her draw him nearer until their lips touched lightly, exploring angles until she found a perfect fit that bridged the gulf between them.

There had been a gap of nearly two decades between her and Owen. In their years of marriage Genevieve had never been swept away by desire. She had always enjoyed novels that spun stories of overwhelming and devoted love, but had little patience with those tales of passion which surmounted all reason and honor.

Though Genevieve had refused to sell love philtres, the nostrums and cures Dale's Apothecary offered had come with the bonus of a sympathetic ear. People dealing with illness often needed someone who would simply listen without rendering judgement. As a result, Genevieve had heard all manner of accounts, most often, sagas of lovelorn woe, marital and otherwise.

Like as not, those stories of lust and desire were accompanied by heartache and loss. Genevieve had always counted herself lucky to avoid the tragedy and drama wrought by those extremes. Despite his perpetual state of sadness, and the pain of his last months, Owen had been a kind man, constant in his fidelity, considerate in his devotion.

Their marriage had been forged of convenience and necessity. Having known no other man before or since, Genevieve had been grateful for the refuge and security he had provided. Although many of Dale's customers had tried to seduce her, she had never been tempted to stray from her vows. A young girl's imaginings of romance and true love faded quickly in the face of the realities of safety and loyalty. Genevieve had never thought she might want more.

Until now.

Calloused hands traced the outline of her lips and she closed her eyes, surrendering to a palette of sensations that took her beyond herself. She stood with Etienne in the lookout of a tower, a fortress much like the one Louis had described. Etienne's lips traced a route along her neck. The turbulent storm raging without reacted with a rumble of thunder.

"Kiss me back," he demanded. "I need your kiss."

She could not deny him. Her tongue tasted his tentatively, as if asking permission. Lightning flashed. Their lips trysted, testing boundaries. She ran her hand along his spine, pulling him closer.

"Mama, are you ready to go home?"

Louis' voice seemed to echo in the distance and the integrity of the illusionary background began to fade.

She felt Etienne shiver, putting space between them as he reluctantly stepped back.

"I cannot do this to you," he said, closing his eyes, trying to hide his regret. "I meant these kisses as a lark, a means to discharge an unasked for obligation." He released her hand and turned away with a gesture directing her gaze toward the storm of chaos at the walls of his inner landscape. "I find it harder to keep the power pent. Yet, when I hold you, the pandemonium quiets. How is this?"

"I don't know," Genevieve answered. "I feel anything but calm when you hold me."

"I don't know how long I can hold back the tide and when it breaks, I feel it will sweep everything before it," he said, his words both sorrowful and bitter. "I can offer you nothing more than friendship, Genevieve. Perhaps, not even that."

"Friendship then," Genevieve agreed. "And there is yet another kiss in the balance due."

"I would not miss it for the world."

His bittersweet smile shattered something deep within her and Genevieve began to understand the enticement of a temptation that surmounted reason. She was learning what it was to be drawn to the edge of love's abyss.

Neither of them could dare the consequences of a fall.

CHAPTER 18

*a*s Lady Morgan's carriage clattered its way back to Dale's, Genevieve contemplated the concept of friendship. Never before had the word seemed so paltry.

Etienne was not at fault. He had accepted this scheme of Lord Wodesby's reluctantly. The entire scenario was made clear from the start. Her family would be rendered less vulnerable by du Le Fey and Morgan protection until Louis won his ring. Etienne would help unmask the schemers and end the charade of betrothal. They would all take their bows and part ways.

As *friends*. But if the kiss they had shared was Etienne's definition of friendship, it was becoming too intimate a relationship to consider with any level of comfort.

Was she so lonely and full of need? A few moments in a man's arms had totally overcome years of good sense. Not even a sorceress as formidable as Nimue herself could transform two kisses, however memorable they might have been, into a true *affaire de coeur*.

It was fortunate Louis was fully engrossed in his book. He had not even attempted to broach the box of treats that Lady Morgan had made a habit of sending,

211

"in case the boy needs a nibble on the way home." Normally, he would have noticed his mother was afflicted with the blue devils and quizzed her upon it.

At her feet, Suzette stretched, and Genevieve realized the carriage was rolling to a stop in front of Dale's. She breathed a sigh of relief when she saw the sign had been turned to *CLOSED*. She had no desire to cavil with customers who were seeking to importune rather than purchase. Jem, Lady Morgan's coachman, slid open the window near his seat. "Have the steps down for you in a minute, milady."

"We are home, Louis." Her son blinked and reluctantly closed the book.

"*Oi* now! What in the—" Jem's shout was cut off by a thud at the door and the sound of someone scrambling up to the box.

Suzette hissed.

Genevieve tried to reach for the door handle and found she could not move. Louis was staring at her in unblinking horror, his eyes frozen open like a statue. He too, was apparently caught in the same paralysis spell.

The coach started moving.

Suzette climbed up Genevieve's shoulder to reach the window, squeezing herself through the narrow opening to the driver's box. The coach had not yet reached the corner when a high-pitched scream rent the air and the vehicle lurched to a halt. "We're free," Louis yelled, shoving the door open. Together they scrambled outside.

"Go round the back and get help!" Genevieve ordered her son, as she saw to the stunned coachman. "Tell Marcel!"

"Cor!" Jem levered himself up to a sitting position and rubbed the rising bump on his forehead, "'ave yer ever seen the like?"

to it," he said, anticipating her protest. "Team is under Milady's spell t'stay put if reins go loose, but they be fretful and blockin' the road. T'ain't safe for the 'orses nor no one else."

Genevieve nodded and sat herself down on the damp ground beside Suzette, trying to shelter her from the wind and the curiosity of passers-by.

"That's your fiancé's familiar, isn't she? A pity that," a sonorous voice remarked with more glee than sympathy in his voice. "Given du Le Fey's current condition, I doubt he will ever be able to attach another companion. My name is Lord Diggory-Jones. I have travelled here from—"

"I don't care if you are the reincarnation of Merlin himself, come direct from the realm of Faerie," Genevieve growled with a glare. The bump of a mage's ring rose beneath his kid glove. Before she could send him on his way, she heard the click of a key being turned behind her and the tinkle of the shop bell. Louis came flying out.

"Mama, what has happened?" Louis knelt beside Suzette, pulling the shawl aside, gasping in horror at the extent of the damage.

"And this must be the boy. Perhaps we had best go inside, so we may talk of this matter privately," he said. It was unclear if his moue of distaste was for the wounded, fallen familiar or for Genevieve's son, who was laying his hands on Suzette. The mage stepped gingerly around them both in a bid for the open entrance. "I am arrived here to offer you the honor of my hand in marriage. Unlike the comte, I have full use of my Gifts and a tidy fortune besides."

Genevieve rose swiftly to interpose between him and the door. She pulled her athame out of the pocket in her gown. "Take one more step and by Hecate's hearth, I will gut you like a pig for the Samhain spit."

His face turned beet with indignation. "Perhaps you fail to understand me—"

"Understand this." She lunged forward, slicing a button off his jacket with a graceful sweep of the blade.

The would-be suitor beat a hasty retreat.

"She's dying, Mama. Unless—" Tears rushed down Louis' cheeks as he looked at his mother in silent entreaty.

"She is very close to the Light, Louis," Genevieve warned softly, coming to kneel beside him and the small body. "We can move her inside and make her more comfortable."

"That would end her!" the boy cried. "She saved us, Mama. You know she did! And the comte loves her." He put his hand on hers. "I can do this."

"You *know* you can." Genevieve realized in shock, feeling a stalwart faith in his abilities radiating from him. Even the short time under the comte's tutelage had made her boy stronger, more confident.

Looking at the agony in his grey eyes, she knew it would be wrong to take this choice from him. "No matter how beautiful or tempting the Light may seem, swear to me you will turn back, even if it means letting Suzette go. Promise me you will stop before you are overcome."

Louis nodded his agreement.

"Whatever may happen, know I love you," she whispered.

"I love you too." Louis gave her hand a comforting squeeze. "By Merlin and Nimue, I swear I will not fail those who love me." His oath triggered the tinge of his magic. Pushing the shawl aside, he cradled a paw in each hand. The stormy steel of his eyes was soon swallowed in the full blue of his Gift.

* * *

LADY MORGAN PICKED her way around the stacks of crates that littered a corner of the schoolroom at Morgan Manse. Etienne rose from behind the mound of papers piled on the battered desk before him.

"Ah, this is where you have been hiding yourself," Lady Morgan declared, taking a seat in an old nursery rocking chair. "What are you brooding over now? Surely this all cannot be for Louis' benefit."

"I had these sent from Yorkshire. It seemed the best place to put them so they would be out of the way." Etienne set aside the papers he had been shuffling through while trying to sort his own feelings. As a result, the documents were now nearly as muddled as his emotions. "I had been hoping my father's records might provide a key to Justice's curse. I've found any number of wrongs, but few that might be righted. In any case, some of these documents need to be destroyed since they can do severe damage in the wrong hands."

He threw a sheaf into the fire and watched them go up in flames. "Pouf! Thus ends nearly a century of old grudges, the fuel feeding feuds which would have died long ago if not for my father's manipulations," he explained, stirring the ashes. "I know that somewhere among these boxes there was something touching upon the Brisbois family. I paid it no heed at the time. Unfortunately, I am no longer able to call something magically to hand with a reference to a word or subject."

"Shall I then?" Lady Morgan asked, lifting a finger to start a spell.

"Would that it might be so simple!" He shook his head with a rueful laugh. "My father would never allow his secrets to fall so easily into the hands of his enemies. He hexed his papers so only he or his heir could access them through magic. Even then, there are some which will be intelligible to no one but me. Hence, I must now sort my way through them as ordinary mortals do, leaf by boring leaf of paper."

"Well, I will gladly help you sift them, if you wish. But first, I am seeking your Suzette," she continued, scanning the room. "Might she do me the favor of carrying a message to Rowan regarding the entertainment we are to attend tonight with Genevieve? Between the weather and the traffic in London it seems to take a dragon's age to get word through of late!"

"You might want to consider attaching a new companion," Etienne commented vaguely, ruffling through a pile of old vintner's bills. "Rowan's Mignon has new hatchlings in her kettle of peregrines and if paws are faster than human feet, wings beat them both," Etienne suggested. He looked up and winced inwardly at his grandmother's sad expression. "Even if you do not wish to do so, I think Rowan would value your opinion of their potential, especially since the Morgans have a noted affinity for avian familiars."

Hastily, he turned the subject. "I'm sorry to say, Suzette is out, accompanying Louis and Genevieve, ostensibly to visit with Marcel."

"Ah *l'amour!*" His grandmother sighed. "I suppose it is just as well you sent Suzette along to watch over them. That invitation!" She shuddered. "Circe is at the center of it, I wager."

"She is canny enough to be certain it could not be traced." Etienne forced himself to tamp down his anger. "It worries me. The Dales are as vulnerable as innocent witchlings in a dark wood."

"I agree. Despite her skills with an athame, Genevieve and her family have no inkling as to how to defend themselves," Lady Morgan declared. "It took me no more than a moment to teach her to shield herself from her Gift, but it will take time for them to learn other offensive skills."

Etienne found himself chuckling, recalling Genevieve wielding her blade. "Perhaps not as long as you think. She is quite fierce, our Genevieve."

"Indeed, she is." His grandmother agreed, regarding him thoughtfully. "A woman of great courage and strength. A man could do far worse."

Etienne was momentarily taken aback. Shaking his head in dismay, he was about to retort when Lady Morgan held up a restraining hand. It was not Morgan magic, but an instinct of self-preservation that kept him silent while his grandmother spoke her piece.

"You have feelings for her. Suzette saw the two of you embracing earlier." She pressed on. "In my day, we would have been posting the banns for such behavior. Given the fact your familiar claims the two of you seemed to be mutually in heat, perhaps a cleric and a special license would have been more in order."

"I had told you about the kisses if you recall." Etienne paced the room in frustration. "She was just fulfilling her obligation."

"Indeed, most enthusiastically, it seemed to Suzette." Her eyes twinkled in merriment.

"She was upset. She was seeking comfort."

His grandmother raised an eyebrow. "From what I am told, a tad more comfortable and I would be contemplating the prospect of a great-grandchild. Not that I would mind, providing a wedding preceded the birth."

"Suzette is a nattering *voyeuse*." With a sigh, he leaned against the mantelpiece staring into the flames. "Genevieve could do far better, Grandmama. You know it is true."

He felt her hand on his shoulder and she directed his face towards her, fixing him in a frank stare, her eyes narrowed in rebuke. "Your father taught you to expect nothing for yourself. Even as a child, you were never good enough, never deserving of joy. Your every act or thought was supposed to be fixed upon the glory of France. *His* glory, that's what it really was!" She took a calming breath, steadying herself before she continued. "I had hoped you would be set free with your father's death, but even as a ghost, the old comte led you into folly. If you allow him to continue to define you, you will never allow yourself to love."

"How can I?" he whispered. "Unless I regain my Gifts, I fear that I—"

"If I could trade my Gifts for more years shared with your grandfather, I would do so gladly." Her fierce aspect softened. "I have few visions of the future these days. Most Seers cannot see beyond their lifetimes. At my age, memories of love past and the prospect of going to dwell in the Light with those who were dear to me comprise much of the sustenance of my heart."

"You are not seeking them soon, I hope." Etienne hugged her to him.

"No Seer can predict death with certainty, especially one's own." Her hoarse chuckle vibrated against his chest. "Pursue love, Etienne, but first you must convince yourself you deserve it." She stepped back, clearing her throat. "As for me, you remind this old woman there is still opportunity for memories to be made. I will talk to Rowan and Mignon about their eyrie of nestlings."

A skitter of paws and a cacophony of voices echoed up the stairwell. Marcel came streaking into the schoolroom, yowling with alarm.

CHAPTER 19

*E*tienne was certain that Lady Morgan was somehow magically manipulating the traffic on the London streets. She was clinging to the seat with one white-knuckled hand while the fingers of the other spun in a spell-casting motion. Though Etienne drove like the devil himself was behind them, not a word of complaint passed her lips.

With near reckless abandon, he guided their vehicle through the crowded thoroughfares. Like a thread plunging over and over through a narrow needle's eye, he slid them through seemingly impossible gaps between pedestrians, drays, coaches and carriages.

As they pulled to a temporary halt at a crossing, there was an unspoken question in Lady Morgan's sympathetic look.

"Not yet." Etienne shook his head, still bracing himself for the inevitable emotional blow of Suzette's death. Though he had never experienced it, he had seen all too many instances of the moment of dissolution on the battlefields. The effect when a magical bond between mage and familiar was severed was often shattering, particularly when either of the linked pair was catapulted violently into the Light.

He had no idea if his pent-up Gifts might be muting the impact of loss. The fact he felt nothing thus far led Etienne to believe there might yet be the chance for a few words of farewell. However, he had long given up throwing coins into the false wishing well of optimism. In his experience, Lady Hope was a far more cruel and fickle female than Dame Fortune. From Marcel's description of Suzette's wounds, Etienne knew there were only two possibilities.

His familiar was either dying or dead.

Etienne had always been reluctant to attach himself to an animal spirit. To care for another creature was to create vulnerability, a means by which others, his father especially, might be able to control him. When Etienne had happened by chance upon a litter of kittens in the corner of the castle stables, the cluster of mewling balls of fur had meant nothing more to him than a heap of potential mousers.

Yet, when Suzette had first opened those sky blue eyes and regarded him with instant recognition, there had been a sense of spontaneous connection, forging a link that had lasted for over a decade. Familiars were prone to live far longer than their pure animal counterparts. With the threat of war ended, Etienne had taken many more years of Suzette's feline friendship for granted.

He glanced at his grandmother, wondering how she had coped with the death of her beloved Nimbus. But he did not dare to ask her. Etienne remembered the brief note of sympathy he had forwarded to her upon learning of the loss of her gyrfalcon familiar. He winced inwardly at the thought, that less than an hour before; he had been high-handedly urging his grandmother to attach a new animal. He would apologize, but he could find no words amidst the profound depths of his own grief.

A world without Suzette.

Another lonely, loveless space in his life.

"Nothing lives forever, my boy," his grandmother said quietly, giving his hand a brief, comforting squeeze before they went on their way again.

The rear door of Dale's swung open as soon as the curricle clattered in to the mews behind the shop. Jem ran out to meet them, sporting bruises on his chin and forehead. Nonetheless, Lady Morgan's coachman insisted he was well enough to tend to their horses. Etienne helped his grandmother to alight and hurried her inside.

He saw Genevieve coming down the stairs and let out a breath he did not know he had been holding. Marcel had stated she was unharmed. Nonetheless, the Chartreux had been focused upon Suzette's injuries. Etienne scrutinized Genevieve from her hair to her heels and only barely kept himself from pulling her into his arms.

"You are unhurt?" he asked, unable to resist a touch to her cheek to reassure himself. "Where is Suzette? Is she...?" He somehow could not bring himself to ask the question aloud, because the words would make it real.

There was a soft hiss at his feet and Etienne gasped, dropping to his knees.

"What are you doing out of bed?" Genevieve scolded, shaking her head in dismay.

Suzette ignored the witch with a full measure of feline scorn as she stropped herself against Etienne's legs, confirming she was on the road to recovery. Submitting to the gentle caresses of her mage companion, she chuffed at Etienne as if he was a newborn kitten in need of comfort, telling him her story in soft mewls.

"Yes, you are the bravest of warriors. A veritable Amazon among cats." Alarmed at the weakness of her voice and body, Etienne was not entirely able to believe she was real and whole. He stroked her lovingly. "You must not exert yourself."

"You were very near death, Suzette," Genevieve chided the feline. "I will be sure to tell Etienne of your deeds while you rest."

Marcel came up behind Suzette and batted her lightly, adding a warning growl. In grudging surrender, she allowed Etienne to cradle her in his arms. With the panache of a feline Cleopatra on her human barge, she was conveyed to rest in Marcel's lair of pillows near the kitchen hearth.

As Etienne settled his familiar, he noted the sleek luster of her fur. The traces of her dire wounds were still visible, but nearly fully healed. "Where is Louis?" Etienne asked in growing concern as he arrived at the only possible explanation that might explain Suzette's survival.

"Marcel told us Suzette's condition was grave indeed, yet she has barely a scratch upon her," Lady Morgan observed, her voice quavering as she reached the same conclusions. "Did Louis...?" She looked fearfully at the hand he had restored for her.

Genevieve's affirming nod was full of concern. Gravely, she beckoned them to follow her upstairs. "*Maman* is with him now. I was warned the pull of the Light is strong, especially close to death." Genevieve's expression was stricken with guilt. "I should never have permitted him do this, but he seemed so certain. Toward the end, Louis smiled at me. *I did it*, he said, *it is so beautiful there* and then he closed his eyes. Your Jem carried him inside."

"How could you?" Lady Morgan's eyes were bright with unshed tears as she eyed the younger woman in indignant accusation. "How did you allow—"

Etienne quieted his grandmother with a look. "You have told me this more than once. Our Gifts sometimes call us to service," he reminded her gently, moving to stand beside Genevieve. "I have learned if we fail to answer, it is hard to live with one's self. She gave her son a choice. That could not have been easy."

Tentatively, he extended his hand to Genevieve in a silent offer of support and comfort. There was a tremble in her touch, as her fingers twined with his. "If I may see Louis? I have much battlefield experience and I may be able to ease your minds."

Warmth enveloped them as they opened the door. Etienne nodded approvingly at the stoked fireplace.

"His skin was chilled, icy as a corpse," Lady Brisbois informed them, her voice quavering. "He is still too cold."

"Not unexpected," Etienne tried to reassure her. "Walking through the Valley of Shadow chills the body as well as the soul. It is good to keep the room extra warm for now."

Moving the blankets aside, Etienne put an ear to the boy's chest. The beat of his heart was steady and his breathing was even-paced and full. Etienne felt his tension calming as he carefully lifted Louis' eyelid and saw the glow of healing Bliss.

The expenditure of power required to elicit that level of continuing recuperative magic was enough to make Etienne quake in his boots. The boy had walked to the very edge. Whatever lure had pulled him back had to have been extremely strong.

"Louis is recovering far faster than many a mature mage thrice his age." Etienne tried to make his pronouncement matter of fact. "He likely over-extended himself, but he is improving nicely. By tomorrow, he should wake. Keep him warm until his skin regains its color," he advised. "I'll send Jem for some of Tante Reina's restorative potions. I would keep him at rest for at least another day. Knowing Louis, I suggest we have a supply of cakes sent over since you may need to bribe him to remain quiet."

Tears of relief streamed down Lady Brisbois' face and she collapsed into one of the chairs beside the bed. Genevieve hovered near her mother, murmuring words of comfort.

"I will stay with Lucille and keep watch on the boy," Lady Morgan whispered to Etienne as they stepped into the hall. "You should see to Genevieve. She has been through the worst of it, yet she is caring for all. Who cares for her?"

* * *

WITH LADY MORGAN and her mother standing sentinel on her son, Genevieve allowed herself to be persuaded to step away. Jem was dispatched to alert the Chief Mage about recent events and fetch a batch of Tante Reina's restoratives and a supply of Louis' favorite cakes.

In the small parlor, Genevieve set aside the box of nibbles and the gateaux retrieved from Lady Morgan's coach.

"For when Louis wakes," Genevieve told Etienne. Her words were both a prayer and an affirmation as she cast a weaving to keep the sweets fresh.

She swung the kettle on to the hob and stirred the coals, seeking calm in the rhythm of routine. After setting out tea leaves and some chipped chunks of sugar from the loaf, Genevieve fetched the china from the cupboard. The mundane, mechanical motions were soothing, helping to ease the galloping thoughts of what might have happened from her mind.

"I see you have become English in your habits now that your family is sworn to Damien," Etienne observed in an obvious attempt to lighten the tension. "Tea is the solution to all problems."

She attempted a bantering reply, but words seemed stuck in her throat. Thus far, she had managed to carry on by keeping the torrent of her emotions at bay. His attempt at humor was the raindrop that burst the dam. The barely withheld flood of fear and panic suddenly came roaring over the inner berm she had built, setting the teacups in her hand to rattling precariously upon their saucers. Etienne removed them from her grasp and set them down upon the table.

"You are shaking," he said, reaching for her. "Would you allow me to hold you?"

She nodded, and nestled herself in his arms.

"Louis is well," he repeated the words like an incantation. "Louis is well. Suzette is well."

If this was his idea of friendship, then it was a state she could grow to accept. The feeling of shelter strengthened her and she found her voice once again. Shuddering, she began to recount the moments of horror.

It was easier to whisper the tale of their terror against the bulwark of his shoulder. The scent of him, the feel of folds of linen against her cheek, the calm reassurance of his voice, were like balms to the soul, slowing the race of her heart as she described how close they had come to disaster.

Louis is well. Suzette is well. She took up Etienne's reassurances and added one of her own. *All of us are safe.*

His hand splayed against her back, bracing her, holding her steady when her knees went suddenly weak. He supported her to the shabby sofa and sat down beside her.

"I didn't need to touch you to know the truth of how close we came to losing him," she finally said. "I saw that reality in your eyes when you examined Louis."

"Even if I could lie to you, I would not," Etienne said, squeezing her hand. "Louis took a great risk. Such is the way of boys on their way to becoming men. We challenge ourselves. *How fast can I run? How high can I climb?* We learn our capabilities. If we are given good fortune, we live through our childhood recklessness to discover the needs for caution and judgement. But those who have never been allowed to stumble? Never have taken the chance of a fall? They often become sad, timid, pitiful creatures."

He leaned forward, his forehead touching hers and she closed her eyes, savoring the silent communion between them. The raging swell of power within him was momentarily still and he sighed before addressing her once more. "Your son has accomplished something few have managed. Louis turned his back upon the glory of the Light. I know of only one other who had the strength to change direction at the brink, and she, a woman without Gifts."

"Miranda," Genevieve whispered.

Etienne eyed her cautiously; obviously reluctant to confirm or deny information disclosed in confidence.

"She told me," Genevieve affirmed. "Her children are also of mixed heritage. We try to help one another."

"Miranda is assisting me in finding out what little is understood of your son's Gift," Etienne told her. "I do not know of a certainty what caused your son to turn around, but he did."

"Love," Genevieve answered. "Louis made a promise to me."

"Miranda too, claims her feelings for her Adam provided the power that pulled her back." Etienne looked as if he was contemplating a deep conundrum. "Whatever the force might be, your son has discovered a means of anchoring himself to life. There is much Louis has yet to learn, but today he proved he already has the discipline of will which he truly needs to gain his mage's ring. I am most grateful, because I did not know how to help him find this lodestone."

"Do not underestimate your own part in this Etienne," Genevieve said softly, cradling his hands between hers. "His control, his confidence in himself is due to your teaching. He did this not just for Suzette, but for you, as well. He cares for you."

"Why do you say this?" Etienne rose up from his seat, shaking his head in agitation. "How could he do this? For the sake of someone he has known for but a few weeks? I would never ask him to place himself in such danger!"

"I know that." Somehow, his distress seemed to soothe her. He truly cared for her son. According to the rumors, the former Chief Mage of France had no regard for anyone other than himself, yet, he had consistently proven otherwise. "Love does not ask. It gives. Even if you helped send him on the journey, you are also the compass that helped bring him home."

"When we are done, we will go our separate ways. This is the agreement we made, no?" He seemed shaken, guilty and he turned away from her as if he could not bear her scrutiny. "He must not form attachments to me. I cannot allow—"

"It is not for you to choose." Genevieve rose, putting a hand on his shoulder. "My son knows you, Etienne. Louis came back for you, too."

"I find that you and your family are addictive, Genevieve. You are fast becoming my balm in Gilead, relief for a festering wound I have no hope of healing. Do not deny that our contact drains you." Etienne voiced his deepest concern.

"I admit I have been left feeling weak in the knees,

but I think you may be ignoring an obvious contributory factor," Genevieve said with a somewhat saucy smile. "Can you honestly tell me you are unaffected by our kisses? Surely a man with your history has experienced encounters which have left you shaken. Even Circe, perhaps?"

"Not like you," he denied hoarsely. "Never like this. I think about you all the time. I crave you, Genevieve. I cannot take the chance of doing you harm. Even if I was willing to use you in this way, the dam within me will someday burst and when it does, I believe it will destroy everyone around me. Once I have done what I have promised, I will return to Yorkshire and people will soon forget your association with a pariah."

"I shall never forget." Genevieve turned him to face her. "Until then, allow me help you, at least. You do owe me the opportunity to repay my life debt and there has been no lasting injury to me."

"Yet," he muttered, trying to ease away.

She would not allow it. "This does not count as the last kiss. Consider this as the gift of a friend."

Genevieve cradled his cheeks between her palms, hoping to calm the desolation in his eyes. "Before you gave Louis the means to shutter himself from the falsehood of others, he saw the truth of your being. Deny it if you will, Etienne, but you are a good man." She drew his lips to hers, fighting the temptation to put her arms around him, to draw him closer, to deepen the contact with tongue and touch.

Genevieve became the butterfly upon the petal's softness as he yielded to her gentle caress. Deliberately, she focused on the tumult within him, treating it much like Marcel's tension in a ruffled fur fit, soothing the raw anger and underlying fear with a comforting touch, consoling him with the reassurance of a love that set no conditions and asked for nothing in return.

Reluctantly she stepped away, saddened by his look of stunned disbelief. He stared at her, shaking his head in denial.

The hiss of water on the coals from the overfilled kettle broke the silence.

"You see," she said. "I am perfectly fine. No weakness."

Compelling herself to be content with a mere kiss when she hungered for far more, she turned to the table and busied herself with the ritual of tea.

Doling out the leaves, Genevieve forced herself to be less parsimonious. They could now afford a richer brew. Carefully, she poured and inhaled the wafting scent of the blend she had compounded. A hint of bergamot, a touch of citrus and a sly insinuation of currant tickled her nose.

As it steeped, she contemplated Etienne's words.

Clearly, he was already perturbed by Louis' growing emotional connection to him. Perhaps they might work out some acceptable means of maintaining Etienne's link with her son, but Genevieve had no delusions about herself. She was a poorly educated witch, a shopkeeper, with neither the influence, nor the dowry a man of his station could demand. She did not even have a naming jewel.

As for Louis, twice-Gifted, as her son was, he would always be considered OutBlood. The relationship of mentor to pupil was far more socially acceptable than that of father to stepson.

Father, indeed! Her presumption was almost laughable.

The cloud this farcical betrothal rested upon was no foundation, not even for a chateau of dreams. Her attraction to Etienne was strong and seemingly, mutual. How much of his feelings were based in her ability to soothe the tumult within him? It was unclear. But no matter what the source of this growing bond between them, she knew a man of his station would never consider her in the role of wife.

Mistress?

The notion of being with him in any capacity was far too seductive for comfort. Even if she was willing to sacrifice her self-respect, she could not countenance how it would affect Louis. It was bad enough her son was considered inferior because of his Outsider father. She would not have the boy branded yet again as lesser because of his mother's behavior, which was a certainty if she were to become Etienne's paramour.

Even if she had the choice of becoming his wife or his mistress, Etienne's association with her had no future in either role.

Etienne's misgivings were correct, but for the wrong reasons. If his magic remained forever frozen, he would inevitably resent any choices forced upon him in his powerlessness. He would come to despise her, especially if he was dependent on her Gift as a magical nepenthe to soothe his inner pain.

She had already seen a drug consume one man's soul. Genevieve had tried to deny Owen the ever increasing doses of laudanum he demanded. Eventually, that craving had driven her husband to hate her. Owen's slavery to the tincture caused his death long before his illness would have.

It required no Seer to envision the outcome of a destiny that held the return of Etienne's Gifts. That to-be-hoped-for event would spell disaster for a marriage. No matter how much she loved him, once his palliative need for her was gone, he would regret the needless sacrifice of his future in an alliance with a woman who had no place in the Highest Circles.

The silence at her back continued. Their embrace had left him nonplussed and he had uttered not a word since. Had her foolish gesture served to intensify Etienne's discomfort? Was he coming to share her concern that the growing attraction between them might be engendering unrealistic expectations on her part?

Genevieve decided to put his fears to rest. There would be no mention of love. She understood they had no prospects and she was resigned to it.

The tea steeped as she tried to find the right words to bridge the growing gap of quiet. When the brew was ready, she poured, letting the ritual of adding sugar, stirring and the soft musical clink of spoons soothe her troubled spirit.

By the time she turned to offer him his cup and her feelings, her hands were steady.

The room was empty.

She set the cup back on the tray and added more sweet to suit it to her own taste.

There was no sense in letting a serving of expensive tea go to waste.

CHAPTER 20

*E*tienne had intended to be gone for no more than a moment or two. He felt like a coward, skulking out the door behind Genevieve's back, but he could not face her. Instead of comforting her in her need, she had somehow managed to turn the tables upon him. Even in the throes of his most passionate encounters with Circe he had never felt as moved as he had by Genevieve's simple caress, her sweet kiss. The woman's tender touch had utterly undone him.

Just the simple domesticity of preparing a cup of tea seemed to rouse a desire that threatened to overcome the ragged remnants of his honor. He had forced himself to step away, or else he was certain he would violate the boundaries he had set for their relationship. Honesty had been promised, but with every minute that passed, Etienne felt less able to face her and confess the truth.

He ached for her.

In his youthful days of daring and stupidity, he had experimented with opium only once. Although a Seer's Gift rarely predicted his own future, his sorcery had woven with the potent smoke in a vivid drug induced haze. He saw a vision of a future self that could be, in thrall to the lure of the pipe, gaunt, hollow, and forever longing.

Now, he felt the same chasm of yearning emptiness at the prospect of a life without Genevieve. He was coming to recognize there would be no cure for him. Without her, it would not take long for the chaos at his core to destroy him. The probability of that end was becoming less of a fear than a consolation. He would not use anyone he cared for in that way, especially not someone he loved.

Finally, he admitted it, if only to himself.

Every time they touched his longing grew.

He wanted more than her friendship.

For Genevieve and her family's wellbeing, he could never allow that to happen.

He charged outside through the back door, hoping the cold air and the drizzle would help bring him back to his senses.

Forcing himself to focus on the attempted abduction, Etienne reviewed what Genevieve and Jem had told him about the event. Someone had obviously been lying in wait for the Dales' return. With the weather remaining so foul all week long, Lady Morgan had been sending them home in her carriage almost daily. Their movements would not have been all that difficult to track and predict.

A vulgar growl at his feet interrupted his musings.

"There is no need for such language, Marcel. Please believe I only wish to protect your mistress," Etienne replied to the Chartreux cat's crude rebuke. "In fact, I need your help in finding the one who attacked Genevieve and her son. I am wondering whether the cap Suzette knocked off the villain's head might still be in out in the street?"

The comte dangled the prospect like a ball of yarn, hoping to distract Genevieve's familiar from delivering a hissing set down. With a cynical cough, Marcel let it be known he would not be so easily deflected. Nonetheless, he charged around the building and Etienne followed to help him survey the street, searching in the growing dark.

Marcel plunged into the midst of the twilight traffic, dodging to and fro as he combed the thoroughfare. With a triumphant pounce, he lunged and snatched an object from the muck, slipping between wheels and hooves until he reached Etienne and dropped the cap at his feet.

Baring teeth and tongue in a wide-open grimace, Marcel inhaled and tasted the odors emanating from the cap. With his mouth curling back, almost as if he were planning to devour the garment itself, the cat employed his considerable array of feline olfactory senses to sort through the scents contained in the fabric.

He hissed in dissatisfaction.

"I am aware you cannot work miracles, Marcel," Etienne agreed, picking up the wrecked cap and examining it closely. "I am not asking you to track him, though if anyone could tease out a trail from this piece of trash, it would be you."

Marcel rumbled agreement. No cat was immune to flattery. *"Tasssted his blood. Know hisss ssstink."*

"An excellent thought," Etienne agreed. "We will find him and draw more of his claret together. In the meantime, if I can ask my grandmother to clean this somewhat, I think we may have an additional thread to lead us through this labyrinth."

* * *

OCTAVIUS WEPT as his brother applied a wet cloth in an effort to peel the dried remnants of a blood-soaked bandage from his back.

"How did you manage to bungle this so badly, Octavius?" Circe hissed as she opened a jar of Dale's Most Excellent Healing Salve. "You were supposed to ask for her hand, not attempt to kidnap her!"

"*Did* ask her, days ago. The witch said *no* when I asked her outright to marry me. Told her she'd have more than enough pin money. Said I would even stand as mentor to her OutBlood brat." Octavius' snivel turned to a shriek. "Ease off, Ollie!"

Lord Pendrake's lips formed a single thin angry line as he applied a liberal portion of the cream to the wounds. It was only brotherly forbearance preventing him from using even more force to rub the salve in.

"I'll take care of him, if you like," Circe offered with a cruel smile that half-tempted Oliver to hand the jar over. "Knowing you and your considerable charm with the ladies, I am certain that Lady Genevieve was greatly impressed with the magnanimous offer."

"Didn't even say '*you do me great honor*' or any of the other things ladies are supposed to tell you to make you feel better when they think they have a bigger fish on the hook." Octavius gave an aggrieved snuffle. "Heard tell at the club there are at least a half-dozen suitors sniffing around her skirts and Lord Diggory-Jones plans to make an offer."

"It was my understanding du Le Fey has already won the fair lady," Lord Cochrane observed, his look a mix of disdain and amusement. "I saw an announcement in The Times."

"Etienne is only using her," Circe said with a dismissive sneer. "Mocking the Chief Mage and Mistress' pet by engaging her affections before he humiliates her is what I hear."

"I wouldna be so sure," the Sea Wolf considered, idly swirling the remains of his whiskey. "The Comte du Le Fey was never a man to squander an asset lightly. A

Truth Sifter? If the OutBlood cub's breeding follows his mama, the boy would be a prize as well."

"There you are, Octy," Lord Pendrake said, patting his brother on the shoulder and eliciting a satisfying wince. "Even Lord Cochrane would concede it wasn't a bad plan, using the boy as leverage to bring his mother to heel."

"Aye, had it worked," Lord Cochrane caviled with a chuckle.

"Your brother had no right to purloin my necklace!" Circe complained. "What if he had lost it, I ask you? I have to return the piece or—"

"No harm was done." Lord Pendrake raised her hand for a reassuring kiss. "Lord Cochrane guarantees us he will return it posthaste to keep Wodesby from suspecting our part in the scheme. Who knows? By then I may be Chief Mage and there will be no need to give it back at all."

"That's why Ollie is taking care of me himself, instead of one of the servants, don't you know," Octavius added, eager to be part of the cabal. "Wouldn't want to have Wodesby or even du Le Fey on our tails." He shuddered and winced again.

"No matter what his true feelings about the woman may be, it wouldna be wise to make an enemy of Etienne, Gifts or none," Lord Cochrane said, eying Circe significantly. "*More* of an enemy, that is. Leastways we now know the Morgan medusa stone works." He downed the last of his dram and refilled his glass. "It should be a simple matter to enthrall Napoleon's guards, get him on my ship and hie off to South America before his keepers even know he is gone from St. Helena."

"And when they do realize all of Wodesby's wards were rendered useless, the Council will be more than eager to replace him with a better mage." Circe clasped

Lord Pendrake's hand and favored him with a triumphant smile. "Will you be attending The Merlin's Ball at Almack's tonight, Lord Cochrane? Lady Jersey suffers no riffraff. Those who lack jewel or ring will not be granted entry. Unfortunately, it seems Octavius will be unable to join us and we will gladly bring you as our guest."

"There's much to be done, but I might enjoy seeing Wodesby prance about as Chief Mage one last time. I'll send ye word if I can come." Lord Cochrane shook his head. "If I canna, I must regretfully decline."

"See! That's how a refusal ought to go!" Octavius declared, pouring himself a drink. "Polite!"

The Sea Wolf topped off his glass. "I only hope Bonaparte is up to the task. There have been rumors about his health."

"Fit or not, what you do with the Corsican is your own affair once he leaves his prison," Lord Pendrake said, frowning at the nearly empty bottle. "Need I remind you that we have an agreement?"

"Aye, I'm a man of my word," the Sea Wolf agreed, his tone growing indignant. "Napoleon may not have Merlin's Gifts, but his military genius is as close to magic as I've ever seen. With me as his Chief Mage, we'll soon have South America and its riches under our control. The plan will work, unless we have any more idiots stirring up a hue and cry." He eyed Octavius significantly. "Now, if I may have the necklace? The sooner the task is done, the sooner I'll be getting the bauble back in yer possession."

Reluctantly, Circe passed him a black velvet bag.

"Need more ointment," Octavius said glumly, holding up the empty jar. "Footman I sent for it says this was the last one."

"Count yourself fortunate, Octavius. Genevieve Dale is still a shopkeeper, despite all her fine airs since she has taken up with Etienne. The woman is not fit to be a sister-by-marriage to the Chief Mage of England," Circe pronounced.

"Dunno bout that," Octavius said morosely. "Could've been a rich man if she'd said a *yes*. Wouldn't believe what that little jar costs. Rumors say that Dale's goods are jumping off the shelves."

"Since we are speaking of rumors, I have heard some other tidbits which might be of interest." Lady Circe steered the conversation with a heavy hand. "You might be consoled to note you were not the only suitor who was rudely given his *congé*, Octavius. Lord Diggory-Jones was telling the most interesting tale when I went to pay a call this afternoon."

* * *

"I DO NOT UNDERSTAND, GRANDMAMA?" Etienne complained. "Yesterday, you were carving Genevieve up with the sharp edge of your tongue for allowing Louis to use his Gift. Then you were demanding she take to her bed and rest after her ordeal. Now you are proposing she attend a ball?"

"As you predicted, Louis is already up and about." The steel in Lady Morgan's spine stiffened her to full height. "I admit, I was a trifle harsh yesterday, but Genevieve has graciously accepted my apology, which *I* have already tendered. Marcel seems to think there may be others who need to beg her pardon. I would tend to agree."

Etienne poked at the coals, muttering to himself about interfering familiars. "This outrage was obviously perpetrated by a mage controlling an immobilizing Gift," he observed, turning the topic.

"Or a medusa stone," Lady Brisbois said as she swept into the parlor and seated herself before the fire.

"Few of the Blood can paralyze more than one victim at a time. Even fewer can do so without their objective in sight."

The comte regarded her curiously. Genevieve was correct. Her mother had changed in the weeks since he had first met her. Their newfound prosperity allowed her to dress with *élégance* to be sure, but the alteration in her was far more than an improvement in style. The timid, fearful lady was transforming into a woman of assurance, a witch to be reckoned with.

"Clearly, whoever it was did not *envisagé* a familiar would be with them. Indeed, we are most fortunate you sent Suzette along, Etienne, or we might now be telling a much different tale and searching for their whereabouts," she posited.

Etienne dipped his head in acknowledgement. "A medusa stone? That, I had not considered because they are so rare. It would explain why Suzette was not immobilized. Such a talisman would not affect a non-human creature."

"I have yet to receive all of the jewelry that Circe owes me," Lady Morgan admitted with a frown, tapping her chin as she reflected. "As I think upon it, a medusa stone pendant may very well be among those items yet to be returned, but I am not certain. Lady Wodesby holds my copy of the inventory, since she is overseeing the matter of the jewelry. And I cannot ask her since she is off in Paris to—" She hesitated.

"To attend the Chief Mage of France's wedding and transfer the regalia belonging to France's next Mistress of Witches. I am aware of it, grandmama." Etienne was surprised to find he felt no remnant of the rancor the statement would have previously engendered. The only emotion he could muster was a sense of relief. One more unfinished piece of that chapter of his life was behind him. "I know my betrothal documents are among the papers I had sent up from Yorkshire. I will search for my copy of the list tomorrow. In the meantime, as you are fond of saying, Grandmama, we might be able to plan upon cooking a number of brews in the same cauldron tonight."

* * *

"THEY ARE DOWNSTAIRS, WAITING FOR YOU," Lady Brisbois told her daughter, reaching up to pin a curl artfully peeking from beneath the gauze of her toque. Delicately embroidered dusky roses were stitched up one side of the headdress, as if making their way up an invisible trellis. "Madame Robard may not be a witch, but her fashions are a form of sorcery."

"Are you certain that the neck is not too revealing?" Genevieve asked anxiously, looking at the tightly cut blue satin, trimmed at the neckline in a corsage of larger satin roses echoing those adorning the toque.

"Pah!" Her mother waved a dismissive hand. "In Paris, such décolletage would be too demure for a convent school. I almost wept, when you insisted upon the blonde lace, but Bouchard has draped it artfully. It draws the eye and accentuates rather than hides!"

Genevieve turned, admiring the slashes of rose in the puff of the sleeves and the rouleaus adorning the hem. She reached down beneath a flounce of lace and withdrew her athame before returning it to its concealed sheath. "I don't know how she managed it but this is undetectable," Genevieve said, looking for outlines or other evidence of the hidden knife.

"I see no sign of it in the drape of the dress, despite its snug cut," her mother agreed. "I still fear a blade at such an event may serve as a temptation rather than a precaution."

"Are you certain you do not wish Lady Morgan to

stay with you and Louis, Maman?" Genevieve asked. "Suzette might also be persuaded to stay behind."

"And deprive the brave feline huntress of her rightful prey?" Her mother shook her head. "Remember, it is *you* who they are after, *mon ange*. You will be well protected. And it is you who must go, if only to show them Brisbois will not be intimidated. It has been weeks since my last attack, so you need not fear for me. Louis and I will manage."

"You have become quite fierce, Maman," Genevieve said, hugging her close.

"I am learning from you and Lady Morgan," she said. "Too many of my years have been spent hiding from the past, as if I might somehow change what has been by the weight of my regret," she said, handing her daughter a shawl of cashmere trimmed with a fringe matching the blue of the gown. "I have come to see that cowering in the dark will not prevent the future."

"Have you had a Vision about us, Maman?" Genevieve took her mother's hand, alarmed at her anxious expression.

"Even when true Seers see the future for strangers, nothing is certain. For those we love? Even less so." She shrugged. "My Gift of foresight was never strong and just weeks ago I came to realize how very wrong I was in my previous interpretations of what might come in your future."

"But what did you...?"

The older woman put a gentle finger to her daughter's lips when she tried to voice the obvious question. "I will not tell you what I saw. In truth, I do not fully remember the details, so long ago it was. There is much to learn from the stories of old about those whose lives go awry when they try to change the fabric the Fates are weaving for them. This though, I will say to you; tonight, you must bow your head to no one."

"I am a Brisbois!" Genevieve declared.

"Yes, you are a Brisbois." Her mother countered. "But even more important, you are also Genevieve Dale. You took a shop which was little better than a market stall and built it into an emporium known both to Outsiders and those of the Blood. An old and honored name did not put food on our table or a roof above our heads. You did."

There was a knock.

"Genevieve?"

Genevieve frowned.

"You must talk to him, *chérie*," her mother said, patting her daughter gently on the shoulder. "Those who have the greatest fears often conceal them in plain sight." Lady Brisbois cracked the door. "Your grandmother and I will be waiting at the bottom of the stairway," she warned the comte. "Do not forget this!"

"I would not dare, milady!" he replied with a short bow of acknowledgement.

As Genevieve's mother waved him inside, Etienne's flirtatious smile faded into a stare of complete stupefaction.

Her mother gave a satisfied nod as she exited the room. Genevieve studied him as he stood in silent admiration.

"You are *incroyable!*" he said at last. "And I am a fool."

Genevieve inclined her head in acknowledgement. "Far be it from me to deny honesty when I hear it."

"I don't want to hurt you, Genevieve," Etienne whispered.

"I know. But any mother can tell you that some joys are not possible without pain," she replied softly. "You too, are looking unusually dapper tonight, Comte. Knee breeches?"

"Even for mages, the standards of Almack's must be maintained," he joked, obviously relieved at the change of subject. "Louis is wearing my chapeau bras and he looks quite comical but oddly debonair. He will break many hearts that one, I am thinking." He cleared his throat. "I have something for you."

Genevieve gasped as the jewelry box seemed to appear from thin air.

The teardrop sapphire pendant almost matched the color of his eyes. Suspended on a simple thin gold chain, the facets caught the candlelight, changing in hue as he lifted the jewel and set the box aside.

"For you," he explained.

"I couldn't," she whispered.

"Only those who wear a naming jewel or mage's ring may enter Almack's tonight," he explained, gesturing for her to turn around. "You are my fiancée. There have been more than a few who have wondered why you are bare of a gem."

Genevieve swallowed her disappointment. His present was given out of necessity. Improper as it would have been, for a moment she had believed she was about to receive a true gift of the heart.

Her mother's words had reminded her of the value of pragmatism and she forced herself to embrace the practical. At least there was no problem in accepting the naming jewel under the circumstances. For a mage's ring or a witch's pendant to have power, it had to be given, not purchased. It was ill luck for witch or mage to return such stones once gifted.

He draped the sapphire upon her bosom and she shivered at the brush of his fingers as he brought the clasp around her bare shoulders. Rooted in place, almost as if she was under a spell, Genevieve remained still while he bent close to fasten the piece of jewelry. His hair brushed her skin and his breath caressed her. Every small sensation seemed to magnify as she watched their reflections in the cheval mirror her mother had insisted upon purchasing.

Nestled in the valley between her breasts, the sapphire's simplicity was the perfect accent for the dress. For a moment, they seemed like a Rembrandt portrait she recalled from childhood. In the lambent glow of candlelight, Etienne's reflection stared at her, his hands resting upon her shoulders. But no artist could have captured the dark hunger in his eyes, the barely restrained flare of desire. Together she and Etienne were potential kegs of powder, waiting for the first spark. Genevieve was determined that she would not be the one to ignite the conflagration.

Her jewel began to glow in response to the Gifts within her. For the first time in years, she felt the steady, amplifying power within the complex crystal, waiting to respond to her command. She cupped the sapphire in her hand, contemplating it. "It feels almost alive, joyous, eager to be of use again," she whispered.

Etienne beamed. "This, I am glad to hear."

"So much power stored within it." She moved it to and fro, watching the play of light, avoiding looking at him, until she had her feelings under control. "It must be quite old and very valuable to contain this much of a reserve." She frowned.

"I see this disturbs you." There was irony in his laughter and pain in his eyes. "How strange. Circe was always willing to take whatever I gave her and always, she demanded more. You are willing to take nothing from me. Yet, I would gladly give you whatever you ask."

"We have already established that Circe was a lackwit to give you up and a greedy thief as well," Genevieve said primly, focusing upon the sapphire winking in the mirror and the shadowed eyes watching her that were a match to the jewel. She wanted to chase those bitter memories away, even if it meant dredging up her own past. "I'm sure you have also wondered why I lack a naming jewel."

"I warrant the circumstances must have been most dire," Etienne murmured, moving nearer.

Even now, the recollection made her ache with grief. Genevieve allowed herself to take comfort in his warmth and closeness. "We had exhausted almost all of our funds soon after we arrived in England. Maman was ill. We had no money for medicine or for food. I pawned the Brisbois jewel to pay for the herbs I needed to help her. That was how I met Owen. He took us in, cared for us." She turned around to face Etienne. "By the time I married my naming necklace was long gone."

"I wish," Etienne whispered. "I only wish...surely with my hands upon you like this, your Gift tells you how I honestly feel. It is so strong."

"No." Genevieve felt the excitement rising within her. "I do not. For the first time since I sold my jewel, my Gift does not even whisper. I have no idea how you feel. I will not, unless you tell me."

For a moment, she thought he would speak. Even though it would change nothing, she still wanted to know.

"Mama, can you help me before you go?" Louis called up the stairs. "I can't find *A Young Mage's Guide* anywhere!"

Genevieve cast her eyes heavenward and sighed. "I told you this would happen. It is in the parlor," she called.

Etienne chuckled. "Now that you have a jewel of your own, I can help you with this, but first, I want to make sure that you are aware, this is *not* the last kiss that you owe me." He bent and touched his lips to the back of her neck, sending a wave that swelled from her spine to the very core of her.

"No," she agreed. "It is not."

CHAPTER 21

$\mathcal{L}$ouis met them at the base of the stairs in the hallway, book in hand. "It was just where you said it was!"

Etienne held out his palm and shamefacedly, Louis placed the book in it. "I'm sorry," he said, his lower lip quivering in dismay. "I'll take better care of it. I was just reading for tomorrow's lesson and with all the excitement I just..."

"Watch and learn youngling," Etienne explained, reaching out to reassure the boy with a hand on his shoulder before giving the grimoire to Genevieve. "Place your jewel against the binding, please."

The pendant's chain extended itself as she drew it forward to touch the leather.

"The book has been introduced to the jewel," he explained. "Now your mother has only to ask where the book is and the jewel will lead her to it. You can do the same once you have your mage's ring."

"So I won't be losing things anymore!" Louis exclaimed.

"Not quite. Your ring is not for keeping track of spinning tops and marbles, vital as they may be," Etienne warned him. "The spell is called a *fetch me* for obvious reasons. Now that it is joined with your mother's jewel, I feel comfortable in revealing another aspect of this particular book." He opened the grimoire to the first page and tapped Merlin's nose thrice. The imbued spell immediately shrank the book to the size of a deck of pasteboards.

"It gets little!"

"Indeed," he patted the cover thrice and the book returned to full size. "Now you try."

Giggling, Louis touched Merlin's nose and on the third contact, the grimoire became small once more.

Etienne tucked the book in the boy's pocket. "A size such as this would be simple to lose. Now your mother may keep track of it and you may take it more easily wherever you go."

"Thank you!" Louis threw himself at Etienne, hugging him fiercely. "I love the book even more now. When will we be reading the ending together?"

"Soon," Etienne agreed, looking down at the tousled head with a flummoxed expression as if unsure how to respond. Tentatively, he raised his hand and patted Louis gently.

Genevieve wondered if he had never before been hugged by a child.

"Very soon," he added. "All too soon."

Only Genevieve noticed the sad expression behind the smile.

* * *

THE STREETS near Almack's Assembly Rooms were still crowded with carriages busily discharging their passengers. Lady Morgan contended their best chance to ferret out the attacker would be at the fete. As the older woman had pointed out, Lady Jersey's annual Merlin's ball was an event no mage or witch who had any pretensions of status would wish to miss. Their assailant, obviously a mage, would either be conspicuous due to his wounds, or notable by his absence.

Despite her recent brush with death, Suzette had insisted on coming with them. She was ensconced in the Morgan coach, ready to verify the scent sign of their attacker. The testimony of one familiar was an accusation. Two cats who agreed upon any matter were proof absolute.

In the meantime, they had their own part of the plan in play. Jem, literally with hat in hand, followed Marcel through the clusters of empty, waiting vehicles, stopping while the cat periodically checked for signs of the scent they were seeking.

Marcel meowed softly and then sped off to fetch Suzette. Jem nodded, his eyes narrowing as he noted the crest upon the particular carriage exciting the Chartreux's interest. The coachman waited a few moments before he stepped forward.

"Oi! This cap belong to any o' ye?" Jem asked.

One of the coachmen's faces lit up. "Never thought I'd be seeing that lid again, and my favorite one. A gift from the missus." He reached out to take it, but Jem stepped back and held it out of reach.

"'ow am I t' know it's really yours, eh?" Jem asked. "Fine lid like this, I'd be sayin' it's mine too. Only reason I'm askin is 'cos of me trouble an' strife. Know 'ow they can be!"

The coachmen and tigers all nodded in sympathy, well aware of why cockney slang used trouble and strife as a synonym for wife.

Jem continued his tale. "Cleanin' it up for me, Betty was, when she saw some woman stitched 'er man's mark inside. Softhearted, my wife! Told 'er I'd ask, but I'm not givin' it over to no one, less 'e gives *evy-dence*."

"How's this for yer proof," the coachman hooted. "P.

B. for Peter Bagley. Puts it on the band of me every topper."

"Aye, it is," Jem agreed with a sigh, handing it over. "'ow'd ye manage to lose it? My woman would 'ave skint me alive."

"Read me the Riot Act, she did, for loaning it out to the young master," Peter Bagley admitted with a chuckle. "Then allowed as there weren't much choice, me being new to me job." He settled the cap on his head and put the one it replaced carefully in his pocket.

"Sounds like 'e's one o' them magic toffs what likes muckin' about *among the lower classes*. Makes sense, given where it was found." Jem winked broadly before imitating the plummy toplofty tones of the gentry as he snatched Peter's hat. "Look at me now, wearing a coachman's chapeau, I am one of you, do carry on while I carry on with you and charge me the commoner's rate for your services."

The coachmen roared as Jem tossed back the cap.

"Got that true, ye do!" Peter Bagley agreed. "Whatever rig he was up to, someone didn't like it, I'd say. Came back, clothes in pieces and cut up like raw meat. Can't say as I was sorry for him, since he came back without my lid and don't I dare ask a penny for it! Else it'll be *out the door with you* and no reference neither! Gentry!"

The word was an epithet.

"Me, I ain't gentry." He pulled out a coin and offered it to Jem. "Here, for your missus, fer the cleanin' of it. Never seen it look better, even new."

Jem waved it away. "Wouldn't 'ave it. Virtue rewards its own, Betty's like to say."

As he strolled off, he was joined by a four-legged shadow.

"*Pendrakesssss! Sssuzette agreessss. Ssssscent was in coach with their ssssigil."* Marcel hissed foul cat curses as they headed back to rendezvous with Lady Morgan.

"Aye, good I didn't take Bagley's money," Jem agreed. "Like as not, 'e might be out o' 'is job."

* * *

"THIS EVENING I have discovered a benefit to being on the losing side of a war," Etienne remarked as he kept a vigilant eye on Genevieve, who was dancing a quadrille.

"Have ye now?" Thomas Cochrane asked, offering the comte a swig of his flask. "Enlighten me if ye would?"

Etienne turned as if to follow Genevieve's progress, but only wet his lips with the potent whiskey before returning it to his former nemesis. The mage had been sticking to him like a limpet for the time spanned by two dances thus far and he had offered his flask with uncharacteristic generosity. Whatever game he was about, Etienne wanted to be certain to keep his wits about him. "Fighting for France means this is the first time that I have been called upon to set foot in this precinct of Hell known as Almack's. If the Italian poet had been forced to dance here, I have no doubt it would have figured as the bottom-most circle of Dante's *Inferno*."

The Sea Wolf's laugh seemed a trifle forced. "Aye, stale cake and orgeat, and here I was thinking the food of the damned would be hardtack and watered down grog." He nodded toward Circe. "To my way of thinking, Justice did ye a favor. That witch would just as soon kill ye for a blood spell, as she would kiss ye."

Etienne nodded his head in agreement, even as he wondered what the connection was between Cochrane and Circe. Usually, Thomas spewed his acid upon those who were deemed to have wronged him.

When Genevieve was, at last, returned to Etienne's side, introductions and stilted conversation ensued. Cochrane made polite queries about her son, his studies with Etienne, and Lady Brisbois' health. It was a relief when the orchestra struck up the opening strains of the waltz Etienne had reserved with her.

"You look puzzled," she said as he led her out upon the floor.

"Cochrane is the last man I'd expect to see at Merlin's Ball," he murmured, positioning his hand around her waist, savoring the feel of her in his arms. "Supposedly, Chile's generals have answered his newspaper advertisement offering his services to create and take command of a Navy. According to Damien, he is getting ready to set sail."

"Might this be a fond farewell to England?" She suggested.

"*Fond* is a word seldom applied to Thomas Cochrane." Etienne chuckled. "He is one of the most irascible mages I know. As for his current feelings toward his motherland, they are less than affectionate."

"He has gone to speak to Pendrake and his party. They are now watching us," Genevieve said deploying her fan in a flirtatious gesture. "Just to make you aware, my previous partner has informed me that your heart is irrevocably devoted to Circe. You are inconsolable and you will be unfaithful to any wife. The French pox was mentioned." Her amber eyes were alight with amusement and her lips tilted lusciously in a mischievous smile. "I have been practicing the steps so you need not fear for your toes. Shall we give them something to talk about?"

"I do believe my broken heart is healing," Etienne declared and realized he had spoken the truth. There was no longer a shattered place within him, filled with the bitter fragments of loss and regret. He pulled her closer than the allowed distance dictated by the patronesses. She looked up, her cheeks still flushed with color from the previous dance, her face framed by clusters of curls escaping from her headdress. With an infinitesimal nod, Genevieve told him she was ready.

As he whirled her on to the floor, he fixed the moment in his memory, framing it as part of the paltry collection he had made of moments of true joy. The sensuous feel of her against him. A light scent of attar of roses. The shimmer of blue satin against her skin. The sparkle of his mother's sapphire as they stepped and spun to the music. The sound of her delighted laugh as he described their watchers satirically.

Her initial tension relaxed as she flawlessly followed his lead.

He catalogued each sensation, but best by far was the pure pleasure in her eyes. He knew she was not dancing to flaunt the perfection of her appearance, her elven grace, or to goad Circe and the other observers. For the space of this dance, Genevieve was with him in every sense of the word, in mind and in body. He allowed himself to wonder for a brief moment if she would make love in the same unreserved way in which she flew with him across the ballroom.

When the music ended, they stared at each other for a moment of breathlessness before he realized he ought to offer his elbow and escort her to the refreshment table.

"Alas for the image of the brooding, dejected suitor," he commented sotto voce. "I suspect that Circe is likely gone apoplectic."

"One does live in hope," Genevieve retorted with a laugh that was a bit too throaty for a giggle. "You dance very energetically for a man whose heart is fractured beyond hope of repair."

He was about to inform her of the newly hale state of that organ and propose his plan to her. Etienne had meant to speak to her upon giving her the jewel, but the moment had robbed him of the words he had so carefully prepared, rendering them wholly insufficient. And then Louis had called.

Once again, Etienne prepared to explain his intentions when his grandmother intervened.

"Both familiars have identified your attacker." Lady Morgan's smile put Genevieve in mind of Marcel's expression when the Chartreux cat was about to pounce on his prey.

The older woman glanced meaningfully at Circe and her party before averting her gaze. "You will notice Octavius is missing the evening's festivities. He was the one who wore the hat Marcel found. It was borrowed from the Pendrake's coachman."

"Grandmama, if you will stay and have a word with Damien? Ask him to make certain Pendrake and Circe do not attempt to leave. He might wish to detain Cochrane as well. My instincts tell me the Sea Wolf is bound up in this somehow. I think I shall pay Octavius a visit since he must be feeling poorly." Only the fury in his eyes gave notice of anything other than bonhomie.

"Marcel and I will be joining you," Genevieve added, her expression like the smoldering heat of a blaze about to consume all in its path.

Etienne bowed. "As milady commands. I would expect no less."

* * *

"BUT I DIDN'T HURT you or the boy," Octavius whined, emerging from his whiskey-soaked haze. "It's me got torn up like one of them Egyptian mummies and gotten snatched half-bald." He held up his bandaged hands as evidence. "Familiar is fine, too, they say. Think your boy could do the same for me? Heal me, like he did the comte's cat?"

"Where did you hear that?" Etienne demanded, taking Octavius by the collar and raising him from the chair.

"Circe. Told me this evening. Got it direct from Lord Diggory-Jones." His eyes bulged as he choked out the words to Genevieve. "Told her you turned him down flat as well. Took a knife to him. Leastways you didn't take a knife to me."

"I should have," Genevieve snarled. "And I will yet, if you give me cause. What did you do with the medusa stone?"

"Gave it back to Circe."

Etienne let Octavius loose and he gasped as he staggered back into the chair. "No need for that du Le Fey! Looks like I ain't even got a bottle left to ease my pain," he mumbled as he peered around in a bleary-eyed search. "Cochrane must've taken the rest of it with him."

"Thomas Cochrane? What's he got to do with this?" Genevieve asked, looking to Etienne.

"Have the boy heal me and I'll tell you all about it," Octavius said, with all the self-confident craftiness that being thoroughly bottle bitten could provide. "If you get to him first."

Etienne's pulled off his kid gloves, baring his knuckles. Octavius shrank into his seat in terror, but it was not the Frenchman's fists that fueled his panic.

Genevieve's athame gleamed in the candlelight. "I think you have given me ample cause to use this. Tell me all, Octavius," she crooned. "Start talking. Or I vow by Nimue that I will carve up your face so it matches what Suzette has already done to the rest of you."

Marcel hissed and leapt up on to the table, scattering the empty glasses and bottles.

"*Au contraire*, Marcel, I would not be so rude as to deprive you of your fun."

With the peculiar smile of his Chartreux ancestors, the cat unsheathed his claws and meowed menacingly.

"In case you do not understand Felenish, Octavius, Marcel has informed me he will be delighted to take care of any areas which might have been previously overlooked."

CHAPTER 22

*G*enevieve, Etienne and Marcel found the rear door to Dale's was closed but unlocked. The trio crept stealthily into the kitchen and found the remnants of a late supper still on the table. Louis' favorite, meat pie, was barely touched and Genevieve found her mother's teacup was full, but her usual lump of sugar had fallen to the cloth at its side.

Even in their current prosperity, she would never have let a precious morsel go to waste.

Only silence answered their shouts, shattering any remaining hopes that Lady Brisbois had been able to successfully hide herself and Louis from Cochrane.

"I was a fool," Genevieve whispered, unpinning her toque to toss it upon the table and collapsing into a chair as they returned from their search of the house and shop. "I was the one who told Cochrane they were alone, without protection. He was waiting to be introduced to me."

"You must not blame yourself." Etienne knelt before her and took her hands in his. "Knowing Cochrane, he had already done his *reconnaissance*. I did not see Thomas when we left Almack's. He must have gone on his way as soon as he determined we were both occupied and diverted from his target."

Etienne rose and examined the room. "The candles are not yet extinguished." He checked the teakettle nesting on its cozy. "Cold. But if he is using the medusa stone, he will be transporting two human statues, by himself. He would not dare to involve another mage in a scheme like this. That will slow him down."

"If he left just after our conversation, it would still give him more than a two-hour start," Genevieve calculated in growing frustration.

Etienne's stricken expression was silent agreement. "We must think. Water is his element. He would head for water. The Thames, perhaps?" Etienne paced the room. "But he may very well want any pursuers to believe that. Cochrane is a brilliant tactician."

"He could be anywhere, Etienne!" she cried, fighting to contain her fear. "I would try scrying, but even if I had the skill, it would not work well for kin."

"A good thought! Damien would help us. Scrying is within his realm of expertise. We will need something belonging to each of them, preferably, something well loved."

"Louis' book and—" Genevieve's eyes went wide with hope beginning to blossom. "If it is still in his pocket." She hastily took hold of her sapphire pendant as she breathed the words. "How far does the *fetch me* reach?"

"It varies with the strength of the one who casts it," Etienne explained, catching her excitement. "I have used such spells to find my belongings a full country away."

"But I am not nearly so powerful." Genevieve shook her head.

"You have more strength than you believe." Etienne

cupped her chin in his hands. "I have felt it. I know it is true. Believe my true confidence in you."

"What if he has left the book in the house?"

"Then we will bring it to Damien, but we will not know until you ask."

She nodded and swallowed to clear a throat suddenly gone dry. "Find me *A Young Mage's Guide to Mastery*."

The sapphire began to sway. For a heart-stopping moment, it seemed to point inward, toward the parlor, but it shifted abruptly and inclined to the door.

Marcel meowed a suggestion.

"An excellent idea," Genevieve agreed. "You will inform Lord Wodesby of what we have learned about the plot to free Napoleon and have Pendrake and Circe questioned."

"Cochrane did not anticipate we would be on his trail this soon, if at all," Etienne said. "He will not want to garner notice or risk his cargo by speeding through the night."

Genevieve started for the door. Marcel hissed, *"warrrrmerrrrr furrrr,"* he suggested.

"A most practical suggestion," Etienne said. "I have some carriage blankets, but you are most deliciously exposed. We will do them no good if we freeze along the way."

"There is an old coat of Owen's on a peg by the door, Louis' coat, and a cloak for *Maman* as well if Cochrane has not taken them with," Genevieve said, marshaling her optimism. "They might need them when we find them."

* * *

THEY CHASED Cochrane through the remainder of the night. Etienne was relieved to discover that

RITA BOUCHER

Genevieve's jewel was leading them along fairly well travelled roads. Cochrane had stopped at one posting inn along the way and they were able to get a description. The Sea Wolf was driving one of Pendrake's closed carriages. Genevieve was heartened to hear the sailor did not appear to be in any particular hurry. The innkeeper and his wife had seen an old woman and a boy, well bundled in blankets against the last of the winter chill.

Genevieve huddled against Etienne for warmth and comfort. If they chose the wrong direction the sapphire would tug the chain like a determined dog fixed on a scent. It soon became apparent Cochrane was headed toward Oxford. A hint of dawn had lightened the sky when they reached a small village along the bank of the Thames.

Many of the inhabitants were already long awake and the wharves were almost empty of boats that had set out to fish, to ferry, and to transport goods along the river. Genevieve's heart fell when the innkeeper informed them that none other than the famous Thomas Cochrane had purchased a fine little sailing craft on a whim, offering coin on the barrelhead. The Sea Wolf was paying a generous bonus to have its former owner sail it to a jetty further along the river. Cochrane obviously had no desire to transfer his unwilling passengers at a public dock.

Etienne took up the reins again and they made their way up the road. The jewel tugged eagerly, its glow indicating they were close to their objective. Etienne and Genevieve covered the remaining distance on foot, concealing themselves when they came within sight of the dock and Pendrake's carriage.

The Sea Wolf had yet to release his vessel from its mooring. Lady Brisbois and Louis were both seated stiffly on one of the boat's benches. Cochrane was setting his oars into their positions and making ready to get underway.

It would not take more than a moment or two for the mage to cast off.

"I could send my athame," Genevieve suggested softly.

"The risk is too great," Etienne said. "His death throes could upset the vessel or send it further into the channel. With both of them paralyzed, they could easily drown before we could reach them." A plan was taking shape in his mind. With a sense of inevitability that was almost as keen as a Seer's Vision, he knew this was where his path was meant to lead. "There is another way."

"Go further up the shore to where it goes flat," he whispered to Genevieve, when he finished sketching her role. "You will need to distract him until I can get in position. Be prepared to defend them if they are still under the medusa stone's influence." Giving him an agonized look, she clasped his hand tightly before slipping away.

Using the false magic skills learned as a child, he projected his voice, making it seem as if he was hiding in the shadows beyond a copse of trees.

"Let them go, Thomas," Etienne demanded.

Cochrane looked up, startled. "Ah, found me then, have ye? Someday, perhaps, ye'll be telling me how. But nae, I willna be handing either of them over. The boy, because I need him, and the auld woman because she is the lever that moves him."

Etienne could hear the genuine regret in the Sea Wolf's voice.

"He is Bonaparte's best chance. The boy will lay his hands upon the Emperor, like yer familiar, and Napoleon will be hale and hearty again. Never fear! I'll be sending the boy and the woman back when I'm done with them," Cochrane promised.

"You will like as not be sending him back in a coffin, Cochrane, if you force him to revive a man on his deathbed. Bonaparte is dying." Etienne realized that the dock, the place where earth, water, and sky met, would provide the most power-laden position and excellent visibility.

"I'm told that yer Suzette was nigh on to the Light the other day, and the boy seems none the worse for it!" Cochrane shouted.

"A small cat is not the same as a sick unto the Light old man and you know it! Do you want to be responsible for the murder of an innocent child?" Etienne could see the growing fear on Lady Brisbois' face as she realized Cochrane's intent.

"Ye always were an excellent liar, Etienne." The Sea Wolf chuckled, pulled loose the knot and cast a wary eye around him. "It almost sounds to me as if yer telling the truth."

"The avatar of Justice will come for you, Thomas, but your fate will be far worse than anything that befell me at the Stonehenge. I was judged guilty of coercion," Etienne declared, still projecting his voice as he moved nearer. "You will be charged with the kidnapping, coercion and killing of a young mage. I swear it's the fact, Thomas, by my mage's ring, by Merlin's tree, and on my mother's grave."

"Prodigious oaths, but without weight, du Le Fey," Cochrane declared as he let loose and drifted. "If ye are foresworn, what more can they do to ye? Steal yer position? That's been done. Take yer powers? Done. Make yer good name into a byword for infamy and ridicule? Done and done again. Much like what England has done to me. Once everything has been stolen from ye, there's a certain liberty in having nothing to lose. No punishment for a broken oath would harm ye beyond what ye have already endured."

As Etienne had hoped, Cochrane could not resist talking, especially about himself, giving Genevieve sufficient time to get into position. There would only be this one opportunity for rescue. Etienne knew from experience that Thomas' affinity with the water was a gift of nature independent of Merlin's Blood. By the time a vessel could be found to follow Cochrane, he would be out into the deep.

Once Thomas was on the open sea, there would be no catching him. Cochrane's claims that his successes owed more to skill than to magic were not just braggadocio. The Sea Wolf had earned his sobriquet with his inborn talents and cunning.

"If you don't believe Etienne, believe me!" Genevieve stepped out of concealment. "And Justice will be kind in comparison to my vengeance if you do not release my son and my mother! I will hunt you down, Cochrane. Return Louis now or you will spend the rest of your days looking behind you."

He reached up and tipped his hat to her. "Milady, it is sorry I am I must do this, but the fate of the Americas rests upon Bonaparte."

"Liar! You care nothing for anyone else's fate! All you care about is the legend you wish to be." Genevieve shook her fist defiantly, deliberately drawing attention to herself. "I warn you Cochrane, even the loudest of crowing roosters has its end in the stew pot!"

Cochrane laughed heartily as he coiled the slack in the rope. "I like yer woman, Etienne, she's a feisty one! I'll do my best to keep yer son and yer mother from harm, milady. Maybe I'll teach yer boy a bit about wind and wave."

Etienne raced toward Cochrane at a dead run as if in a last desperate effort to stop him, but the Sea Wolf used his oar to shove his vessel unerringly into the current. The small boat rapidly pulled away from shore.

Etienne took a deep breath when he saw that Cochrane was preparing to unfurl the boat's small sail.

It was the moment he had been waiting for.

He cleared his mind of all distractions and deliberately began to breach the barrier built since he stood facing Judgement at the henge of stones. As he tore down the wall, he felt power filling him, demanding release. He flexed his Gift, feeling it respond sluggishly, like a muscle complaining it had been unused for far too long.

That might be a problem, he thought, as the tremors of warning began, reminding him of the consequences of tapping his forbidden magic. The events he was about to craft required some delicacy. He forced his trembling hands into a graceful gesture, sending his Gift soaring into the ether. The signal of impending danger cascaded from a cautioning pinprick into a rushing torrent of pain.

Ignoring the growing agony, Etienne began the delicate dance with the wind. With his feet firmly on the dock, he took control of his long-denied Gifts. A pattern of air and water appeared, like a map in his mind's eye. He found a passing breeze and caught it, diverting it to subtly drive the dinghy closer to shore as he quickly assessed his ability to marshal the precision that would be necessary.

When Cochrane caught sight of Etienne, standing on the dock with his hands extended outward in a seeming gesture of futility, the Sea Wolf guffawed. His laughter floated across the water. "Too late, du Le Fey!" he crowed in exhilaration. "Even with those braw Outsider shoulders ye've grown, ye canna swim fast enough to catch me."

Etienne's fingers delicately wove his net of weather, preparing to cast his spell.

"Perhaps there is another way." He heard the voice of Justice warning in the air beside him. *"You will lose your Gifts."*

"Better my Gifts, than Louis and his grandmother," he said dismissively.

Justice remained silent.

Thinking himself beyond reach, Cochrane was ignoring matters on shore and devoting his attention to hoisting the dinghy's single canvas. All the while, the sea mage's magic was being funneled through the medusa stone which kept Lady Brisbois and her grandson in thrall.

Gathering the wind in his hands, Etienne drew the breezes toward him. He focused the forces on one nearby tree amidst a small grove. As soon as Cochrane had his sail unfurled, Etienne deliberately toppled the trunk, producing a loud crash, while leaving the others around it fully intact.

Satisfied he was sufficiently adroit to accomplish his goal, Etienne was pleased to find the din had achieved his secondary objective. Thomas had momentarily taken his hand from the tiller, leaving the vessel without a helmsman. Taking advantage of his distraction, Etienne crafted a zephyr. The light wind filled the sail with just enough force to drive the boat back towards shore. Buffers of air surged around the hull, preventing it from heeling and tipping its occupants into the water.

Frantically, Cochrane tried to tack and then reef the sail. But even though he ultimately managed to lower the canvas entirely, it was too late to slow their rapid glide towards the jetty. The mage rose to his feet, his back towards his prisoners, facing the wind with his hands outstretched in a spellcasting gesture.

As Etienne had hoped, the Sea Wolf was trying to use his Gift to prevent the boat from reaching shore, but his magic was of no use against a tidal wave of suppressed power. Cochrane's change of focus allowed Louis and his grandmother to get loose of the medusa stone's influence and they were already on the move, edging to the bow.

"Hold fast!" Genevieve screamed as the boat beached, plowing its way through the mud and up the shoreline before it came to an abrupt jarring halt.

Cochrane was thrown into the shallows by the impact.

Louis and his grandmother scrambled to dry land. Lady Brisbois grabbed the boy's hand and the two of them instantly vanished.

"What have ye done?" Cochrane rose from the water, sputtering. "Have ye won back yer Gifts and none of us knowing it?" he demanded, anxiously scanning the murky water around him. "Where are the boy and his Gran? Have ye gone and pitched them in the drink to drown, ye daft French fool?"

"They are safe!" Genevieve shouted. Her expression was a combination of jubilation and sadness as her eyes met Etienne's. He felt himself filling with the glow of Bliss, probably for the last time, as the remnants of his Gift began to leach from him.

Cochrane turned tail, but instead of running away, he raced toward Genevieve with a burst of preternatural speed, drawing a knife from his waistband as he ran.

"Call back the boy," he ordered, grabbing her by the wrist and brandishing his weapon. "Gifted or not, du Le Fey, I have yer woman. Give me the boy, and I will do my best to return them both to ye unharmed as soon as I am done with them."

The Sea Wolf's astonishment was patent when Etienne began to hoot with laughter. "I think it is the other way around, Cochrane. My woman has *you*."

The sailor opened his mouth, but before he could get a word out, he felt the bite of a blade at his throat.

"As you see, Lady Genevieve can take care of herself!" Etienne smiled and bowed in salutation.

"Drop it and let me loose or by Nimue's hand, I will end you now, Thomas Cochrane," Genevieve threatened. "On second thought, don't bother, because it would please me no end to slice you throat to spine, for daring to lay your hands on my son and my mother."

Cochrane's knife thudded to the ground. Her wrist was freed and she levitated his weapon to Etienne's hand.

"Or perhaps I will give the comte the pleasure of choosing what to do with you, Sea Wolf," Genevieve purred mockingly. "How do you keelhaul someone, Etienne?"

"I believe it requires a large vessel, certainly larger than what we have here," Etienne mused, watching Cochrane turn pale. "Then we attach him to a rope and drag him from stem to stern or port to starboard. Given the magnitude of his lordship's planned treason, I am sure Damien and the Admiralty might manage to oblige us with a large barnacle encrusted vessel for a lengthwise haul."

There was a racketing of wheels and Lady Morgan's curricle raced to the dock in a cloud of dust. Jem assisted her from the vehicle. "It would seem all is under control, and you have not yet killed the scoundrel," she said, disappointment in her voice as she surveyed the scene. "And here I am rushing to the rescue, planning to save the day, but I am arrived too late."

She smirked at the sight of the famed Sea Wolf, standing rigid as a statue with Genevieve's athame hovering at his throat. "Rather uncomfortable, isn't it,

Cochrane, being forced to stand stone still," she observed her acid tones laced with honey. "Lucky thing for you, to have had some practice in the stocks."

"Beg pardon for nae greeting ye with a proper bow, Lady Morgan," he spat out the words slowly from between tight lips. "Doing the pretty would mean the end of me, like as not."

"And no less than you deserve!" Lady Morgan fumed, anxiously scanning the area around them. "Where are Louis and Lucille?"

"We are here, Lady Morgan." Louis and his grandmother popped into view, startling them all.

Cochrane gasped, his eyes widening as the athame drank a thin ribbon of blood. "Might ye not think of dropping yer blade, milady?" His agitated burr became more pronounced as he addressed Genevieve. "Could be yer finding it a wee bit difficult to keep steady, with the rough night's ride we all of us had. Is nae simple to keep yer grip steady on a pitching deck, as it were."

"Tired as I am, it *is* becoming difficult to maintain," Genevieve agreed. "You are correct, Lord Cochrane, this is the way accidents happen, and much as I would like to facilitate one, I am sure there are others who have precedence in the matter of punishing you." She let loose her hold upon the athame and gathered Louis and her mother in her arms.

Cochrane gulped in dismay as the blade remained hovering at his throat.

"Speaking of pitching decks, Lord Wodesby and I have just waved our farewells to Lord Pendrake and his new wife," Etienne's grandmother announced. "He and Circe are off on an extended honey journey to the Jamaicas to visit Pendrake's estate there. And to their great joy, Lord Pendrake's mother and his brother have decided to join the voyage. They are expected to remain there for the foreseeable future."

"Truly a *bon voyage!*" Etienne laughed.

Lady Morgan turned at the sound of her grandson's voice. The sudden look of joy on her face was painful for him to see, knowing he would have to dash her hopes. The blue touch of the Bliss in his eyes had yet to fully fade away and it was likely she mistakenly believed his Gifts had returned.

He folded her in his arms and hugged her close. "I had no choice," he whispered. "*C'est fini.* My Gifts, they are gone for good, Grandmama." He felt the sharp heave of her chest at his whisper, as if she had received a stab to the heart. "It might be best if Cochrane continues to believe otherwise."

Characteristically, by the time she stepped back, there was no sign of her disappointment. The old woman drew herself up and regarded Lord Cochrane with the harsh glare of an Oxford don about to dress down a recalcitrant pupil. "As for your fate, it would seem Lord Wodesby has seen a Vision of your future, Cochrane. I have been charged to carry his message to you."

Her voice deepened with magic to match Damien's timbre exactly, and for a moment she assumed the mien and gravitas of England's Chief Mage, meting out a verdict. "You are banished from the realm of Albion, Thomas Cochrane, for the next decade. Be gone by summer's end!"

Lady Morgan's voice became her own again. "And before you go, Lord Cochrane, you will return the last of the talismans stolen from my family." The chain bearing the medusa stone floated from his pocket into her reticule.

"Now hear *my* warning to you, milord," Genevieve added, beckoning her blade from his throat. It flew back to her hand and she held it up to the early morning light, letting it absorb the traces of Cochrane's

273

blood. "A Brisbois athame has tasted you. Threaten harm to me or mine again and it will seek you out, no matter how far it must travel."

"Understood, milady." The Sea Wolf bowed. "And by your Gift, know this for truth." He held out his hand and Genevieve reluctantly touched it. "I meant no lasting harm to you or your son."

"You speak honestly," Genevieve agreed. "But what we mean to happen is not always the outcome of what we do. You would have risked my son's life and my mother's. That is not something I can forgive."

Cochrane looked to Etienne. "Ye may nae believe this, du Le Fey, but it is glad I am, ye have yer Gifts returned to ye. Now if ye would do me the favor of whipping up a wave and floating my vessel, I'll take my leave."

"I think not," Etienne said softly, deciding to sit on the tree trunk he had uprooted rather than fall on his face. With the last kiss of the Bliss, the torrent of power that had passed out of him was having its effect.

"Bless me blue! Yer shaking! All for a mere puff of wind ye could have managed with a wave of yer little finger in the old days," the Sea Wolf declared in astonishment as he studied their faces with the powers of intuition which were the foundation of his naval genius.

"Nae, I canna believe it," he murmured, coming to a belated realization. "It is nae because ye willna, but ye *canna*, else ye could hae stopped me with the use of a few spells. But ye had only one throw of the dice, did ye? Ye dinna heed the warning of Justice and used yer Gift before times. Ye gave up yer power? For the sake of an OutBlood boy? And here I'd thought ye were a canny man!"

"Silence yourself, fool, else *I* might use Genevieve's

athame to cut out your tongue!" Lady Morgan ordered, the blue flooding her eyes in a wave of fury. "If not for the parole offered you by Lord Wodesby, you would find yourself lying full fathom five, as Shakespeare so eloquently put it, and there would not be enough left of your bones for the coral to build upon. Test me further, and I vow by Nimue I will sink you to the bottom of the sea with none the wiser. I was merely told to deliver Lord Wodesby's message. He did not require me to heed it!"

With an imperious wave of her hand, Cochrane's boat shot into the water. Judging the rising tide of Lady Morgan's rage, the Sea Wolf hurriedly splashed his way aboard and applied himself to the oars without so much as a backward glance.

Louis regarded Etienne with a stricken look. "Is it true, what he said?"

"I commend your control, Louis. I know I would be most tempted to violate another's privacy under the circumstances," Etienne said. "Yes, it is true. If you would see my inner walls, you would find them crumbled. The power they contained is gone."

"It is my fault!" Louis shook his head, his face contorting in grief and guilt. "It is all my fault!"

"Remember how *A Young Mage's Guide to Mastery* spoke of choices?" Etienne patted the place beside him, bidding the boy to sit. "I knew what I was doing. I chose and I would make the same choice again given the circumstances. Look inside me Louis, when I say this to you and know what it truly means."

Etienne solemnly offered his hand to emphasize that his innermost thoughts were open to his pupil. "You saw the chaos within me, the struggle to keep it contained. Sooner or later, it would have destroyed me and endangered all I hold dear. That threat is now gone." Etienne grinned, finally acknowledging his own feelings. "I am free, Louis! For the first time in my life, I am truly free!"

"And you are...happy?" Louis seemed surprised by the answer he saw within his mentor.

In reality, Etienne was still somewhat astonished by his own reaction. He had expected bitterness and perhaps, sadness. He acknowledged those feelings might yet come, but he had never felt so much at peace. Within his newly found inner harmony, Etienne made a decision.

Louis was ready to move forward.

Etienne looked towards the light rising into the eastern horizon, and recognized the time he had been secretly dreading had arrived. "If you would excuse us for a private moment, ladies, Louis and I must take a walk before this sun fully rises."

Lady Morgan understood immediately and nodded, with a smile that was bittersweet. "We will wait near the dock." She shepherded Genevieve and her mother away, whispering explanations as they went.

"Shall we read the final chapter together now?" Etienne asked, smiling as Louis pulled the grimoire from his pocket and tapped it thrice. The book blossomed on his lap and they leafed to the final chapter.

"Shall I read it aloud?" Louis asked.

"Not this time," Etienne explained. "The last chapter must be read silently, as each mage must draw their own lesson from the conclusion. What I may assume may differ from your understanding, but each will be valid."

"But don't you already know the ending?" Louis asked.

"No," Etienne said, "my grandfather and I never finished the book together. Even if we had, the moral I might learn now would likely be very different from the one which I would have drawn as a child. I think you will find this is so someday, if you take it up again. My grandfather told me the story itself is subject to change depending on the need of the reader."

Louis nodded and began tracing the print with his finger. They finished the last words together and the boy tapped Merlin's nose and placed the book in his pocket, waiting for Etienne to speak.

"It is good," Etienne said, taking a deep breath and contemplating the end of the story. Should the mage continue his quest alone or join forces with the witch?

By the time they closed the book, the debilitating effect of Judgement's punishment had passed and it was time for the last step.

"Come with me now, Louis Dale, to end and begin a journey," Etienne requested, rising to face the East. "Let us walk together, so you may walk alone."

Louis eyes widened in recognition of the ritual words. There was nothing secret or complex about the ceremony. The only true mystery had been the *when* of it.

That *when* had become now.

"Now four elements will be summoned. As I name them, you will call them to you." He paused, conveying confidence with his gaze. "Fire."

Louis quickly produced a flame at the tip of his finger.

"Water."

A stream of droplets gathered, extinguishing the flame with a hiss.

Showing off a bit was permitted.

"Air."

A breeze ruffled playfully at Etienne's hair, causing him to smile.

"Earth."

A cloud of dust rose at Louis' feet, coating his muddy shoes.

"Do not think yourself done with your studies, Louis Dale. You have ended the voyage of childhood. Now you begin that journey which will last until you walk into the Light."

Etienne was about to reach into his pocket for the long unused mage's ring he had been holding in anticipation of this moment. Instead, he hesitated, and slipped the jeweled sapphire ring from his own finger.

It was not a Vision that moved him but the choice felt right. "This belonged to my grandfather, Lord Morgan."

Louis looked up in confusion.

"He wore it with honor and so will you, young mage," Etienne declared. "Do I have your oath?"

"Yes, sir," Louis vowed, embracing his teacher. "It fits me now," he whispered in wonder. "A moment ago, it was too big, but now it is perfect."

"As it should be. It will grow as you do. Now raise your hand and catch the light, child of Merlin!" It was difficult to keep the quaver of emotion from his voice as Louis' hand glowed blue, illuminated through the facets of the ring's jewel.

"Is this the end then?" Louis asked as the magic faded.

"Yes and no, young mage." Etienne rose, hugging the boy close. "New beginnings are defined by endings and this ending is happy. Do not dare to be sad for me, especially on such a day. You are safe. The people who love you are safe. You have earned your ring. Go show it off!"

Still, Louis hesitated.

"I must warn you as one man to another, have these ready." Etienne pulled three snowy handkerchiefs from the ether. "The lot of them will likely cry."

"Happy tears!"

"Indeed, a fine start," Etienne said. "You see? Already, you know far more than I did when I received my ring." As the boy scampered off, Etienne sat on the log and prepared to watch the sun rise upon his final day as a mage.

* * *

THE MORNING SUN painted Etienne's hair with a glint of gold. He remained silent as Genevieve sat herself beside him.

She deftly pulled a handkerchief from the air, causing him to give her a weary, wan smile. "Louis has been giving you lessons, I see."

"I am told he had an excellent teacher," she said. "It would appear you have no need of it. Although, truth be told, I wouldn't blame you if you did. It was a noble act, Etienne."

"I am sitting here, going over every moment inside my head," he admitted. "I even heard the voice of Justice, telling me there might be another way. But still, I can determine no other action which would have better kept your mother and Louis from harm." He shrugged. "I suspect defying Judgement might have become necessary eventually in any case."

"I don't understand."

"I would not have been able to deny my Gifts much longer without risk to all those around me," he explained reaching up, smoothing her hair back and gathering a pin that was dangling precariously.

"But I could have helped you contain them," Genevieve offered.

He put the pin in her palm, wrapped her fingers around it and brought up her hand for a kiss. "You are a generous soul, Genevieve. But how best to explain? Ah! It is like these curls of yours. Constantly, you are restraining them, forcing them to remain in an order that is not natural, like so."

He took the pin and gathered up a coil of hair, deftly fixing it into place.

"As the tangled chaos of power within me grew, you would have constantly been attempting to control it with your emotions, trying to persuade something which is meant to be free to remain pinned even as it struggled against its confinement." He combed his fingers through her curls, pulling out the remaining pins one by one, until her hair tumbled down her back in a sunlit chestnut stream, hanging loose to her waist. "Inevitably there would not be pins enough. It would overwhelm you. I could not ask you to do this."

"Ask me to dress your hair?" Genevieve clasped his hand, attempting to lighten the moment.

"Make you my keeper. Before, I met you, I had chosen to isolate myself and hope for a miracle before my Gifts destroyed me. But I am a most selfish man. The slim hope of redemption is worthless compared to the promise of a life with you."

He took the crumpled handkerchief from her hand and made it disappear. "So, I made a plan. I would ask you to marry me. On our wedding day, I would have deliberately violated the dictates of Justice with some spectacular last touch of magic before we took our vows. Without my pent up Gifts, I could do no harm to the people I love."

Genevieve sniffed. "I may yet need that handkerchief, Etienne. All the others you gave Louis are quite soggy."

"An accurate prediction! A fitting finale for my last day as a mage. I had warned Louis that a bout of feminine tears was about to fall and he might have been disappointed otherwise." Looking out over the water, Etienne ran a nervous hand through his hair.

"You could do far better than an infamous scoundrel who no longer has any chance of regaining his Gifts, Genevieve." Etienne met her eyes at last with a look of apprehension and sadness. "Before there was a slim hope. I confess, I had thought the use of my power against Cochrane might be permitted, but that was not to be. Now, my Gifts are gone for good and I would not have you tied to an impotent mage."

"You forget, Etienne. We have kissed. We have danced. I have seen absolutely no evidence of this impotence that you speak of. Quite the contrary, in fact," she said, her prim tones belied by the heat in her eyes. "And then there is the matter of the one kiss that is owed. A Brisbois always pays her debts in full." She moved closer, drawing his lips to hers.

Without his Gifts, their kiss was a different experience entirely. The looming presence of power had dissipated, leaving only her and Etienne together in his inner landscape.

Although she did not use her own Gift, there was no need. His heart was open, proclaiming his most guarded truths. His feelings for her were so much more than she had ever imagined. He loved her. He wanted her and needed her. He had been driven by love and necessity, but he truly felt a strange mixture of sadness and satisfaction at his loss.

Tentatively, Genevieve accessed her Gift, using the jewel to focus her power in a way she had never done before. She opened the door to her own emotions, revealing herself in an intimacy she had shared with no other. He would know without doubt that his lack of magical Gifts did not matter to her. There in the deepest chambers of her heart, she showed Etienne that she had magic enough for them both.

Etienne's smile rivaled the dawn for warmth. "May I have your answer, Lady Genevieve?"

"First, you must ask the question," Genevieve reminded him.

"Will you marry me, Genevieve," Etienne asked. "Pending your mother's consent of course?"

"And if my mother refuses?"

"Then I will set my grandmother upon her. Lady Brisbois ought to be forewarned though. My grandmother is in the habit of getting what she wants and she has made it clear she wants you!"

"Has she?"

"Abundantly clear." Etienne raised her fingers to his lips again. "She would not have given me my mother's naming jewel to gift to you, were that not the case."

"This belonged to your mother?" She cupped it in her hands, letting it sparkle in the light.

"I had intended to ask you last night and explain my plan before Louis interrupted us. I was less than pleased, I admit, but if he had not—"

"We might never have found them in time," Genevieve completed the thought, staring at the pendant.

He nodded. "I realize that it is rather simple, but if you want another, I would—"

She put a finger to his lips. "I want no other. No other jewel, no other man. Only you, Etienne, always. Only you."

"I assume this means you are accepting my offer of marriage?" Etienne asked.

"And here I'd thought you were a canny man!" Genevieve parroted Cochrane's words and confounded expression.

"A truly canny man confirms," Etienne said. "Now regarding that last kiss, I believe there may be a matter of interest on the debt between us."

"Indeed," Genevieve agreed, inclining her head.

"There is definitely interest. What did you have in mind?"

"I think the terms are negotiable, but shall we begin with a small surety payment?"

Neither one of them heard the rustle of leaves behind them.

Louis eyed his *grand-mère* and Lady Morgan curiously as they returned to the curricle. "It took you an awful long time to find them."

"The comte and Lady Genevieve will follow us later in their own vehicle," Lady Morgan told Jem. "I will drive the carriage and you will drive the Pendrake coach."

"Shouldn't we wait for Mama and the comte?" Louis asked. "We can all go home together."

Lady Brisbois' smile spread from ear to ear. "In their own good time. They have some important matters to discuss."

CHAPTER 23

SIX WEEKS LATER

The bell above the door to Dale's tinkled loudly as Lady Morgan charged into the store, her new familiar, Zephyr, perched on her shoulder.

"What has you ready to belch smoke and breathe brimstone, Matilda?" Lady Brisbois asked. "The look upon your face is fit for a dragon. Has Louis been accidentally setting things afire again?"

"No. Louis has behaved beautifully since Etienne and Genevieve left to put the house in Yorkshire in order." Lady Morgan slapped a scroll of parchment on the counter. "Did you know anything about this?"

"It would help if one might be informed what *this* is," Lady Brisbois withdrew into formality.

"Allow me to explain, Lucille." She untied the dusty ribbon binding the roll. "Forgive me if I seem somewhat overset. I will start by saying that I was searching for a copy of the list of the Morgan bridal jewels. Lady Rowan still has mine and I had no wish to trouble her."

"I had thought everything was returned," Lady Brisbois said. "And even were it not the case, you know Genevieve cares little for such things."

"That is the very reason why I want to make certain your daughter is given her due. Etienne had mentioned he had a copy of the list among his papers, so I went searching through the documents regarding his betrothals." She unrolled the parchment. "I was only aware of two such contracts for Rowan and Circe. This precedes either of them."

Lady Brisbois sighed and went around the counter to lock the front door of Dale's and turn the sign to "Closed." Her friend followed her to the recently refurbished parlor. The battered sofa had been replaced by a luxuriously cushioned nile green library seat from Ackermann's. A new inlaid marble table provided ample space for the preparation of tea.

"I confess I much prefer heating water by magic, but until Genevieve had a jewel of her own, it didn't seem right to remind her of what she had lost by her sacrifice," Lady Brisbois declared as she lightly tapped the kettle with her gem. The steam rose up as it boiled.

"You are doing a very poor job of procrastinating, my friend, and you know me not at all if you think I will wait for an explanation while you muck about with the tea!" Lady Morgan's eyebrow rose along with her temper. She took a piece of raw meat from her reticule and offered it to her peregrine. "Zephyr is getting upset."

"My apologies to you and your familiar. This is not an easy story to tell," Lady Brisbois began. "As you have obviously concluded from the document, my husband had sealed a betrothal agreement with the late Comte du Le Fey. In time, his son, Etienne, would have wed our daughter. Even though Genevieve was barely of age to walk when this was signed, part of her dowry was handed over to prove our good faith. It seemed a most excellent match of two Gifted and powerful families."

She shivered and poured herself a cup, regarding the liquid bleakly as if viewing an image of those terrible times within. "Then, *poof*, in an instant all we had was gone. I managed to save only myself and Genevieve. Other than my witch's gem, and the one which my daughter wore, I sold what little jewelry I had upon me. I journeyed to the chateau of the Devil Comte with my daughter."

Lady Morgan's irritation was replaced by sympathy, as she guessed what was to come. "That is why you were afraid of Etienne the first night we met? He has the look of his father."

Lady Brisbois affirmed with a nod. "The old comte denied the bargain. An alliance with the Brisbois family was no longer desirable. I asked for the return of Genevieve's dowry so we would not be penniless."

"He turned you out?"

"Not quite," Genevieve's mother said with a humorless smile. "Thinking me weak and defenseless, he tore off the mask of nobility which had deceived us all. He offered me a roof over my head if I would remain as his mistress. Using my Gift, Genevieve and I fled as fast and as far as we could go. We roamed the Continent for many years, always on the move for fear he might be seeking us."

She sighed and stirred her cup. "We were getting by, until one night, I had a terrifying Foreseeing. I saw a Vision of my daughter as a woman grown, embraced in the arms of the Devil Comte. It was then we fled to England." She lifted her tea in an ironic toast. "Now I know it was not the Devil Comte, but Etienne I saw in Genevieve's future."

"You were wise to fear the old comte and you ought not to blame yourself. My husband and I were taken in by him as well. We both rued the day when we accepted his suit for our daughter Delphine's hand." Lady Morgan shook her head. "He was an evil man."

"The Fates weave and spin as they will." Lady Brisbois shrugged in resignation and added sugar to her cup. "But they have led us to this place. Without those events, there would be no Louis. Etienne might have married Circe—"

"Pray, there is no need to go any further." Lady Morgan held up her hand, begging her friend to desist from further detailing her catalogue. "I will have that cup now, if you would not mind."

As Lady Brisbois prepared the tea, Lady Morgan unrolled the document, setting it to hover before her while she perused the particulars. "Hmm, I had only given this a cursory glance before." She ran her finger over the terms. "That was no paltry sum the Devil Comte stole, the greedy swine. Etienne is trying to redress as many of his father's evils as he may. Unfortunately, they are numerous, but I know my grandson would gladly repay you"

"But why would he need to repay us?" Lady Brisbois asked. "They are married. The terms of the contract are complete, are they not?"

Lady Morgan skimmed down the page. "Not quite. There is one detail not yet fulfilled."

Genevieve's mother set her cup down and looked at the contract. Her eyes widened in amazement. "The balance of Genevieve's dowry is still unpaid. Could it be possible?"

"He has already given away what he would keep, if his Gifts are what Justice meant," Lady Morgan reminded her excitedly.

"And he used his Gifts to save us from evil," Lady Brisbois added.

"If this is the meaning of *Promises broken must be mended*, I would gladly gift you the funds," Lady Morgan offered.

"Nonsense! Your grandson forced a most generous financial settlement upon me. Dale's is doing very well and my daughter shares her profits with me. I am, in fact, a comfortably wealthy woman once more. It is best, I think, that I pay this as a Brisbois. You know how *geas* tend to be."

"Indeed, you are quite right, Lucille, curses can be pernickety by their very nature," Lady Morgan agreed. "Jem is around back with the curricle."

"I shall fetch my hat and we shall visit the bank *tout de suite*."

* * *

YORKSHIRE, TWO DAYS LATER

In a sunny room adjacent to the master bedchamber, Etienne and his comtesse were enjoying a very late breakfast when there was a knock. Tying the belt on his banyan, the comte cracked the door and was surprised to find Jem standing in the hallway.

"Everyone is well," Jem said holding out two letters. "'er ladyship says I'm to say that first. Lady Brisbois and Lady Morgan said to give these both, direct to your 'and."

"Why don't you go down to the kitchen, and have a bite to eat," Etienne suggested. "We will let you know if there is a need for a reply."

"Was that Jem's voice I heard?" Genevieve asked as her husband seated himself once more.

"It was. All is well he says, but he carried these from London." He broke the seal on the first envelope.

"I don't know why I'm so hungry these days," she said, applying herself to her toast. "This is my third slice."

"I do," Etienne said with a risqué grin. "Good country air, plenty of activity, such things give me an appetite."

It only took a second for her to apprehend his

meaning and blossom into blushes. The comte took a moment to appreciate his wife before returning to the mystery of the missive.

"This is puzzling," he said. "This contains a bank draft from your mother. A rather large amount, I might add."

"Is she attempting to return her settlement again?" Genevieve asked. "She is quite proud and rather stubborn."

"A hallmark of the Brisbois women, it would seem," Etienne said, searching the sheet of vellum that had wrapped the note for an explanation. "There is only one line written here. *Balance of the dowry promised for my daughter, Genevieve Madeline Celeste Brisbois paid in full to the Comte du Le Fey, as stated in the terms of her betrothal contract.*"

"That is most odd and cryptic, even for my mother," Genevieve mused. "What does the second letter say?"

Etienne broke the seal and scanned the document. "Ah! Grandmama says she found a document I had been seeking before we were married." His finger slid along the lines of script. "There appears to have been some sort of a betrothal agreement, between my father...and yours, it seems. You and I were promised to one another, almost from the cradle. This is a final disbursement on your *dot* as promised by your father in that contract." He waved the draft. "The amount pays off the remaining balance of that dowry due to the du Le Fey family upon your marriage."

"I hope this does not mean another session with your man of law to get this all made right! Does your grandmama say anything else?" Genevieve asked. "Can you please pass the jam pot?"

Distracted by his examination of the letter, Etienne attempted to pass the jam.

With a preoccupied wave, he sent the crystal jar of

strawberry preserves floating across the table. Genevieve looked up from her toast, her eyes widening in amazement as the container hovered before her, waiting for her hand to grasp it.

"Etienne," she whispered, hardly daring to raise her voice. "Etienne, *mon cher*, look."

Etienne glanced up. The question caught in his throat as he stared transfixed at the floating piece of glassware. "You?" he finally asked.

Genevieve shook her head.

Slowly, Etienne flexed his fingers. The jar remained aloft but tipped upside down, sending its top and its contents spilling to the table.

"It would seem that your dexterity may need some work," Genevieve said with a growing grin.

"My grandmother does say something else," he said, taking a deep breath. *"Lucille and I sincerely hope that this means that broken promises have finally been mended."*

EPILOGUE

ONE YEAR LATER

*T*he sound of wood being chopped echoed from the garden.

"Aunt Genevieve!"

Louis was holding his sister, Delphine, when Giselle dashed in, her pixie-shaped face bright with excitement. Were it not for the sleeping baby in his arms, he would have left the room without delay. Though Giselle du Le Fey was his father's sister, she was extremely annoying, and always pretending she knew more about everything than anyone else.

"Most of Suzette's kittens have opened their eyes and my familiar just introduced himself."

"Congratulations, Giselle," Louis' mama said, looking up from the book she was reading. "Your *maman* and I must plan a celebration!"

"With all the grandmothers?" Giselle asked. "Lady Lucille, Lady Matilda, and Lady Adrienne?"

"But of course," Louis' mother agreed. "So tell us about your new friend."

"His name is Gaston and he looks much like his Papa, Marcel," Giselle informed them. "Gaston smiled at me."

"All Chartreux cats look as if they are smiling,"

Louis explained, trying to be kind in spite of her obvious ignorance. "Their appearance is due to the nature of the breed's facial structure. The peculiar muzzle shape often gives that false impression."

"Well that may be what *you* think, *Nephew*," Giselle said. "But *I* know Gaston's smile is special just for me."

"You. Are. Not. My. Aunt," Louis told her firmly.

"Etienne, my brother, is now your Papa. Delphine is your sister and my niece. That makes you my nephew, *Nephew!*" Giselle laughed, tickling her niece's feet before running off to go back and become further acquainted with her new familiar.

Louis sighed. He might have tried to discuss the situation, but his mother was wearing her *Louis be a gentleman look*. At that moment, his Papa strode into the room, slipping his shirt back on because it was proper to do so, even though Louis had noticed his Mama was not at all offended at seeing Papa without it. He had been chopping wood, a useless endeavor, since he could easily charm the axe now to do it by itself.

There was no use complaining to him about the girl's behavior. Papa had already informed him that Giselle's teasing was a female form of affection.

No wonder women were difficult to understand. Their confusing conduct began at a young age.

"Smiling Chartreux!" Louis shook his head, looking down at his own familiar, who had been born as part of Suzette's first litter. There was no question at all about when Desirée was smiling since she resembled her mother.

"Sssssilly girl," Desirée agreed.

Delphine chose that moment to wake up, her face screwing up into an angry howl.

"I think she is hungry," Louis said, hoping that it was not a dirty nappy that was upsetting her. His Papa insisted he learn to chop wood. His mother demanded he learn to change diapers.

Thank the Merlin, he could not feed his sister, or he suspected they might ask him to undertake that task as well.

"I will take her upstairs for you, Genevieve," Papa offered. "It sounds as if she is hungry."

Mama laughed for no reason at all. "We definitely ought to feed her."

"Meet me in the garden in an hour, Louis, and we will practice swordplay," Papa said.

Louis gave a quiet sigh. He had yet to discern what possible assistance his father could provide in feeding Delphine. In her older brother's experience, the baby tended to be especially voracious when their father was present during her feeding. Postulating from past months, Louis knew it would be well over an hour before their father returned downstairs.

Delphine opened her gray eyes wide and stared up at him. A toothless grin blossomed and she gurgled with a gummy grin of adoration.

Louis had to admit she was a sweet little mite, especially when she smiled. He knew it was not merely a matter of facial configuration. Unlike Giselle, Louis knew a genuine expression of love when he saw one.

His sister was, most definitely, smiling at him as their father swept her up into his arms.

AUTHOR'S NOTE

Until Mike Duncan's *Revolutions* podcast introduced me to Thomas Cochrane, the 10th Earl of Dundonald, I was unaware that S.C. Forester's *Horatio Hornblower* series, and Patrick O'Brien's *Master and Commander* novels, are partially based on Lord Thomas' legendary exploits.

Unfortunately, the naval genius, who Napoleon nicknamed *le Loup des Mers (the Sea Wolf)* possessed a volatile and irascible personality. Cochrane's conflicts with authority, and contempt for the English Admiralty, helped to hasten the wreck of his career and his self-imposed exile from England. Cochrane's loose cannon reputation was a likely reason for the credibility given to the rumors that he was plotting to free Bonaparte from his prison on St. Helena to help conquer, and eventually rule, South America.

With his career and fortune in ruins, Thomas Cochrane and his family sailed for South America in August of 1818 to take command of Peru's navy. Although the Sea Wolf was not actually a mage, given the scope of his amazing exploits, it was easy to imagine that magic might have been involved.

ALSO BY RITA BOUCHER

DESIRE IN DISGUISE
Miss Gabriel's Gambit
The Devil's Due
A Misbegotten Match
The Scandalous Schoolmistress
The Poet and the Paragon

ENCHANTED HEIRESSES
The Would-Be Witch
Lord of Illusions
A Touch of Magic

ABOUT THE AUTHOR

Rita Boucher is the author of eight novels. If you'd like to send her a message, please feel free to write her c/o Oliver Heber Books @publisher@oliver-heberbooks.com